SACRIFICE
FOR THE
STANDING STONES

BREE MOORE

For Tyler, who is my Theo.
Thanks for always doing the dishes.

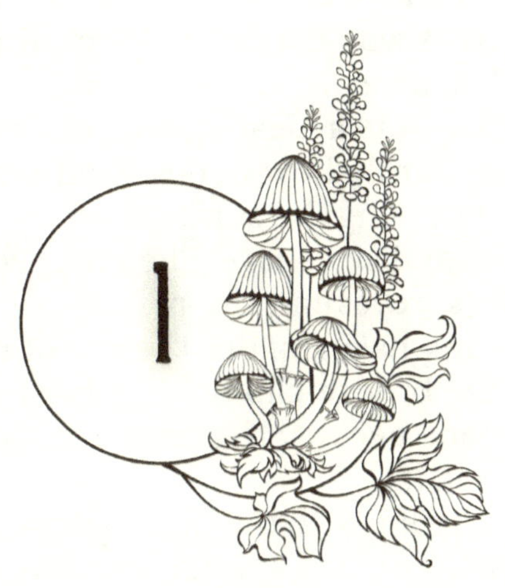

BRIA

HAD IT BEEN THE last day of her existence, Bria would have taken more pleasure in it than all the past days of her life.

She filled her lungs with crisp, bright air, enjoying the slight nip it gave her as a breeze brushed across the skin of her arms and face. Yes, today would be a good day for her last if Tala willed it to be so.

Lifting her skirts, she stepped over a fallen log, spotting as she did the bright yellow mushrooms dotting its surface, barely in the young primordial stage. In a few weeks, they would make a delightful meal.

Patches of crystal blue sky peeked at her between the trees, the bright spots becoming further apart as she entered the deep woods. She breathed in the musty forest scent of rotting things and new growth, admiring the gold and orange leaves mixing with green. The Gathering was upon the forest, the third season as the world turned, and soon the trees would wear their new dresses and the leaves would fall, dancing, to the ground.

Bria stopped beside a clear spring. The tiny waterfalls on the far side burbled over rocks and branches, their rushing waters rippling the surface and breaking the image of the trees and sky above. She stripped off her over and underlayers, revealing the rest of her skin, tanned from days basking naked under the eye of the sun. Then she removed the bronze clip holding her red hair out of her face and made her way to a large rock at the deepest end before diving in.

Her skin sang to life with the tickling of bubbles and the plants at the bottom of the spring. She kicked her legs and brought herself back to the surface, breaking through and taking a large breath, laughing at the sky.

The forest exalted with her, and as her heart beat in sync with the breathing of the land, everything came together in a moment of perfect harmony, and Bria thanked Tala for another day in the Morwood, and for entrusting her with the care of it.

Footsteps shattered the peace of the woods, crashing through delicate undergrowth and frightening birds who called their warnings down to her.

She swam behind the rock that protruded into the spring, hiding in the shelter of its shadow. She could see enough of the forest to spot the strong, male legs that appeared at the edge of the spring as they had the last five days.

Ever since Magnus Ironcrest discovered that she spent her mornings in the spring.

"Bria Glenraven, I know you're here. I heard your splashing from across the forest. Come now, don't hide from me."

Bria suppressed the groan in her throat. She pressed her forehead against the rock, borrowing its quiet strength before she pushed away from it. She sank further into the water until only her head was visible, her red hair spreading behind her as she drifted out into the center of the spring.

"Magnus. I've said you are not welcome here."

"And I've told you that I will not be swayed," Magnus replied, settling onto a rock and removing a brown leather boot from his foot. He grunted with effort until he tugged it off, then pulled at the other.

He wouldn't dare bathe with her. She had rejected him time and time again, made it clear she had no desire for his advances, but here he was, delusional as ever.

"Do they train you to have no respect for a woman's privacy in that fancy palace of yours, human?" Bria called, swimming further back towards the waterfalls. Their splashing gave her confidence and the rushing of their waters gave her strength. Like sisters who would help her chase off this unwanted suitor.

"They trained me to be the most skillful of lovers, if you'd allow me to show you. But since you refuse, I am left to reveal my desperation," Magnus replied, his voice muffling as his shirt passed over his face. He stood, hands going to the top of his breeches.

Bria swam beneath the nearest waterfall, climbing out of the water onto the ledge of rocks that had formed beneath it in years of erosion.

"That's quite enough clothing removed. This is your final warning, Magnus Ironcrest," Bria called. Goosebumps broke out on her skin, and she trembled. Through the narrow curtain of water, she could see that the earnest suitor had ignored her, and his bare skin flashed pale in the sunlight before he dove into the spring. His arms windmilled, bringing him closer to her hiding place at an alarming pace.

Bria climbed across the rocks, toes gripping and hands guiding her to the upper ledge where they could grasp and pull her up. Silently, she dragged herself to the place above the waterfalls, crossing over at a still spot, while relying on the fact that her pursuer would be too focused on swimming to look up and find her making her escape.

She glanced down, noting the man's progress. The sun gleamed off his impressive physique. She could appreciate the work he'd put into his body. Unfortunately, his personality didn't impress her. He'd nearly made it across the spring before he stopped and stared at the waterfalls where Bria no longer hid.

Dashing the last few steps into a copse of trees, well-hidden from below, Bria watched Magnus's confidence turn from confusion to frustration. He slapped at the water, his face contorting. He swam a few strides away, calling after her.

"Bria! Don't hide from me."

Bria couldn't resist a giggle. Fortunately, the noise of the waterfalls on the water hid the small sound from Magnus's ears. He was human, after all. He didn't have her keen senses. The forest might as well be dead to him.

She left her clothes on the large rock where she'd taken them off, walking naked through the forest. She'd spent most of her time communing with the forest this way since she was a child, at least until the outward expansion of the realm of Dunholm pressed closer and travelers became more frequent. Also, she'd matured enough that her father had insisted she cover herself. For her own protection, he'd said, but he didn't understand that she had Tala to protect her.

The breathings of the goddess surged beneath her feet, supporting them with a carpet of leaves and moss. Tiny whisperings from the trees rubbing against each other, sending messages through their boughs and roots, tickled the inside of her ears. She had the notion that if she sat long enough she would understand what they said. Perhaps they spoke of her passing, a daughter of Tala, the one who protected them and cared for them.

But she was only one druid, a lone daughter, and she would be the entirety of her days, unless she broke the curse that rushed through her blood. The curse that would kill her the day she bore a child.

Hunger gripped Bria, so she snacked on the tiny, orange, citrusy currants and fatty nuts that Tala provided until she reached her cottage nestled amongst a group of tall, grandmother-like trees.

Reluctantly, she donned a set of cream-colored underthings, then selected a brown underskirt and a green linen kirtle. Tightening the laces at her bodice, she adjusted her skirt layers and put an iron kettle over the fire, heating the rainwater she'd collected the day before for her morning meal.

She chopped sweet, fragrant leaves and took her honey pot down from the shelf, busying her body while her mind buzzed with anxiety.

Magnus would come around shortly, once he'd realized that she wasn't toying with him in some flirtatious game, and he would be in a sour mood. She was tired of the games, tired of his advances, and tired of the clueless way he came day after day, knocking on her door and destroying her peace. He showed not a modicum of understanding nor respect for her feelings. Not unlike the past several suitors that had come, sent by the human queen of Dunholm.

They were sent to test her, to see how well she resisted them, to spy on her for signs of her fertile time arriving. Because despite all of their deficiencies, the humans had the good sense to realize that if the druids died out completely, the forest, and their realm, would perish.

It was unfortunate that they hadn't realized it until after they'd started the war that had destroyed her people.

Bria chopped down on the pile of nuts on her wooden board, the blade going awry and slipping out of her hand. She jumped back, yanking her hands out of the way as the knife clattered to the floor. She calmed her breathing before she retrieved it, then grabbed a thick rag to grip the kettle's hot handle with, pulling it off the fire.

The menial tasks of pouring boiling water over dried grains calmed her. She watched them slowly swell, then added the chopped leaves and nuts, breathing in the fragrant aroma. Last, she drizzled in golden honey. Licking the last drop from the spoon before using it to stir the gruel, Bria took the bowl to the rocking chair by the fire, turning it so her hair would dry while she ate.

Halfway through her breakfast, the door to her cottage burst open, and Magnus strode in, his red hair sticking up every which way, his eyes ablaze.

Bria set her bowl on the floor and braced herself on the arms of the chair.

Magnus's shoulders heaved, and he raised one hand, pointing accusingly at her. A harsh chuckle erupted from his throat. "You are a little minx. Teasing me with your words, your body, then disappearing and leaving me frustrated. I grow weary of our games, druid."

"They are not games to me," Bria replied coolly. She crossed her arms over her chest, her heart taking on the quality of an ironwood tree. She would not be moved to compromise herself, not for this man with his childish tempers. He didn't deserve to claim victory over her.

Magnus licked his lips, taking a step forward. "Let me show you what I came for," he said, his voice taking on a husky tone as his eyes roved over her. "I can show you things—"

The laugh that came from Bria held no humor. "I've had one of your kind out here nearly every month, and any time I've let them 'show me things,' as you put it, it's been underwhelming. So you'll excuse me if I don't jump into bed with you."

His expression darkened. "I'm not asking anymore, druid daughter. The others failed because they were weak. They gave up too soon. But an Ironcrest does not yield, as I will prove to you." He moved towards her, arms reaching, intent on grabbing her.

Bria widened her stance, wishing the cottage had dirt floors instead of wood so she could feel Tala's power more acutely. But it didn't matter. In the end, she was surrounded by her sisters and brothers, the trees and wildlife. Even the tiniest worm wriggling in the dirt could be felt if she concentrated hard enough.

Wind rushed through the door to her cottage, making it bang against the inner wall. The wind tugged at her skirts and lifted her hair, whipping around Magnus. Bria spread her arms, letting the wind spiral around her, and sent a request for the earth to shake—just a little bit. She grinned as Magnus's eyes widened at the fury of the Mother of the Earth.

"You insult me, Magnus Ironcrest, if you presume that I am some weak-kneed female who will give in to your demands. Since you have not taken me at my word, you will take me at my power. You will return to the men the queen has selected to pursue me, and you will warn them of exactly who they are dealing with. Perhaps the next man they send will be prepared to respect a daughter of Tala the way she deserves."

Bria drew in the power of Tala, asking the goddess to put her fear into this man who presumed to take what was hers.

The room darkened, and Magnus stumbled away from Bria, running into the doorway. The wind rushed back towards him, snatching the door and slamming it into his face. He cried out and fell onto the ground outside.

Bria walked towards him, summoning the trees. They bent to and fro as if possessed, their branches reaching for the terrified suitor. She reached downward and called the denizens of the earth forward. Ants, millipedes, beetles and snakes all crawled forth and climbed up the man's fancy clothes.

"No! Agh! Call them off!" Magnus screeched, clawing at his clothes and flinging the little creatures every which way as he scrambled to his feet. Red-faced, breath heaving, clothing rumpled, the first-born of the seventh generation of the Ironcrest clan pointed an accusing finger at her.

"You are mad. Being alone in the forest has turned your head. What will the queen think when I tell her that the last druid is unfit for any man?"

Bria laughed, letting the wind lift her hair again. "You'll tell her I have no need for weak human men. I will break the curse, and never again will a druid daughter be used to keep your crumbling realm alive."

She sent another surge of Tala's power at the sneering man—birds dove in with their talons and beaks. The attack wiped the snide expression from his face and Bria relished in the yelp of fear he released as he sprinted away. As a final gesture of power, she willed Tala to pursue him until he left the Morwood for good, then released her own grip on the goddess's power and stumbled back to her chair to eat and replenish her strength.

There was a time when her people had populated the Morwood, made it thrive, and kept it safe from those who would overharvest its resources. But there hadn't been more than a single druid in generations. Her mother, and her mother before her, and her mother...all held the title of the Last Druid—the lone surviving daughter after the war that had wiped out most of druid-kind. And each one had birthed a single child, a girl to bear the burdens and the gifts of continuing the druid line.

What Bria didn't understand was why Tala had cursed them in the first place. How could the earth goddess have allowed her own priests and priestesses to nearly die out, to be forced to rely on human men to sustain them? To sustain her? The forest suffered, and the people that relied on the forest grew angry and suspicious of Bria, accusing her of withholding the forest's goodness. But the truth was, Bria was alone. She could not sustain the forest herself. And she could not accept that her only purpose was to bear a child and die, leaving the same burden on her own daughter.

Which was why, when the time of her first fertile cycle arrived, she would not yield herself up as a sacrifice to the selfish whims of men. She would break the druid curse, or she would die trying.

THEO

T HEODORE BLACKWIN LEANED BACK in his chair, eyes closed as he tried to forget his mother's latest lecture and focus on Master Graymont's lesson. The ancient mentor had gone off notes as usual, droning about his failed conquest with the druid woman named Sorcha. The mother of the current last druid.

Theo sat at the back of the class, leaving the front seats for those eager-to-please and the younger ones starting their training. He remembered being fifteen years old, pimple-faced and occupying the front-row center seat, eager to learn everything he could and be chosen as the next suitor for the mysterious druid coming of age at the same time he was.

The more he'd learned, however, the more he'd determined to let others go first. Let them fail. Let them make their clumsy attempts. He would hold back, learn from their mistakes, and learn everything he could from the books that lined the walls in the classroom in one of the palace towers.

He had failed everything else in his life, including gaining the physical experience everyone deemed necessary for a suitor of the last druid. "Practicing" on dozens of women paid from the realm's coffers hadn't appealed to him, and though the others made fun of him for his lack of obvious prowess in bed, Theo couldn't help but feel there would be more needed to win a druid's heart.

A stiff breeze blew in through the window, bringing with it the scent of the forest. The legs of Theo's chair thumped on the ground as he came forward, and he stared out the window, breathing in again, deeper. Unmistakably, he could smell the forest, though it was a day's ride away. The scent sent a shiver through him, and he gazed out the window until a hawk flew past with a shrill cry.

Master Graymont coughed loudly.

"Master Blackwin, did you have some revelation on the titillation of a druid that you'd like to share with the rest of the class?"

Theo rubbed his eyes under his glasses, then glanced over the amused and mocking stares of the ten teenage boys that filled the first two rows of the class, then over at the three men that remained from his own class. He would get it in the corridors later.

His face flushed, and he murmured denial and an apology, rubbing the back of his head and picking up his quill again, trying to appear engaged until Master Graymont released them for the middle-day meal.

But the old instructor never got to finish. Footsteps rushed up the stairs, and hoarse cries rang out through the corridor.

"She's mad! She's gone mad!"

Theo sat up straight, recognizing the voice of Magnus Ironcrest, the one who had most recently gone to win the druid's affections. He'd been pursuing her for nearly a month and had given all of them the impression that she was responding to his advances. A matter of time, he'd said, until he had the druid in bed.

Of course, the real trouble wasn't getting her to bed them. She'd bedded several over the past few years. The trouble was catching her during her fertile time. Unlike humans, druids had three fertile periods over thirty years, each a month long. The rocky human and druid relations didn't help matters, and as a result, only one druid remained as keeper of the Morwood.

Magnus rounded the doorway and stumbled into the nearest desk, belonging to his best mate Hugo, who yelped and leaned as far away as he could manage.

Dirt was smeared across Magnus's normally impeccable face, and twigs and leaves cascaded from his hair. There was even a tear in his doublet, but what interested Theo most was the look of abject horror on the man's face.

"Master Ironcrest, be a man and tell us what you saw," Master Graymont demanded, adjusting his robes, his own face flushed with excitement.

"The forest came alive," Magnus said in a rush, making a noise of disgust as he flung a beetle off his arm. He recovered and continued. "She commanded it. It was like...like magic."

"Yes, they do have quite a lot of power. As I always tell you, it is something to respect."

"She used it against me, Master. To drive me away. All I did was talk with her, try to woo her as you taught me. But she wouldn't hear it, and she turned the might of the earth against me. Things...came from the earth." Magnus shuddered and gazed at his hands, which were cut and bleeding. "Even the fowl of the air came against me. And she commanded the wind. You never said they could command the wind."

"The ways of the druid are still a mystery to us," Master Graymont replied. "We do not know all they can do, though many of the ancient texts are exactly as you describe. They are denizens of the one they call Tala, a spirit of the earth and sky. Do not tell me you insulted her."

"I did not!" Magnus said, indignantly drawing himself to his full height, which wasn't much to speak of. Even most of the gangly youth at the front had surpassed him. "I praised her. I practically worshiped her. And she not only rejected me, but she also threatened the realm. She said to choose carefully who we send next, because they might not be so fortunate."

"That's hardly a threat to the realm," Theo pointed out, shocking himself with the bold statement. "She said to choose wisely who we send next. Perhaps if you tell us where you went wrong..."

"I told you; I didn't go wrong!" Magnus slammed his hands on the desk in front of him, spitting the words across the room at Theo. "The druid is mad. Years of isolation have turned her mind. She is unapproachable. Measures should be taken."

"What kind of measures do you suggest?" Master Graymont asked sharply.

Magnus tugged at his doublet, straightening. "She should be eradicated. Removed from the forest. She is a danger to suitors and travelers alike. I hate to think what might happen to our queen should she venture through the Morwood to visit Askeland, for instance."

Theo's blood chilled.

"You don't mean to suggest we *kill* the last druid?" Gareth Drayke, one of the younger students, said.

"Yes, I do," Magnus said stiffly.

Silence filled the room.

"We can't kill the last druid. The forest would die, and so would our economy," another student argued.

At least Theo wasn't the only one horrified at Magnus's mad suggestion.

Master Graymont folded his hands into the sleeves of his robes, seemingly content to watch the exchange.

"Then we force her to bear a child and bring the child here to ensure they aren't raised wild and go mad like she has," Magnus sneered. "We've let this go on too long, leaving too much to fate and the whim of these druid women. Why not raise them from birth to accept our kind, living in the city itself?"

"It is part of our agreement with the druids," Theo shot back. "After the war, we swore the forest would remain their home, and later, when the Conception Accords were drawn up, we promised not to remove any druid child from the forest."

"It's time for that to change," Magnus argued. "Because it has led to the unchecked power and feelings of malice towards humans. I pity the fool who attempts to make her theirs after what I just saw. She could have killed me." His voice went up in pitch, and he covered up the fearful tone with a cough.

Could have, but didn't, Theo thought, stopping himself before he wished it had happened. Magnus had been one of his greatest tormentors growing up. It was difficult to have any sympathy for him, especially after the way he talked about the last druid as if she were an animal to be hunted and put down.

"Thank you, Master Ironcrest, for bringing this to our attention. Though I wish you had chosen a more appropriate time, place, and audience." Master Graymont looked pointedly at the young crowd before him, the adolescent boys who now had looks of terror on their faces. They hadn't had the lesson on druid magic yet, and many of them looked entirely shaken at the thought that they had signed up to pursue what could be one of the most powerful women within reach of the realm.

Theo remembered the feeling—the awe, the fear, the respect. He didn't feel the fear so much now. In fact, he felt the opposite.

"I will bring this up with Queen Runa and her council. Meanwhile, get yourself to the dispensary to have those wounds treated. In light of these things, it may be some time before we send someone else—"

"I'll go," Theo said, shooting to his feet so fast the chair behind him fell.

Over a dozen shocked gazes fell on him, but he didn't back down from the scrutiny.

Master Graymont seemed to have lost his words, mouth moving without sound.

Theo cleared his throat again. "I'll be the next suitor."

Laughter broke out near the doorway. Everyone looked to Magnus, who stood leaning against Hugo's desk, shaking his bowed head.

"You're as mad as that druid wench. Maybe you're perfect for each other, but more likely you're signing your death warrant."

Master Graymont coughed. "Yes, Master Blackwin, perhaps you are being a bit hasty. In light of recent events, it would be prudent to wait a month or so until things have calmed down and we have a chance to repair whatever misunderstanding occurred here."

"No, I'll go," Theo said, his heart pounding. He didn't want the druid's encounter with Magnus, which he was certain they weren't getting a full picture of, to poison her against men forever.

"I can't allow it," Master Graymont said, shaking his head. "Not until I've spoken with the queen."

"Then I'll take it to the queen!" Theo insisted, grabbing his bulging pack off the floor and shoving quill, inkwell, and parchment into it. "She'll listen to me. After all, I am her son."

Her failed son. But that didn't matter to Theo as he stormed across the room.

Magnus stepped in front of him, so close Theo could smell his stale breath.

"You think you stand a chance with her? When you've never even seen a woman's bed?" Magnus tsked softly. "If you're hoping she'll take pity on the poor virgin prince, you may want to reconsider. She can be in your arms one moment, at your throat the next. Are you certain you want her to be your first?"

Theo shoved past Magnus, face burning as he left the classroom. He didn't need the reminder that he was a virgin. He'd tried, and failed, to bring himself to utilize the women paid by the realm's coffers for the suitors' training. Something about the whole thing felt wrong to him, and he hadn't wanted his first time to mean nothing.

But Magnus had a point—did he really see himself as a match for a powerful druid woman who reigned over the forest? A princess—no, perhaps a queen—in her own right. And he was a whelp of a prince in comparison, the youngest son of a matron queen who still hadn't born a daughter to be her heir and neither had either of her married sons.

If Theo bore a daughter with the last druid, she would technically have first claim on the throne of Dunholm.

And if he sired the next queen, his mother would finally have a reason to be proud of her youngest son.

His feet quickened their pace, taking him down the stairs and closer to the central area of the palace, where his mother's private chambers stood and where his fate would be decided at last.

BRIA

Sending the suitor packing put Bria in a fantastic mood for the next several days. It had never felt so good to tell a man no; hopefully she'd sent a message to the rest of the realm of men that she wouldn't put up with any nonsense.

Ideally, she wouldn't have to put up with any more suitors either, though she doubted they would accept her blatant refusal forever, considering the terms of agreement made between their people after the war.

But that war had been over three-hundred years ago, and the rest of her people had long ago passed away. Perhaps it was time for new terms. Terms that allowed her to choose who she would make a child with and surrender her life for. If at all.

Voices on the road made Bria's scalp itch, but she fought the urge to hide in the trees. The voice of her father echoed in her mind. "Ye need them, Bria. As much as ye dislike the thought of being dependent on anyone, a life of solitude is no life at all. Trade with them, celebrate with them. Get to know the humans of the forest. It'll prevent the worst of the rumors from being born if people know the truth of ye."

She hadn't done much to dissuade the rumors as of late. She'd been too obsessed with ridding herself of relentless suitors, and the death that awaited her if any of them succeeded in impregnating her. Which they wouldn't, of course, but she still wasn't certain she could condemn the forest to losing its only steward in the event that she should die before bearing the new priestess of Tala.

Gritting her teeth, Bria slowed her steps to a stroll and plastered a welcoming smile onto her face. No, too many teeth. She softened her expression, keeping her lips closed tight.

The humans came into view—three of them, a man and two women, dressed for light travel. Moving from one of the villages into the city for some business, no doubt. One of the women pulled a small handcart that jingled promisingly, and Bria perked up. She could trade with these folk.

"Hail," Bria called, raising a hand.

The conversation between the two women died almost immediately, and the man looked Bria over with a pleasant-enough face at first. Bria saw the transformation gradually overtake his expression as he took in her bare feet, wild mass of untamed curls streaming over her shoulders, and the obvious druid marks in her clothes and the bracelet she wore.

His lip curled in distaste, and he said something quietly to the two women, who nodded and steered themselves to the other side of the road without acknowledging Bria's greeting.

Rude. And odd. Mountain people and village people alike tended to be more welcoming to her than the city folk. But perhaps it had been too long since Bria had gone among them and shared the gifts of Tala.

Or perhaps rumors of what she had done to the suitor a few days prior had already circled far enough to include those who didn't live near the palace. That seemed a stretch, but she couldn't understand why these travelers would give her such a cold greeting.

She would have moved on and given these people their space, but the forest reached out to her in warning.

If she left these people alone, they would die.

She dashed towards them. "Something stalks you. Get down."

The man and two women exchanged glances.

"Is this some kind of trick to make us look like fools?"

"No, of course not," Bria said, her brow furrowing. Why would they think she would trick them?

"The forest is quiet today. Let us go on our way. No need to make things up to frighten us away," the man replied, adjusting his grip on his walking stick.

Bria hushed them, scanning the trees. She reached deep into her magic, opening her sight further. There, as still as a tree itself, sat a creature of shadow so tall and dark that if she hadn't been looking for it, she never would have seen it—an eldritch creature from the southern forest called an umbrawraith.

The umbrawraith had no solid form, and it stalked the living and drained its essence, sucking it in like a hummingbird took nectar. They rarely came out this far, having plenty of food in the deep woods, but something must have drawn this one out.

Bria drew a quick symbol in the air as she ran towards the nearest tree. Her exhale sent the symbol towards the shadow beast.

Sleep, Bria urged.

The umbrawraith startled as the symbol touched it. But instead of falling into a peaceful slumber, it emerged from its hiding place, reaching its amorphous limbs towards Bria and the travelers.

The humans behind her shrieked and cowered together. Of course, they didn't have the sense to run.

If Bria had any, she would abandon them. But the forest, and all who dwelled in it, was her stewardship, even if they were only travelers. Not to mention the rumors that would fly if more people disappeared under her care. Humans would come to destroy the forest they deemed so dangerous. She couldn't let that happen.

Summoning her strength and muttering a quick prayer to Tala, she leapt at the nearest tree, climbing to a safe vantage point almost on level with the top of the umbrawraith. She drew the runes needed to bring forth the Great Staff. Glowing with blue-green light, the outline of a staff appeared with a hooked top, resembling the kind shepherds used while tending their gentle animals.

The umbrawraith *was* a gentle animal, at least when unprovoked. The screams of the humans and Bria's confrontation seemed to have agitated it. It let out a low moan, like something out of the worst nightmares, and thrashed about, making the trees creak. It opened its great dark maw and leaned towards Bria as if to swallow her.

She whirled the glowing crook above her head, inching her way out on the branch.

The umbrawraith followed the circling staff, its head moving back and forth as if hypnotized. It had no visible eyes, but Bria knew she had it when its shapeless limbs relaxed down by its sides, its mouth went slack, and its attention trained on her. Pride rushed through her. She had corralled smaller shadow beasts before, but nothing with this much will. She had to send it back to the southern forest where it couldn't harm people.

Still spinning the staff, she sketched more symbols in the air with her free hand, shoving them forward. The glowing marks leapt towards the umbrawraith and multiplied, circling it in a rotating band. A second band appeared, moving the opposite direction.

"Return to your place," Bria shouted, gesturing with an illuminated finger.

The umbrawraith followed where she pointed, turning its massive, amorphous form away from the cowering humans. It seemed to swallow the forest floor as it moved, leaving rotten vegetation in its wake. It couldn't affect something as old and strong as the tallest trees, but the brush, moss, and other less rooted plants succumbed to its influence, leaving a brown trail where it passed.

Bria's shoulders slumped in relief as the umbrawraith passed out of sight. Her breath still came in quick gasps, as if she'd run a mile. The Great Staff burned in her hand, reminding her to release the runespell before it consumed her. She drew the banishing runes, sending another prayer to Tala, this one of thanks for her guidance and protection.

She jumped to a lower branch and swung from there to the ground, landing in front of the humans, who glanced around the forest and clutched each other, still trembling.

The man licked his lips. "W-will it return?"

Bria shook her head. "No. It will return to its home in the southern forest and likely sleep for a hundred years or more."

"Are there more like it?" A woman asked, her voice shrill and her eyes wide.

Bria hesitated. If she told the truth, would they spread the word and petition to have the forest burned? Humans were unpredictable at best and more destructive than any natural phenomenon could ever be.

"They have their place in the forest," she said carefully, gesturing at the ground. "They help make way for new growth. Watch."

She walked over to the rotted path the umbrawraith had left and knelt down, waving her hand over the ground, whispering to Tala. A surge of power went through her, smaller than when she had wielded the Great Staff, but no less magnificent. Tiny green sprouts wriggled their way out of the soil, leaves and buds forming, then blossoming with tiny white flowers.

Bria's breath caught at the beauty of life renewed. These tiny flowers would eventually fill this area, a carpet of green and white.

She looked to the three travelers, all of whom had mixed expressions of awe and terror. She tried on a smile, to look less threatening, but it was no use. They might now be more afraid of her than the umbrawraith, and all she had done was save their lives and grow some flowers for them.

"We best be going now," the man stammered, waving his staff down the road, in the direction of Dunholm.

"Tread lightly in the forest and you'll have nothing to fear," Bria replied, though she knew they wouldn't believe her. "Tala protect you," she added.

The humans all but fled from her, walking as fast as they could, glancing occasionally up at the trees as if they would come to life and chase them from the forest.

Bria was tempted to make their nightmare come true, but she restrained herself. They were harmless, after all. She just hoped they would remember her kindness when the fear left them. Those were rumors she could handle.

Her mind puzzled over everything that had happened as she left the road and wound through the trees towards her destination. It had once been a thoroughfare, where people from all around were welcome to visit as they came from the mountains and other rural parts of the realm. But the roads had long since been claimed by Tala's influence, covered with fallen trees and overgrown so they had become nearly impassable. Only this secret road, made by the footsteps of Bria's ancestors, remained as a clear way to get to this particular place.

It was not a place Bria visited often.

Bria hitched the strap of her bag over her head to keep it more secure as she climbed over a crumbling stone wall and made her way around moss-covered towers that were built with such craftsmanship they once might have appeared to blend into the trees that now wrapped around them.

It was all that remained of the home of the once-great Morwood Druid clans.

Her stomach hollowed out, aching with echoes of the pain that haunted the once-vaulted halls. Her feet shuffled almost imperceptibly on the leaf-littered path, the decaying plant matter carpet now dotted with new gold and red leaves fresh-fallen from the boughs above.

It felt both sacred and eerie. More eerie when Bria's eyes roved over the rotted, lichen-covered bones of the dead. Human and druid remains alike sprawled across the ruins, the human bones blackened with decay, the druid ones filled with fungi and even flowers at times, Tala's gift from beyond the grave making them useful and beautiful even in death.

They almost seemed as if they might come to life, to again tend and guard the forest. But that was wishful thinking. And insane thinking, at that. Could she be so desperate for the company of her own kind that she would wish for re-animated skeletons to talk to?

Father was right. I do need to talk to people. Someone other than those empty-headed suitors, anyway.

Her heart twinged with a familiar longing, and her feet slowed. She trailed her hand along the stones, considering the last time she'd seen her father.

In her twenty-first year, almost four years ago. He'd kissed her forehead and chuckled when she insisted he stay.

"You don't want your old man mucking up your chances with the parade of suitors you are to receive. Your first one will arrive soon. If I'm here, I won't let any of them get close to you. Not when I know their intentions towards my daughter, duty to the realm be damned."

It had made Bria laugh, too. A naive laugh. She hadn't known how trying it would be to entertain man after man intruding on her space in the woods. They'd come far apart at first, every six months or so, growing closer together as she reached her mid-twenties. As if they expected her fertile time to happen any moment. But her mother hadn't been fertile until her late twenties, and Bria expected she would be much the same.

She wished her father had stayed. Wished she could go to visit him, but he hadn't told her where he was going, which hurt more than anything else. He claimed she came first and duty second, but when the time had come, he'd followed the rules to the letter. Leave the druid in her wilderness and don't look back.

She might as well be property of the queen for how much control she had over her own life and destiny, and deep down, it terrified her. What future would her child have if she didn't break the curse? The same one Bria faced now. Perhaps worse, if human and druid relations faltered further.

Bria would never let that happen. She just had to find the missing link, the cure for the curse that would kill her when she bore her first child.

Her encounter with Magnus's desperation had renewed the urgency to seek out a secret location. According to her father, her mother had looked for it nonstop leading up to Bria's birth. The crystal caves, he'd said it was called.

The few writings available in the modern vernacular that she understood claimed that the caves were a sort of well for Tala's power, and that if anything could heal the druid's fertility, stopping the senseless deaths of each mother as she was made, it would be this place.

But Bria, as her mother before her, had roamed through every part of the forest, using her druid powers to sense places where Tala's power gathered, and still it eluded her. She had prayed to Tala, begged her to reveal the cave's hiding place, but the goddess remained silent. Loving, but silent.

Bria had come to the ruins to plead again for freedom from her fear of the curse. Surely Tala wanted her daughter to remain safe. If the queen sent more men like Magnus, impatient and pushy and self-indulgent, Bria's hand would be forced to take a life to protect herself.

As a druid, she swore to hold life sanctified. She would not take a life unless Tala blessed the taking, even for her own sustenance, which is why she ate only that which did not disturb the thriving life around her. Occasionally, in times of deep winter and famine, Tala provided an animal.

It seemed unlikely to Bria that Tala would kill a man for Bria the same way she sometimes took the life of a deer to feed her priestess. Unfortunately.

Bria stopped at the beginning of the labyrinth to the center of the ruins. No walls encased the labyrinth. Instead, flat, rune-covered stones wound around in a spiral, representing the continuation of life and the non-linear path to enlightenment. She could have strode in a straight line across the stones, but doing so would defeat the purpose of contemplation and intention one was meant to carry following the spiral.

She stepped onto the path and leaves swirled about her bare feet, running across her toes. Around she went, keeping her mind focused on her intent: to speak to the goddess Tala, and be heard.

Tightening her grip on her satchel, Bria reached the center of the labyrinth. A wide-rimmed bronze bowl, weathered by decades exposed to the elements, rested on top of a stone pillar, bringing it to the height of Bria's waist.

Bria pulled her satchel forward and rummaged within it, pulling out ingredients one at a time. She fumbled with the herb bundle for a moment, almost dropping it before she placed it inside the bowl. She sprinkled flower petals, and the tiny piece of rabbit bone she'd procured, creating the patterns she'd seen explained in the rituals in her books.

Communion with the goddess was a sacred rite with specific guidelines to be observed. She pulled her hood up over her hair, covering the wild red curls, and bowed her head before beginning the fire chant.

She drew flint and steel from her satchel and struck them over the ritual offerings in the bowl, the fire sparking hungrily and quickly covering the bundle of dried herbs. Bria chanted until the offering had burned away, leaving the bone alone in a pile of hot ash. Her feet ached, but she remained, watching the smoke curl without form.

She dipped a stick into the ash, bringing some out to cool before using it to draw a rune on her forehead and two others on each cheek, then tossed the stick to the side and took up a new chant, hands pressed together, face raised to the sky.

A shift of energies occurred within her, something clicking into place. She lowered her head, watching the smoke that billowed now, against reason since the fire had gone out some time before. But the smoke flowed, forming a ring in the air, and Bria could not see the other side of the labyrinth and ruins that she knew stood opposite the pedestal.

Instead, a vision moved, somewhat blurrily within the smoke ring.

Dark shadows, shifting and clashing. Bria squinted, barely making out the forms of humans and druids coming together in battle. The image faded into blackness, and the sounds of women screaming—no, not screaming. Moaning? Bellowing?

Bria didn't have a word for the sound, as if the women were going through something arduous. The image revealed a woman kneeling, skirts hiked up, pulling a baby from between her legs and kissing it softly before she lay on the ground and did not stir again. Hands took the infant from the dead mother. Again, and again, and again.

She forced herself to watch, even though fear gripped her heart. This would be her fate if she did not break the curse. Why show her the fate she already knew?

The image went dark, and she expected the smoke to clear, but then a sun broke through the darkness, parting it like water around a stone in a river. Golden light filled the vision, and Bria's heart surged with hope.

This was it—proof that this curse of death would end. It would end with her. It had to.

"Show me the caves, Tala. I am ready!" Bria cried.

The smoke broke apart, fading so rapidly Bria barely blinked and it was gone, just a wisp floating up from the charred offering in the bowl.

Anger and agony flashed through her in equal parts. She clenched her hands, resisting the urge to knock the bowl from its stand and scatter the offering. It would be disrespectful, sacrilegious, even. Not to mention an immense ingratitude for what Tala had given her.

A vision of the past and a sun breaking forth. Hope. But what did it mean? Could there have been a clue hidden in the vision? Something Bria had been too distracted by her intentions to see?

Why couldn't she have the answer now instead of these vague images?

Bria sat cross-legged at the center of the labyrinth, meditating on the vision until dusk descended and the birds sang their evening songs. There were fewer of them around now, a sure sign that the time of the Gathering had crept up on her, and the days and nights were beginning to reverse, until the Sleeping would be upon them, and even the goddess Tala would take her rest beneath a frigid coating of ice until spring broke forth.

She had work to do before the cold season descended. She would have to seek out the cave on another day.

Joints and muscles complained as she unfolded her legs and stood, brushing off her clothes before unwinding the path out of the labyrinth. She walked home in contemplative and admittedly confused silence, grateful that she didn't have another unsettling encounter with any travelers on the road.

THEO

L IKE A RAT ABOUT to enter a wyvern's den to steal a scrap of its dinner, Theo waited at the entrance to the reception hall where the queen, his mother, took audiences with her citizens and dignitaries alike.

She knew he was there. The page had gone inside ages ago to announce his presence. Either she was caught up in some negotiation, or she was making him wait, a trick she often utilized to put her opponents on edge.

But her youngest son was no opponent. He represented the singular biggest disgrace to her rule since she'd taken the throne—she hadn't born a daughter. And his birth had nearly killed her, so it was decided that she would not bear any more children.

Even taking his time changing his clothes and freshening up before seeking her audience hadn't quelled the nerves that gripped him in a stranglehold.

The doors swung open in front of him and Theo jumped, then straightened, jamming his loose shirt tails into his pants at the last second, adjusting his glasses on his face to be certain they were straight, and giving his wavy brown hair a once over using his fingers as a comb.

A man stepped out, hands in his pockets, an expression of smug satisfaction spread across his chiseled face.

Magnus Ironcrest, looking far more put together than he had the hour previous in his frantic state.

Theo raised an eyebrow. "What business do you have with the queen?" *And how did you get here before me?*

"Someone had to inform her majesty of the druid's betrayal of our contract."

"Her mother refused far more suitors than she has. I think you're just sore she saw through your charm to the snake underneath," Theo replied. What emboldened him in the face of a bully like Magnus, he didn't know. The man had tormented him all the years they'd been under Master Graymont's tutelage together. But something about thinking of how Magnus had tried—and failed—where everyone assumed he would succeed seemed to put them on the same level.

Magnus was a failure now, too.

The man tossed his head. "It was her attitude, more than the number of her rejections, that led me to this conclusion. She's dangerous and needs to be put down or reigned in."

"And you're the best one to do that?" Theo remarked.

"No," Magnus drawled, crossing his arms and grinning wickedly at Theo. "You are. I have...other duties, set upon me by the queen herself. I no longer pity you for the role you must play."

"What are you talking about?" Theo asked. Inside the reception hall, the herald called his name, formally announcing him. The queen might have made him wait, but she wouldn't show him the same patience.

Magnus smirked as he strolled away.

Theo rushed into the reception hall a few steps before realizing he looked undignified. He slowed, striding until he halted at the center spot where countless others had stood before, looking across at his mother on the slightly-raised dais where her throne resided.

She seemed...out of sorts. Her face was paler than usual, though her cheeks were flushed, and a few strands of hair that were normally slicked back against her head had fallen free. Looking delicate and almost vulnerable, his mother stared out the window, hardly seeming to notice his presence. Not at all like her militantly focused self.

And the places on either side of her, normally occupied by Theo's older brothers who acted as counselors, were empty. In fact, the entire room was empty, except for the herald, who stood in position at the doors. Even the guards were absent.

How had seeing Magnus put her in such a state? Had the news about the druid upset her so much?

Theo cleared his throat. He wasn't meant to speak first, but the sight of her worried him so much he couldn't resist.

"Are you well, mother?"

The queen glanced at him, her hand trailing on her throat, which Theo realized looked red, as if it had been grabbed. But surely no one had put a hand on her in her own castle.

"I will forgive your insolence, youngest son of mine. Your inquiry is, I hope, without guile. I don't expect political intrigue from you; you've never shown any ambition for it. Unlike your brothers."

She finally looked at him, a long, hard stare with her steely green eyes that on many days, like today, seemed more gray than green, reflecting the overcast sky that currently covered the sun.

Theo swallowed. "Have you...sent them away?"

The queen laughed. "No. Innocent boy. I could not. Not yet. But if they make any move against the throne publicly, I'll see to it. I simply—" she waved one fair, thin hand in the air. "—sent them away for a moment. I'm tired of their arguing. They will be angry if I make them sit out of this conversation, however. They have been sent for and should be here shortly."

A stiff silence fell over the hall. The queen seemed content to sit and stare out the window, occasionally glancing at him, fingers moving from trailing down her throat to resting in her lap.

Theo, as usual, didn't know how to navigate this situation. He could start speaking before his brothers got there, but his mother had made it clear she would wait until they arrived before continuing. He could speak of something else, of his hobbies and pursuits, but she held no interest in what he did in his spare time, unless it was of some advantage to her. His studies were useless, unless he had some information that gave her an edge over the neighboring realms. He'd learned long ago how little she valued what he had to offer.

So he remained silent, hands clasped behind him, until the loud voices of his brothers exchanging affectionate insults echoed down the corridor outside, and the herald moved to let them in, only to be thrust backward as the doors swung open, admitting the two brothers.

Like night and day, one with raven-dark hair—that was Damien, born of the queen's union with one from the Nightfist clan. And the other with long golden-hair, not unlike a mane, the tell-tale genetic trait of one from the Goldenvane clan. Felix, the oldest.

The two jostled each other a moment before composing themselves, bowing to the queen, and pausing a moment to let the herald announce them before they descended on Theo.

"Theo!" Felix cried, ruffling his hair.

Damien nodded to him, the smirk that seemed a permanent fixture on his face growing more amused than smug.

"We haven't seen you in ages. Thought you'd gone and holed up somewhere in the atheneum and died," Felix joked.

"I haven't seen you much yourselves," Theo replied, his entire body rigid. He hated these men who had once been boys, older than him by years, each from a prominent and respected clan, each seen as a success in their own right.

Damien had betrothed himself to a princess from Askeland, allying them with Dunholm and bringing peace and the best trades seen in decades. Their wedding would happen soon—Theo hadn't cared enough to recall the date, but it was soon. These things took years to settle.

Felix, despite his joking nature, had made a name for himself in the queen's military and was considered something of a prodigy. They were in a time of peace currently, but he'd cleaned up her soldiers and they were more organized, skilled, and more efficient than ever.

Theo looked them in the eyes and realized with some shock that sometime in the past few years, he'd finally reached their height. Exceeded it with Damien, who actually had to look up at him.

"You still studying druid-seduction?" Felix asked with a wink at Damien.

"Master Graymont must have taught you everything he knows by now. It's time you studied in the Red Hall," Damien added.

Theo flushed. "I have," he mumbled, glancing away. The men and women of the Red Hall were paid prostitutes, commissioned by the queen to pleasure those who resided with her. She didn't hold for sexual tension causing mischief within her walls, and the students of the class Theo had taken were famous for their frequent visits. It was no secret what Theo had been trained for—to get into the druid's bed.

It frustrated him that so much of the class had focused on physical matters when he was certain that any respectable woman cared about far more than how good a man was in bed. He hadn't spent much time in the Red Hall, especially compared with suitors like Magnus, and none of them let him forget it.

"There is a matter of great importance to discuss today, my sons," the queen said.

Theo couldn't have been more grateful for an interruption than in that moment. If they'd been allowed to continue, as they had in the past, it would end with them dragging him down to the Red Hall and selecting a lady that came highly recommended from each of them, then they would lock him in a room with both—it had happened before, and they weren't memories Theo liked to revisit.

Then again, it had been years since they'd tormented him that way. Eventually, they'd gotten bored, when Theo got over his adolescent emotions and had learned to figuratively play dead, making him far too boring for them to spend their time on.

Felix gave him another slap on the shoulder and sauntered to the dais, sitting in a chair to the right of his mother.

Damien took the left, and together, the three of them seemed a complete set. Theo wouldn't fit anywhere in that picture, as had been made painfully obvious last year when his mother had commissioned a family portrait, and Theo, standing awkwardly aloof, had stood out like a sore spot on a lady's face.

It wasn't his lanky build or his sandy hair. No, when compared with the stark contrasts of his brothers' almost exotic features and his mother's commanding presence, he simply disappeared into the background, a mere shadow. Perhaps that was why the artist had depicted him nearly as one, blending him in with the scenery like a piece of furniture.

He wished he were furniture now, with three predatory gazes focused on him, as if each one were puzzling how to best use him for their gain. He wouldn't put it past them. They were all strategists, moving pieces about the realms like pawns in a game.

He just wanted some peace to read his books.

"Your brothers might not have heard the news, so I will congratulate you publicly on putting yourself forth as the next suitor of the druid," his mother said.

Theo startled at what sounded like *praise* coming from the queen. She never said anything positive to him. He reflexively adjusted his glasses.

Felix shifted in his seat with excitement. "Truly, Theo? And you didn't tell us? You rascal."

Damien's eyes widened. "Congratulations indeed. A conquest on the horizon at last. I was beginning to think ambition passed you over in the womb."

"The recent failure of Magnus Ironcrest to procure the maiden's attention seemed to have sparked the fire at last. Competition does wonders for a young man."

"A pretty girl helps, I'm sure," Felix said with a grin.

Theo swallowed his discomfort at the suggestion in his brother's voice. Everyone saw him that way—trained as an escort, almost like those who occupied the Red Hall. A fair number of his classmates had joined them, after all. But Theo wasn't like that, and they knew it made him uncomfortable. They reveled in it, even.

"Thank you," Theo said awkwardly. "I aim to serve in whatever capacity I can."

"Question is, have you spent time learning outside your books?" Felix asked, raising his brow. "You won't stand a chance if you haven't got a clue what you're—"

"Enough, Felix," the queen said with a sharpness she rarely used with her oldest son. She used a hand to slick back some of the strands of hair that had fallen free from her bun and straightened, some of the flush gone from her now, looking more herself than when Theo had first walked in.

"Theodore Blackwin, I have reservations about the attempt you wish to make. Your life is yours, and if you should like to forfeit it, I have no argument. But the loss of the druid would be too much for this realm to bear, and I am concerned that sending another suitor so soon after the recent incident would drive the druid daughter further into madness."

Damien and Felix shared glances, whispering. Apparently the rumors hadn't caught up with them yet, which was unusual. Nearly an entire day had passed, after all, and their sources were usually quite proficient at keeping up with the rumors.

The queen paused, as if listening to the whispering of her advisors.

"Magnus Ironcrest was attacked by the druid yesterday morning," she said quietly. "He claims she mistook earnest pursuit as a threat and told him to warn the realm against sending any others. He believes she has violated her contract with us, and that action should be taken. I have some mind to send a contingent to the forest to teach her a lesson." Her eyes flashed, and fear took hold of Theo's mind.

He cleared his throat. "Magnus is a...passionate fellow. Perhaps he intimidated her. The druid, I mean. He doesn't know the art of subtlety, of biding one's time."

"He was with her for nearly a month," the queen replied. "Some would call that patience."

"Not if she is predisposed to mistrust. She must be handled with...delicacy," Theo finished weakly, uncertain what he was even saying.

"And you believe that you can handle her?" Damien asked, one eyebrow raised.

"I believe..." Theo said, struggling to find the words, "that I can offer a different approach than has been tried before." If he was correct in his theories, earning her trust and friendship first would take time. Months. But no one would miss him. They would hardly notice his absence. And the longer he spent with the druid in the woods, the more the rumors would spin that he had succeeded.

The queen tightened her lips into a thin line, her fingers tapping the arm of the chair beside her.

"I sense your eagerness, and as I said, I will not stop you. But I require something more, Theodore Blackwin."

Theo's relief vanished at the queen's words, and a chill settled over him, sinking deeper than a draft from the window could.

"You will bring her here to meet me. At the palace, in three months' time, pregnant with your child, or you will be enlisted in the army under your brother's tutelage. You will make something of yourself, he will be sure of it. No son of mine will be seen as a failure."

"And if I succeed," Theo blurted, sending the entire room into shocked silence, "you will build an atheneum in the Morwood. A place with thousands of books one can study in peace. And you will let me reside there all of my days, undisturbed."

Theo nearly fainted when the queen inclined her head in agreement.

"Very well. Perhaps I have overlooked your potential. May it be as you have said."

Trembling with adrenaline, hands sweaty and shaking, Theo bowed and strode from the room. The moment he'd crossed through the doors, what he'd done sank deep into his heart.

He had sold a woman's soul for a library.

BRIA

BASKET IN HAND, BRIA stood at the edge of the riverbank, plucking berries with a vengeance. She still had no insight into her vision from the previous day, and she'd woken up irritated, her mind spinning with possibilities and wondering at hidden symbols.

Two birds swooped past overhead, twittering their love songs to each other. They landed on a branch nearby, and the male postured, flaring his bright blue feathers as if trying to impress the female.

"Shouldn't you two be headed towards Askeland for the Sleeping? The Morwood isn't a friendly place for lovers this time of year," Bria said aloud.

She watched the couple for a time. Such odd behavior for birds when the frigid months were coming. She shook her head and returned to berry picking. She wanted to make jam and dry the fruit into strips. These particular berries grew during the Gathering, and they made a delightful addition to stores for the cold season. She could, of course, ask Tala to produce anything she needed at any time of the year. She wouldn't starve by any means, but it was considered respectful to use the resources that freely grew in the forest and not waste the goddess's offerings.

That reminded Bria that she needed to pray for a wild goat offering of milk later, so she might make cheese.

Almost the instant she thought of it, twigs crackled, and a horned head appeared from the flaming red brush across the river. It was a magnificent white buck goat. Several brown and gold females stood with him, foraging.

Bria nearly dropped her basket. She stared open-mouthed at the goats as they came down the embankment and drank from the river, before spreading out on the grassy knoll above the water.

The buck raised his head and sniffed the air, and Bria noticed one of the nearby does wagging her tail rapidly, and then she urinated.

Sniffing with curiosity, the buck stuck his head in the urine stream.

Bria made a face. It was entirely natural, but she was grateful her kind didn't need to smell the pheromones in their urine in order to find a fertile match. There would be signs when her body was preparing for its first month-long fertile period. The fever she would get before her cycle started didn't sound fun, and plants blooming wherever she walked would be embarrassing. But she hadn't caught sight of either yet, and she was more than halfway through her first decade.

Every druid woman had three fertile periods, one each decade, each lasting a month. Perhaps she wasn't fertile at all, though that was likely a false hope.

She popped a few berries into her mouth, absently picking and occasionally glancing at the goat herd, watching with curiosity as the buck chased the female through the trees while she flagged him with her tail, until eventually he mounted.

Conquest successful, the buck went back to grazing, though occasionally he wandered close to another female when she urinated, sniffing curiously.

Typical male. Two seconds with one, and he wanted another. Bria snorted to herself, but more amused than anything. They were animals, driven by the singular need to multiply and prevent the dying out of their species.

That thought filled her with guilt, and she stopped a berry mid-way to her mouth. Why didn't she feel the same? She was a mammal, same as the goats, and the last of her species. Surely it wasn't healthy for her to be so against the continuation of her kind?

But then, the goats weren't self-aware. The does wouldn't likely die when they dropped their kid. They would multiply, their herd would grow. They would thrive.

Bearing a child would kill Bria unless she found the caves and unlocked the curse.

She abandoned the berry bush, setting down her basket and making her way to the river edge. She dipped her feet in, relishing the deliciously cold water, then washed sticky berry juice from her hands. She kept the goats in her periphery. None of them seemed to have a kid currently, though there were more moving further in the trees. She needed a nursing mother to get milk. She would have to fetch her bucket, as well, and properly ask Tala to provide.

She splashed water on her face, then took up her basket and headed back towards her cottage.

The trees thinned somewhat as she spotted the sloped, tiled roof. Grunting caught her hearing, and as she crested the hill, she caught a glimpse of two black bears bumping into each other, one jumping up as if to mount...

Bria groaned internally. It seemed Tala had a message of her own to send. Three mating couples in the space of half a morning? And at the time of the Gathering, no less? Bears, as Bria knew, mated at the height of the Warming. They had no business coupling so late in the season, not when they should be gearing up for the Sleeping by eating their fill to get ready for their long, isolated hibernation.

She leaned her back against a tree trunk, listening to the bears snuffle and wrestle, hoping they would leave soon so she could return home and grab her bucket before the goat herd moved on.

You don't need to be so heavy handed with the hints, Bria said in a half-serious prayer, trying to keep the scolding she felt out of her thoughts. She didn't want to make her creator think she was ungrateful, but surely Tala understood why Bria didn't want to find a mate at this time.

The wind brushed her cheek, and Bria leaned into the gentle touch from her goddess, listening carefully to the leaves. But they were just leaves, not some divine voice whispering to her.

Reveal the location of the caves. Then I'll find a partner. Surely you don't intend for us to die out completely?

The sounds of the bears faded, but Bria stood a while longer, listening to the trees and other sounds of the forest. A lone bird called out, and another answered, their unique songs moving back and forth among the trees.

When it became clear that Tala wouldn't grace her with a response, Bria peeled herself away from the comforting bark of the oak and retrieved her milking bucket, determined to not waste the day simply because her goddess was being mysterious.

Fortunately, she found the goat herd where she left it, and as evidence that Tala was not angry at her insolence, Bria found two females with nursing kids among the herd. They allowed her to squat at their sides and take some of their milk, which Bria did gratefully and thoughtfully, ensuring there would be plenty for the goats' babies.

Milk pail full, Bria went back to her cottage, watching warily for the mating animals that had been coupling in front of her all morning. If Tala were a goddess predisposed to cruelty, Bria would have thought the whole thing a joke.

But her goddess seemed to be in earnest, perhaps not wanting Bria to be alone during her fertile time.

Bria had no personal experience with the raging hormones that the books and journals on her shelf warned her of. The fertile month was apparently a highly volatile time for a druid, driving women and men alike to coupling with abandon, even in public.

The thought made her blush. Except for the few travelers and villagers she'd encountered now and then, she'd lived alone with only her father for company, since her mother had died at her birth. She was reserved in conversation with strangers as a result of her isolation, and felt far more comfortable talking with Tala and the plants and animals of the forest than with human beings.

It was difficult to imagine, as she strained the hairs from the goat milk and started preparing it for cheese making, that there would come a time when she would willingly throw herself at a man without reservation.

A sort of thrill went through her at the thought. She'd been with men before, taking advantage of the willing suitors who visited to ensure she fully understood what went into the mating process, but always on her own terms. Always controlled, measured, and well-thought through.

She shuddered to think what might happen if someone like Magnus came along while she was in a vulnerable, suggestive state. But what protections could she put into place? She had no weapons other than her magic and a single dagger she barely knew how to use. It would be useless if hormones overrode every rational thought in her mind out of a need to fulfill her biological purpose.

For now, she would stay busy, hope her threats to the realm were enough to keep the next suitor away for some time yet, and pray to Tala that she would have years more to find the cave and break this curse before she became with child.

6

THEO

OBSTINATE. CONTRARY. IMPROPER. LAUGHED *at me.* Theo scanned down the list of entries in the experience log kept by those who had attempted to win the druid's affections. The entries were tinged with the bitterness of embarrassment and failure.

Closed-minded, stuck-up individuals the lot of them.

The more Theo read, the more the words seemed to morph, their meanings, though not always written out distinctly, coming off the page and sinking into his mind, forming a greater picture of the druid daughter named Bria Glenraven.

Hides her hurt with amusement. Desperate for a cure. Untrusting of men or humans in general? Likes bread and being barefoot. Lonely.

Theo made some notes. One of the problems with the current suitor system was that while they knew an incredible amount about the woman they were meant to solicit, she knew hardly anything of them. It didn't seem like a good way to earn her trust, to start out revealing how much they had studied her, like she was a specimen, rather than a person.

Perhaps a better approach would be to feign a lack of knowledge, to discover the hidden parts of her the way one might learn of anyone or anything?

Theo gazed off in the distance, tapping his chin.

His thoughts were interrupted a moment later by the sound of the door to his private room clicking open. The knock came after, followed by a muffled cough.

Theo closed his eyes, sighing. "Come in, Master Graymont."

"Ah, you were expecting me," Master Graymont said, shuffling into the room and closing the door behind him. His gaze roved over the books and papers sprawled across Theo's desk, and he tsked, as if disappointed.

"I know you are a man of book learning, Master Blackwin, but I would think there wouldn't be much left to learn now. Aside from getting out there in the woods and putting all that knowledge to the test, that is."

Theo took his glasses off his face and made a show of cleaning them to settle his nerves at the implication in Master Graymont's tone. "There is always more to learn. This is my third time through these documents, with the addition of Magnus's notes, and I've filled five pages with new conclusions and information. How could that not be valuable?"

"Bria Glenraven is a flesh and blood woman. A druid, yes, but she is no simple creature you can woo with words on a page."

"Yosef tried poetry. As did Ames. She showed an appropriate amount of disdain for their attempts, I believe. Six others ran a flattery campaign, including Magnus. Two tried the straight-forward approach and attempted to create a contract with her. One bribed her with land. I can clearly see what hasn't worked, Master Graymont. The picture has been painted quite clear. Bria Glenraven is not opposed to casual relations at her discretion, but she will not promise away her child. The question is, why?"

"Casual relations are exactly why I am here," Master Graymont said. Theo rubbed his hands down his face, failing to suppress a groan. His mentor raised his voice. "As the druid nears her fertile time, she will become more difficult to manage, as she realizes what is happening, and then she will melt like butter under any sort of attention. It is a matter of patience and diligence so she doesn't throw you out of her forest fortress before her hormones make it impossible for her to refuse you."

"Precisely what I'm concerned with. Her tolerance level has seemed to max out around six weeks. Magnus failed in two."

"We all knew Magnus would fail," Master Graymont said coolly, hands tucking into his robe sleeves. "You, on the other hand...I've looked forward to the day when you would try your hand."

Theo blinked in shock. "Me?"

He'd been the butt of every joke made in class. A skinny, acne-covered teenager who bloomed far later than the others. The one who would not—could not, in fact—bring himself to "practice" one of the most important aspects of the class. How could he be the one his instructor looked forward to watching make his attempt?

"Yes, you," Master Graymont said, his eyes widening and his hands emerging from his sleeves to gesture energetically at Theo. "You know more about the druids than any of the others, but that isn't the advantage I see. You are patient, biding your time. And you are naturally likable. It's almost impossible to hate or distrust you. You've cultivated this persona of someone who can have insults hurled at you, yet you return again and again. It's precisely the kind of idiocy needed to win over the druid."

Theo scoffed, placing his glasses back on. He glanced down at his notes again, frowning as the words appeared blurry. His shirt had smudged his glasses more than cleared them. "So I can talk to her. She might not throw me out, but when she does get to her fertile time, she'll find out how woefully unprepared I am. All the books in the world can't teach me that."

"Once she is fertile, she will care about nothing else but taking you to bed until she is with child. You'll see—your inexperience may do you some favors. But, even with your patience, I fear our friend Master Ironcrest is right, to some degree. The druid has turned against us."

"Or against dying in the name of continuing the curse," Theo said, not entirely certain how he'd come to that conclusion. Then again, it was written here, in snippets of recorded conversation, told by spited men.

She seeks caves like a hound put out to flush the hills, but there are no caves in the Morwood. We searched for days on end, to no avail. And they are on no map that I've requisitioned from the cartographers' records, one entry said.

"Master Blackwin? Are you quite all right?"

"We've been blind," Theo muttered. He ran his hands through his hair, almost certainly making it stick up like one of the raging self-proclaimed prophets that collected coins on the streets of the city. The caves were the key. They were important to her in some way. What if he helped her find them?

"Yes! I've been trying to convince the queen of this for years," Master Graymont said, clapping his hands together.

Theo looked at him in confusion. The man couldn't read his mind, so how could they be thinking the same thing?

"We've ignored the most critical information. I knew you would see it too. There is a much more efficient way to make the druid...more agreeable." His instructor struggled to get his hand from his pocket a moment before producing a piece of parchment and slapping it on the table, partially unrolled.

Theo tugged on the edge, and Master Graymont drew out the opposite side, exposing the contents.

"This is...what is this?" Theo asked, looking at the equations filling the parchment. It didn't seem to have anything to do with caves.

Master Graymont pointed to the bottom corner, where scrawled handwriting detailed what looked like measurements.

"It's a recipe?" Theo asked, shoulders slumping. His teacher hadn't had the same idea. In a way, it gave him relief. Someone had probably tried helping the druid find the caves, anyway. It was obvious.

"Yes!" Master Graymont said emphatically. "A recipe to the druid's heart. Or rather, her womb. I've studied their biology extensively. You hear me talk about it in class, but even there I don't share everything." He jabbed at the scroll. "This is my life's work. For years, I worked late into the night, eschewing all else so I could answer one question—what would we do if a druid one day refused to entertain the suitors the queen sent? And I've cracked it. Well, I think I have. The only thing left is to try it on a druid."

"Try what, Master Graymont?" Theo asked, dread forming in the pit of his stomach. Nothing good could come of this, he was certain.

"Bringing on the druid's heat, lad," Master Graymont's voice cracked, and his eyes seemed to spark with a mad energy. "All it takes is a tea brewed. It's been extremely effective on the human women who have tried it, bringing on their monthly menses more predictably. And they fall with child very quickly. I've only had a handful of failed cases—"

"You're talking about drugging her into a hormonal state where she won't refuse to have intercourse with me?" Theo asked, horrified.

"She could still refuse, of course. We're not altering her state of mind. None of these herbs do that. These simply bring on her fertile time. I've tested them extensively, and it's possible we might induce fertility more frequently. Instead of once every ten years, what if it were once every five? Or once a year, even? Failed suitors and failed attempts wouldn't jeopardize the realm and drain resources the way they do now. Instead, we could simply give the druid this tea and induce the fertile cycle again, sooner."

Theo understood what the man was saying. The logical side of his mind agreed—it was much more practical than waiting until the druid came into her time naturally, especially if she was unwilling. But it was underhanded and dishonest and it made Theo's skin crawl.

"What do you think, lad?" Master Graymont asked, a note of uncertainty creeping into his voice.

Theo spoke slowly and clearly, trying to ensure that his words were not misunderstood. "Not only does it seem dangerous to mess with a woman's biology that way, experimenting on her without her understanding or consent, but it is manipulation to the highest degree, and I won't participate in it. I do this on my own merit, or I don't do it at all."

"You simply haven't caught the vision yet. I thought you had—never mind. Take it with you. Then, if you change your mind, it's at hand." Master Graymont drew a metal tin from his other pocket, dropping it to the side of the scroll, which he then rolled deftly and tucked into his sleeve. His expression was neutral, but Theo sensed the man's disappointment.

"I am sorry, Master. I–I can't bring myself to do it."

"Not even for that atheneum you want built?" Master Graymont raised his eyebrows. "The druid would come to no harm, and you would get everything you wanted."

Except dying upon the birth of her child if she fell pregnant, Theo thought. He kept the words to himself and shook his head.

"Using this...method...it would be like cheating."

Cheating her of her dignity, and me of my integrity, Theo added in his mind.

Master Graymont's lips tightened. "Best of luck then, lad. And mind the trees."

The instructor swept from the room, leaving a cloud of frustration and disappointment in his wake.

Theo trembled with a confusing jumble of feelings, frozen at his desk staring at that metal tin. He wanted to prove himself, to escape the manipulating reach of his mother.

But not like that.

There was no more putting it off. It was time to pack.

Theo gathered up the books and papers, organizing them into neat stacks, placing papers together and rolling them up, and tying them in a leather holder for protection and ease of transportation.

His gaze drifted to the tin sitting on his desk as he rounded the room collecting items of clothing, boots, and other supplies. He made a trip to the kitchens to check with the cook about his rations, swung by the armory to get his sword, ducking under the swordmaster's disapproving stare and feeling guilty that he had neglected his swordplay lately in favor of more time in the record hall underneath the palace.

Arms full, he staggered up the stairs and back to his room, dumping the load on his bed.

His eyes fell again on the innocent-looking circular container, traitorous thoughts skirting around the edge of his mind.

If he failed...well and truly failed...could he bring himself to use it?

As much as he wanted to be the kind of man who would never consider such a thing, his hand moved with some secret, dark compulsion, putting the herbs with his other things.

Guilt followed him the rest of the evening until he sank into sleep. It was there again when he woke in the morning, a shadow that followed him as he loaded his horse, mounted, and left the comfort of the city walls for the uncertain fate that awaited him within the Morwood.

BRIA

Bria lifted the ax above her head and brought it down with a grunt, splitting the log partway. She braced a hand against the wood and tugged her blade out, resetting the log so she could go at it again.

She hardly dared glance up from her work, lest the sight of yet another animal copulation met her view.

Tala hadn't let up the past several days, despite Bria's pleas. The goddess would not heed her.

She had considered that it might be a warning of things to come. Tala often provided symbols and patterns in nature, warning of storms, of bandits, or of other trouble that might disrupt Bria's safe haven.

But mating animals wasn't one of the signs the journals mentioned, and Bria had kept a sharp eye out for those. She definitely hadn't experienced any unusual hunger, the first sign of her fertile phase, not when she often forgot to eat these days.

Bria tossed the split logs onto the growing pile some feet away, wiped the sweat from her brow, and readied another log. She put all her force and frustration into it, driving the ax straight through the piece of wood.

If only she had someone, anyone, to talk to that she could trust. She was alone in the forest among the animals and a silent goddess.

She needed her father. He'd always been a steady and reassuring man. But to leave her woods, to go into the city to find him...it would take far greater distress for her to abandon her safe haven, even if it did give her a break from suitors and her fruitless searching for the sacred caves.

Raising the ax again, she breathed deeply, focusing on the wood before her. A bird cawed from a tree overhead.

She brought her ax down as she registered the call as a warning.

"Greetings, maiden,"

Her head turned, twisting her torso, and the ax glanced off the log. She nearly dropped it, but recovered, holding the ax at her side and turning towards the voice.

A man with dark chestnut brown hair tied at the nape of his neck had entered the copse of trees around her cottage.

How had she missed sensing him? Or had Tala not warned her?

Bria recalled the bird and scowled at herself. She should have heeded the bird, though the warning could have come before this stranger was upon her.

She took in his fine clothes, the health of his steed, and the packs on its back, and tried to present a pleasant face. She didn't need to feed any more rumors about her wildness.

"Hail, traveler. What brings you this deep into the forest?"

The man ducked his head, eyes on the reins in his hands, before he glanced up again. "I seek the druid of the Morwood. Do you know her?"

Bria rubbed the inside of her cheek with her tongue and cocked her head. Did this man truly not know who she was at a glance, or was he playing with her?

"Aye, I might know her. But men should be warned to steer clear. She hasn't the patience these days for that kind of attention," Bria said vaguely, as if this druid were a distant acquaintance, rather than standing right in front of him.

A suitor, no doubt. Sent so soon? She'd barely had a weeks' reprieve! Apparently her warning hadn't been enough...but then again, she could be jumping to conclusions.

The man dismounted. "I'm simply a scholar interested in preserving druid culture. I have questions for her."

"The castle at Dunholm has extensive records on human interactions with the druids, I'm sure," Bria replied. Her skin crawled at the thought of being interviewed, of all things.

"I've read everything they have at Dunholm. The only thing left is to come straight to the source, I'm afraid." He smiled, a not-unpleasant smile. He had a kind enough face, but her recent encounters with one Magnus Ironcrest had left a bad taste in her mouth, and she didn't wish to be in the company of a man for a long time.

"As I said, the druid is busy. Come back later," Bria replied, her mouth betraying her desire to not encourage the conversation to continue.

"You're her, aren't you?" the man breathed, his eyes lighting up in wonder. He moved closer, tugging on his horse's reins so the animal followed him. "I've waited a rather long time to meet you."

Bria tensed as he drew nearer, holding her free hand at the ready, prepared to draw the symbols in the air to summon the spirits of the forest to her defense.

"You aren't just a scholar, I take it. You're a suitor," Bria accused.

The man laughed, rubbing the back of his head with a free hand. "You catch on quick. I had no intention to mislead you. I am a scholar, and I would like to know more about you, your life and customs. But yes, I am also a suitor sent by Queen Runa."

Bria set the ax down, leaning it against her splitting log, and grabbed several chunks of wood. Balancing the pile in her arms, she stomped over to the shelter where she kept her chopped wood and tossed the fresh-cut pieces onto the stack.

"Didn't get a chance to talk to Magnus, did you?" she called over her shoulder. "If you had, you wouldn't be here."

What kind of man would the queen send after someone like Magnus? Another foolish man driven by the desire for recognition and power? Someone skilled in the art of romance to put her off her guard? An assassin?

She snorted at that last thought. No, he hadn't come to kill her. The queen wouldn't risk angering Tala, even if she didn't believe in the goddess of the earth and sky.

She whirled around and froze, finding him within striking distance.

He scanned her form and backed up a step, perhaps noticing the fire burning in her eyes.

"You don't intend to harm me," he said, a hint of a question in his voice, hands raising defensively. "If you give me a chance..."

Now that he stood closer, she could more clearly make out his face. More soft lines than chiseled features, and his hair had a slight wave to it. They had certainly sent a disarming sort of man, the kind you didn't suspect of anything.

She crossed her arms over her chest, leaning into one hip. "I gave him a chance, and if I'd been a weaker woman, he would have taken advantage. I have no confidence you won't do the same."

The man spread his arms and lowered into a bow. "We started off on the wrong foot. My name is Theodore Blackwin. I didn't come to challenge you, but I would like to be friends."

"No one wants to be friends with me," Bria said. The words caught in her throat, feeling as if they would choke her. "Either you are trying to fool me or you have succeeded at fooling yourself. In any case, I will be merciful and provide you with a warning. Leave now, before I change my mind."

She turned away, walking towards her cottage. She needed to sit down, drink some tea, and eat something grounding after this furious encounter. A good, rich soup would do nicely.

"I have good reason to believe you would not harm me. Your people are pacifists. There is no record of them harming another living creature except out of protection," Theodore Blackwin called out after her.

Bria turned her head and body with a jerk, fists clenched, breath coming in shallow, heaving gasps she could barely contain long enough to speak. Being pacifists had gotten her people slaughtered when the humans came to steal their sacred secrets. The secrets the druids protected for Tala. She would not lay down and let anyone rub her own life creeds in her face while they threatened her well-being, no matter how kindly their tone as they did it.

She raised her hand and drew the first line of the first symbol of protection that would activate Tala's power and send the ignorant human running and sniveling back to his queen, but something stopped her. An inner knowing that if she moved against this man, she would violate her agreement with her goddess to cause no harm. Sufficient warning, it would seem, had not been given. Or, as she did not want to consider, the goddess disapproved of Bria's violent thoughts towards him.

"I will assume you are a threat to my safety until you prove otherwise, human. If you know what is good for you, do not approach me again." She finished with a snarl and turned so hard her neck strained, storming off into her cottage, slamming the door between her and the infuriating trespasser.

She set a kettle on the fire and started chopping nuts and vegetables to make a soup. The knife hacked up and down on the board.

Certainly Tala did not approve of this man. She had stayed Bria's hand to test her, that was all.

Nuts went into the pot first to soften, then carrots and tubers, followed by aromatic herbs and wild onion. She stirred them with a bit of goat milk butter and salt until the onions went transparent, then poured in part of the water she had boiled and added a bunch of waxy watercress.

Setting a lid on the pot to let everything come together, Bria poured the rest of the water into a stoneware mug. The herbs inside bloomed, herbs that would calm her nerves and relax the strained muscles in her neck.

She tidied and fussed as the tea steeped, occasionally glancing towards the window and wondering if the man had gone. She refused to check—he mattered little to her, and she would ignore him until he left, simple as that.

The water in her mug changed from clear to brown, and Bria took it to her chair. Breathing in deeply, the painful knot inside of her chest relaxed somewhat, and she used a spoon to mix in honey and a bit of cream. As she drank the tea, everything loosened, until the pounding of rock on metal disturbed her state of mindfulness.

Bria gave in to her curiosity and left her mug on the floor, walking to the window at the front of her cottage to look out.

The man crouched outside, pounding a stake into the ground as he erected a tent at the edge of *her* circle of trees.

Bria bristled. How dare he intrude on her privacy! She had a mind to make the earth sink beneath his tent or send the trees bending to frighten his horse, but again, there was a sensation of strong disapproval that sank in her gut like a stone. If she called on Tala's power, she would bring the ire of her usually benevolent goddess.

From the look of the clouds above, it would soon rain, and that would be enough to make the soft nobleman think twice about camping outdoors. She would let Tala send the man away herself.

Bria fetched a shawl and returned to her soup, removing it from the fire. She retrieved the last of a loaf of bread from her larder, spreading a thick layer of butter over a slice and relishing in the fact that she was indoors, eating a warm, savory dinner, while the wind picked up outside and the unfortunate suitor struggled with his tent.

Storms in the Gathering season weren't nearly as nice as the Warming ones in the Morwood. He would pass a cold, miserable night and be gone by morning.

THEO

RAIN SEEPED THROUGH THE fabric of Theo's hastily set-up tent, and he spent half the night trying to find something, anything, to prop his bags up on so his precious books wouldn't get wet. He shouldn't have packed so many of them, but he couldn't bear to leave them.

In the end, he slept with his bag on top of him, huddled in his cloak and listening to the sound of his tent trying to rip its way out of the ground. He prayed to whatever gods might be listening that it wouldn't collapse on top of him.

Incessant birdsong woke him in the gray hours of dawn. He peeled his eyelids open, rubbing away the crust that had accumulated, cursing nature. Surely the druid had sent those birds to sing him awake at the barest hint of sunlight.

Damp, cold, and aching from being unable to change positions all night, Theo hauled his bag off, holding it up as he stood, and carried it out of the tent with him.

Everything was wet. The ground, the sticks he gathered from beneath the trees, the rocks he piled in such a fashion to indicate a fire pit, and his socks. He hated wet socks.

At least he'd found a place for his books—a dry patch of ground between a bush and a tree trunk where it wouldn't get dripped on too terribly.

After his fifth attempt, he got the spark from his flint and steel to catch on the tinder he'd been able to scrounge up and the dry wood he'd somewhat shamefully borrowed from the druid's sheltered pile. He would replace it, he promised himself, as he got a merry little flame going to stave off the morning chill.

He rubbed his hands together, crouched in front of the flame, watching the orange tendrils reach higher and higher, until he realized he needed more wood, and ideally, something to eat.

Rummaging in his other pack, the one he'd left on the ground and allowed to get soaked through, he found the small, upright kettle and tin cup he'd brought with him, along with packets of grains, sugar, even butter wrapped in an oilskin. He could make a nice, warm breakfast of these.

He used the kettle to boil some water, taking advantage of the wait to gather more dry-ish firewood and make his own stack.

Once the water was boiling, he poured it into the cup along with handfuls of grain and let it sit until the individual kernels had softened, then added a pat of butter and a spoonful of dark brown sugar. He would have killed for some cinnamon and milk, but he hadn't brought any, so he blew on the mixture, stirring it and watching steam rise into the air.

The warm breakfast was the highlight of his morning, and he cheered right up after, setting about making his camp more livable. He left the flap of his tent open, hoping the sun would dry things out, including himself, and then, cup and spoon cleaned out, he settled on a log he'd dragged next to the firepit with his notebook and pen, eager to take notes about the night before.

The druid—Bria, he must think of her by her name—seemed to have woken as well. Smoke drifted out of the cottage chimney in earnest, and he heard the occasional clang of a pot. At one point, she emerged from the cottage, grabbed some firewood, and returned, closing her door without a single glance his way.

Their conversation the previous day had been both enlightening and infuriating. She dodged every attempt at congeniality and did not even pretend politeness. It seemed that a few years of constant unwanted attention, or perhaps a life lived away from society, had given her cause to strip away false pretenses and get straight to the point.

She didn't want him here. She would, in fact, rather he be dead than here, she'd made that much clear. Except she hadn't attacked him. Right at the end, he could have sworn she had activated her powers, but no trees had swayed towards him, no rumblings had shaken the ground, and no animals had surrounded him to chase him away.

Why hadn't she attacked?

Druids were known to be peaceful unless provoked, and they only attacked first in the most extreme situations. Otherwise, they had kept to themselves, leaving their lands to generously attend to the crops of surrounding areas, to heal cursed areas of land, and to do the work of their goddess, Tala, Theo supposed.

Curiosity bloomed within him. He wanted to rush down to the druid's cottage and pound on the door until she opened it to ask her the questions swirling around in his mind. What sort of beliefs did she have about her goddess? Did the deity speak to her audibly, or in her mind? Had she ever seen Tala? Were her powers connected to the goddess?

He clamped down hard on the urge and settled for writing the questions down, excitement dimming to a simmering frustration. To get her to answer these questions, she would have to trust him enough to talk with him without threatening him, and that would be an immense amount of work in itself.

The door to the cottage swung wide sometime later, and Bria emerged, carrying a basket with several tools inside, dressed in fresh, dry clothes that Theo found himself envying. He certainly would have worn a dress if it meant he were dry.

Smothering the fire with a wet pile of leaves and some dirt, Theo tucked a smaller version of his notebook into the pocket of his breeches, along with a pen, and took off after Bria through the forest.

She lost him within a few hundred feet, vanishing between the trees without a trace. He searched for any sign of her all morning, then gave up when the sky emptied more drizzling rain on him.

Soaked through and exhausted, Theo stumbled into his tent, defeated.

It rained for two more days. Theo didn't bother going out, despite noting Bria left around the same time each morning. He considered giving up more than once but gritted his teeth and thought of the atheneum full of books he would hold his mother to build for him once he'd succeeded at winning the druid's affections.

On his tenth day in the Morwood, the sun shone cheerily through rain-wet leaves and Theo emerged from his tent to stretch. Curling up in a damp tent for several days made facing the ire of the druid much more appealing.

She emerged from her cottage just when he anticipated she would, glancing at him with a single eyebrow raised. Impressed or simply surprised he'd lasted this long? It didn't matter, he wouldn't lose her this time.

He stepped in line behind her. She didn't spare him another look, even with the sound of him clumsily crashing through the underbrush.

Theo was no foresting expert, despite the fact that the class he'd taken had sections on forestry and survival, but it seemed the druid changed directions an awful lot, often not following even a game trail to her destination. She stopped at random to touch a tree and commune with it in some way, pressing her forehead against the trunk, occasionally making gestures in the air, as if blessing it.

Theo kept a respectful distance and made a note in his book whenever she stopped. If nothing else, his time spent with the druid in the woods would allow him to potentially add to his peoples' knowledge about them.

Sunlight streamed through the gray clouds above, illuminating every drop of dew like a thousand jewels of ruby, orange, and crystal. Every color brightened a hundredfold, the saturation so bright and beautiful, it almost hurt Theo's eyes.

The scene before him put every other image of beauty in his mind to shame. And at the center of it was Bria, her flaming red hair gleaming down her back, her smile infectious as she turned to face the sun.

Theo stared unabashedly until Bria faced him and her lovely expression morphed into a scowl. She put her cloak hood up and moved hastily ahead on the path they followed.

Theo stumbled over a tree root in his rush to catch up. The druid woman moved faster than he thought possible, her bare feet flowing over the ground more than walking. She never tripped on a rock or root or got struck with a branch, whereas he seemed to hit every single one, getting mouthfuls of wet leaves and snags in his cloak. His booted feet ached from striking various hard things sticking out of the ground.

It was like the world molded around Bria, while it actively worked to keep Theo out. He gritted his teeth and pressed on, the way becoming more tangled and difficult to pass than before, and pretty soon he had to keep his eyes more on the ground than on Bria, and before he knew it, she was gone, vanished into thin air like a specter.

Theo let the curses flow once he thought Bria was out of earshot. He wanted to appear a polite gentleman, but these damned tree branches and the damned rocks and the—

On his next step, his foot sank ankle-deep in mud, and he yanked it out with a suctioning sound, groaning at the thick yellow-brown sludge that coated the fine leather. He glanced up, realizing the trees were as thick as ever, but the ground seemed...not solid. The plants had changed, and frogs filled the air with their chirps and croaks.

A marsh. They had entered a marsh. He hadn't even known there was a marsh in the Morwood, but here they were. Unless the druid had manipulated the land somehow and created this with her magic. More likely, humans hadn't explored enough of the Morwood to know about places like this.

Theo pulled out his notebook and took a sketch of the area, squinting through his mud-spattered glasses to try to see the end of the marshy area. When he finished, he moved to take a step and found his feet locked into the ground, having sunk down to his ankles, even standing on what he'd assumed was solid dirt.

Tucking away the notebook and pen and cursing up a storm, Theo yanked at each leg, getting no further than feeling his socked foot start to emerge from his boot. That wouldn't do.

He glanced up at the nearby trees, cursing them again, this time for not having branches in his face, or even near enough for him to grab.

"They can hear you, you know. It isn't wise to curse a tree." Bria stepped out from behind a thick, gray-trunked tree up ahead, her hand stroking the shaggy bark.

"Did you do this?" Theo asked, despite his intention to not come across as antagonistic in any way. Accusing her wasn't a great start to their relationship.

Bria didn't bother to hide her amusement at his obvious frustration. Her green eyes sparkled, and the corners of her lips turned upward. She shook her head, as if afraid to speak and let out a laugh.

"The marshes claim those who tread too heavily. You haven't learned how to walk as if you are part of the forest, so it recognizes you as an intruder."

Theo struggled to pull one foot upward. It made a slight sucking sound, and he got excited, yanking harder, but the boot still didn't budge.

"How do I make it see me as a friend and let me go?"

"Not saying obscene things to the trees and rocks would be a good start. But you've already dug yourself in pretty deep there. Maybe...an apology?" Bria suggested, taking a strand of her hair between her fingers and fiddling with it.

Theo grunted, trying not to get distracted by her beauty. Letting his guard down earlier had led to this mess.

"You expect me to apologize to some trees?"

"They are living things. They can hear you, understand you. Better than you understand yourself. Their energy communicates with your energy. Just by being here they can influence you, improving the functioning of your body. You humans never recognize it for what it is—the trees offering you a gift of healing. So many of your issues would improve if you spent more time among them and less time cursing them or cutting them down for your own use."

"Your cottage is made of wood," Theo pointed out, not sure why he felt so irritated, like a boy being lectured. Somewhere inside, he recognized she was probably trying to be helpful but in a way that was somehow degrading to his pride.

Bria bristled. "My cottage was made using gifts from Tala. Trees who willingly gave of themselves to give us a place of protection. Haven't you noticed how the wood is not cut but molded? My people do not cut living wood."

Theo looked up towards the sky and closed his eyes, wishing he were back in the castle with a fat stack of books and something warm to drink.

An image of his mother's disapproving face floated through the pleasant vision.

If he failed at this, he would be sent into military service, and he could kiss his personal library goodbye. Suddenly, apologizing to a bunch of trees didn't seem so bad.

"I am sorry for my thoughts towards you, noble trees. I am ignorant to your ways, but I will learn to watch where I step and what I think," Theo said, gazing at the branches and feeling in every way a fool.

Bria snorted and waved her hands, and the ground seemed to rise under his feet until he stood on solid ground once more.

"You did that," Theo said, accusingly.

"I speak for Tala. I am but a servant of the trees," Bria said, bowing slightly.

Theo didn't miss the smirk on her face. It irked him, but it also made her more appealing somehow. He wouldn't want to be coupled with a woman who did whatever he asked, and her blatant honesty was refreshing compared with the women of the castle who played flirtatious games and connived their way into the beds of those with more power.

He knew where he stood with Bria. He stared at her for a long moment, until she turned up her nose and pivoted back into the trees.

"Stick more closely this time. The path I take will remain solid," she said.

It was the first kindness she'd paid him since his arrival, unless not attacking him with all the force of the goddess of nature counted.

Theo grinned and shook out his legs, which were feeling a bit cramped after both the hike and struggling in the mud, and he followed Bria, being sure to draw as near as he dared. It might have been doubly foolish of him, but he had caught a glimpse of the druid's better nature, and he was fairly certain that despite her big words, she didn't actually want to see him dead.

9

BRIA

THE SUITOR FOLLOWED BRIA each day, a silent shadow as she went about her rounds, checking on the health of the forest and infusing trees and patches of land with healing energy where needed. He didn't attempt conversation, simply kept pace with her, notebook in hand, his glasses glinting in the sun.

What was he scribbling? Things about her? About her powers? Bria wondered if she should worry she was showing him secrets he could use to exploit her, but he seemed sincere enough. His blunder into the marshes had disarmed her enough that she startled when she realized she felt *comfortable* around him.

She was actually enjoying his silent company. It filled a place in her that had felt frayed and tense ever since her father left.

Lonely? Dare she admit that she longed for the company of others? And why had none of the other suitors made her desire their company?

Bria knelt beside a creek and scooped the crystalline water into her mouth, relishing its cold touch. She splashed her cheeks, flushed from the morning's exertion, and stared at her broken reflection in the rushing water.

Theodore knelt a few feet away, partaking of the water, and Bria sensed his eyes on her.

She froze, wondering how he saw her. If he wanted *her*.

Have some sense, Bria, she scolded herself. *Don't lose sight of what you need to do.*

Theodore cleared his throat. "I'm going to return to my camp now. If you'll point me in the right direction, I'd be most grateful."

Bria gestured. "We're quite close. Through the aspen grove due north and over the hill. You'll see the roof of the cottage."

"Thank you," he said, tilting his head. He stood and walked away without another word.

Bria watched him go, uncertain of her feelings. When they had first met, she had wished him ill and wanted nothing more than for him to leave her alone. Today, he had irritated her, yes, especially the way he had offended the trees, but he hadn't pressed for her attention, pleaded to get her to accept him, nor had he advanced at her with any intentions other than, it seemed, to observe her and get to know her better.

It was almost enough to make her feel bad for the way she'd treated him before, but no, whatever his intention, he was still a suitor, trained for one thing—to manipulate her to bear the next last druid.

She mustn't forget it.

When the sun rose to its peak in the sky, Bria headed home, trailing her hands along mossy bark and gripping the soft, damp ground with her bare toes. The trees whispered to her, their sparser branches allowing more sunlight to filter through as they lost more leaves by the moment, creating a carpet for her to tread on.

Soon, she would have to don shoes to protect her feet from the elements. Soon, but not quite yet.

The sound of an ax on wood echoed through the trees, increasing Bria's heart rate. She paused, trying to sense if any spirit of the forest were being harmed as was often the case when humans were around, but she sensed nothing.

Picking up her pace, she emerged from the trees at the top of the hill and came upon a rather startling scene.

The soft-skinned nobleman, who likely had never picked up an ax in his life, hacked away at a piece of wood that kept slipping off the block.

Bria stifled a laugh, but she couldn't keep the smile off her face. He was shirtless, the skin on his back glistening in the golden daylight. Some muscle, but not as much as some she'd seen, and he was certainly pale. The work would do him good.

She breezed past him without glancing up, the basket on her arm brimming with goods she'd found in the forest. She had enough merdle mushrooms for a good stew, and the leeks she'd found at the riverbank would make a delightful addition. If she started now, she'd have time to make more bread before dinner.

After the midday meal, Bria spent the afternoon elbow-deep in bread dough, making enough to eat as well as offer up to Tala the next time she petitioned the goddess. Leaving the shaped dough to rise, she realized the sound of the suitor's chopping had stopped. She glanced out the window, and sure enough, he was nowhere in sight.

And neither was the ax.

Bria opened the door, glancing anxiously in every direction. Where had he gone?

Then she felt it. The splitting pain of a spirit's bonded form being destroyed.

She lifted her skirts, hiking them to her knees, and took off at a run into the forest. A vision sent by Tala pierced her mind. A man with an ax, standing over a fallen log, raising the weapon and swinging it down. From the spirit's perspective, he looked terrifying, and Bria sensed that the spirit would do anything to protect her bonded form—after all, they were raising a host of new spirits in that log.

The spirit surged forward in the vision, and the last thing Bria saw before it cut off was Theo's terrified face.

The foolish man deserved the spirit's ire, but he didn't deserve to die. Cursing at herself for not watching him closer, Bria picked up speed, crashing through the underbrush, apologizing to the bushes and trees for passing so violently.

Some of their branches moved out of the way when they noticed her haste. They wanted her to aid their sister as much as she did.

"Put the ax down!" Bria bellowed, skidding to a halt and sending gold leaves scattering under her bare feet.

Theodore had the ax raised in defense as a billowing blue-green cloud approached him, a snarling, delicate feminine shape forming from the gathered essence, her face contorted in a hideous, furious expression no mortal could ever manage.

Theodore didn't so much as glance at Bria, his eyes fixed on the angered spirit of the forest.

Bria formed several symbols one after the other and cast them at the spirit.

"Rest, sleep, calm. I will give him the punishment he deserves," Bria muttered.

The spirit shrieked and surged towards the cowering suitor, who reflexively swung his ax. It went right through the spirit's essence without a mark, angering the spirit further.

"Drop the ax!" Bria shouted.

This time, Theodore glanced her way and fumbled with the weapon, letting it thud to the ground. He put up his hands defensively and backed away from the pulsating, ever-changing form of the forest spirit.

Rushing forward, Bria threw herself between Theodore and the spirit, planting her feet in the earth and putting her hands up in the channeling mark.

Tala, help me! she cried in her mind.

The goddess moved within her, stretching like a slumbering giant, and sent a surge of power through her limbs and out her hands.

A spiral of golden light burst into the air like golden sparks from an ethereal fire. The forest spirit stopped its approach and leaned into the sparks, a look of peaceful awe descending over its face.

Bria's hands were coated with golden light. She touched the spirit's essence, shrinking it down until it was little more than a puff of green and blue mist between her palms, and she pressed it back into the fallen tree.

Theodore made a strangled attempt at speech.

Bria ignored him, turning to the hacked portion of the spirit's home. A wide, splintered gouge exposed the fresh wood beneath.

She closed her eyes and ran her hands over the wound, the remnants of Tala's power leaving her skin as she knitted the wound in the bark back together. Her skin lost all evidence of the goddess as she finished, leaving the wound still raw and exposed, but mending. She had used everything the goddess had given her. Time and nature would do the rest.

Breathing deep to keep her tone steady, Bria opened her eyes and turned towards Theo.

"Do you remember nothing from our conversation in the marshes? No living wood."

Theodore gestured helplessly. "The tree is on the ground. How is it alive?"

Bria stormed over to the tree's roots, which were firmly planted in the ground. "The tree fell in a storm and a spirit took pity on it, using its essence to grow the roots back into the earth so the tree might live. Now they are bonded, and in gratitude, the tree acts as a nursery for the spirit's young. Does this look like dead wood?" Bria gestured at the raw wound, which wept with golden sap.

Theodore kicked at the ground like a chastised child. "No," he admitted. "I just wanted to do something kind for you."

"Well, stop. You have no idea what you're up against here. If I hadn't been near enough to interfere, that spirit would have consumed your life force and used it to heal the tree and feed her young. You'd be a husk rotting on the forest floor," Bria found herself shouting and took several heaving breaths in an attempt to calm down.

Theodore stared at her, the surprised expression and round lenses of his glasses giving him an owlish look. "You...saved my life."

Bria rolled her eyes. "I shouldn't have."

"You don't want me dead," Theodore said, mouth widening in a grin.

"Don't think anything of it," Bria snapped, leaning forward and grabbing the ax from the ground between them. She examined it for damage and fortunately, found none. She should have let the suitor get consumed by the spirit. Then she could have returned to her search for the caves unbothered for another month or more before the queen realized the man she'd sent had failed.

Instead, he glowed as if she'd kissed him, looking pleased as a mother hen on a fresh clutch of eggs.

Bria pointed the ax handle at him, working hard to hold her anger at a reasonable level. "This isn't the forest that you know. The spirits have abandoned their homes near high concentrations of humans. You are deaf to their cries and those of their children and elderly, so they fled and came here to the deep woods. The heart of the Morwood is home to many such creatures, and they will not hesitate to kill you if you jeopardize their safety. If you misstep again, I will let them."

Bria turned and fled back towards the cottage, shutting herself inside. She paced for a time, checking the window frequently to make sure the human had returned to the camp at the edge of her grove, hating herself for caring.

At last, he lit a fire outside his tent, poking at it and glancing at the cottage frequently.

She remained hidden in the shadows, peering out at him but not allowing him to see her watching. And then she went to the shelf holding the few books and journals she had of her people, trailing her finger along their crumbling spines. She pulled several out, turning fragile page after fragile page, looking for the few words of the ancient druid language that she knew and longing with all her heart to understand what was scribed there. The secrets these words held would lead her to the caves her mother had sought, and they would reveal the answer to healing the curse that had destroyed her people.

If only she could read them.

As tears of frustration and fear fell down her cheeks, she cried out to Tala and every part of her trembled.

The goddess had responded when the forest spirit was in trouble. Why did she remain silent when Bria needed her most? Why didn't she reveal the path to the caves and allow Bria to heal the curse over her womb and her people?

Bria was tempted to throw the books in the fire, for all the good they did her, but instead she clutched the one she held to her chest, wishing her ancestors would appear and speak to her the wisdom she desperately needed.

THEO

For another long week, Bria evaded Theo entirely. He woke at the crack of dawn to find her cottage empty, smoke barely wafting from the chimney into the frost-bitten air.

Theo drafted a letter. Apologizing for his ignorance, pleading with the druid to forgive him, asking if she could find the patience to teach him how to avoid doing the same in the future, promising he would heed her words.

His fingers nearly froze as he wrote it, despite his gloves, but he carefully penned the note with his best handwriting, something he'd always been proud of, and slipped it under her cottage door after dark before stomping back to his tent and bundling up with every layer he had.

He passed the coldest, most fitful night he'd ever known and woke in the morning to the cottage door slamming.

The light of the sun wasn't even a thought on the world yet. No birds stirred, and darkness surrounded him so completely he wondered if it might still be the middle of the night and where the druid might be going with the moon still in charge overhead.

He could wake up and catch her, follow her as he had before. Possibly blunder his way into another unforgivable crime against nature. He knew that to someone who valued life above all things, what he'd done was truly horrendous, first offending the tree spirits on their hike through the woods, then riling a forest spirit to the point of it emerging to defend its young.

And she'd had to save him both times. He looked and felt like a fool.

And now he huddled beneath several layers of clothing, his cloak, and his blankets, shivering and wondering if he was cut out for this. He should have waited until spring, at the very least. He couldn't feel his toes. His glasses fogged with each breath he took.

Surely the realm could wait until the forest thawed for the next last druid to be conceived.

"*You have three months,*" his mother's words echoed in his mind. Almost one month gone, now. Two more months before he would forfeit his mother's approval, the atheneum she'd promised if he succeeded, and his freedom. He would be forced to train in the military. No more cozy days reading by the fire in his room, no more long afternoons spent researching.

Faced with his ornery queen of a mother and the threat of military enrollment, Theo would rather take his chances with the cold and the obstinate druid.

He rolled out of bed, tossing off layers but keeping his cloak, hat, and gloves. He fumbled with the flap of his tent and half-crouched, half-crawled out of it, noting the spider-web-like touch of frost that coated the fallen leaves and branches on the forest floor.

He straightened and then hesitated, gazing across the forest clearing at Bria, who stood between his camp and her cottage, her feet bare and her red hair framing her pink-cheeked face as her breath puffed out in visible clouds.

Theo didn't dare do more than breathe, and he did that shallowly, until she moved first, turning away from him.

He wanted to ask if she'd read his letter. Perhaps she'd stepped over it as she walked out that morning. Perhaps she'd thrown it in the hearth without even opening it. She hadn't wanted anything to do with him from the moment he arrived, and he'd done nothing to convince her otherwise.

Stomping his feet to get his blood moving through them again, Theo moved to the firepit. He'd warm up, get some breakfast, and go over his notes for something else to try so he could get back in her good graces. Well, get into them in the first place, since he'd failed to do even that.

"Did you mean what you said? In your letter?" Bria called out.

Theo startled, nearly tripping over his own feet as he looked up. His heart quickened. "I did."

She glanced at the forest, clenching her fists as if she were considering taking back her words. Then she turned back to him.

"Come on, then. And take off your shoes."

Theo almost objected. His toes certainly did, curling at the thought of being exposed to the frigid air. He could have argued that he wasn't a druid, and he didn't have the same affinity for nature that she did, and it was possible that the frost would pose a grudge against his appendages the same way the trees had it out for him before.

He rather wanted to keep his toes. But he also wanted to prove himself to this stubborn druid woman and gain her trust.

Gritting his teeth, he unlaced his boots, wobbling the entire time as he tried to stay upright, fully aware of Bria's eyes on him. He tugged them off one at a time, yanking off his sock before he could change his mind.

The cold bit into his feet the moment his skin touched air, and it worsened when he walked and little sticks and rocks poked at him. He walked towards Bria, expecting some sort of mocking, but she only watched him with an expression akin to wariness.

"How do you manage in this weather? Do you ever wear shoes?" Theo asked, prancing on the ground so his feet didn't have to remain in contact.

"Yes," Bria replied simply, then she turned and trotted off into the forest.

They walked for what felt like hours, the sky brightening to a pale blue, but no sun burst forth through the trees yet.

Bria spared him the experience of walking through frigid water, skirting the stream which burbled too actively to have iced over from the previous night's frost.

Theo's feet soon grew numb. He checked on his toes occasionally, reassuring himself that none had fallen off. They looked red, and every step felt like needles prodded the surface of his foot, but otherwise they remained intact.

They stopped at a seemingly random spot. Trees loomed, like anywhere else in the forest, their nearly bare limbs like spiderwebs as they criss-crossed overhead.

Bria sat down cross-legged and motioned for Theo to do the same.

"Er, what are we doing exactly?" Theo asked, speaking for the first time since they'd left his camp and the cottage behind.

"You weren't born with the ability to hear the voice of the forest, but it's something I'm told humans can learn. So today, we practice," Bria said, her voice sounding reedy and thin in the cold air. Perhaps it did affect her, then, despite the show she put on.

Theo glanced at her feet. They looked red, too. As did her hands, which were bare. He was grateful for his gloves.

"Center yourself here. It is an active place, brimming with life, and the trees whisper loudly. Don't try to hear them, the noise in your head will overwhelm their voices. Just be. Feel yourself becoming one with nature."

He tried. He truly did. At first, he thought it might be like reading. He gazed up and down the tree trunks, memorizing the patterns of bark, thinking there might be a key to hearing the trees there. He considered their roots stretching far underground and wondered what they might feel having lost their leaves. Did they accept and embrace the change in seasons or mourn what they no longer had?

Thoughts spun and whirled in his head, and he glanced at Bria, noting how serene her face was, how still she remained. His entire head was buzzing with thought. What had she said? Don't try, or the noise will overwhelm their voices?

Theo stopped trying. Or rather, he tried to stop trying. Thoughts came and went. A few times, he succeeded in having no thought, and then his head held a disconcerting emptiness.

The sun broke through the trees at last, and the day filled with more tangible signs of life.

Bria sighed and made little moaning noises.

Theo opened his eyes to find her stretching her limbs and standing. She noticed him watching.

"I don't expect you'll get it on your first try. Let's find something to eat. It's a learned thing to concentrate on an empty stomach, and I suspect you aren't familiar with that, seeing where you're from."

He hated to admit it, but she was right. The only time he'd ever gone without a full meal was during the three-day survival excursion Master Graymont took the class on every year to prepare them in case they ran out of provisions and got lost in the forest during their attempts to woo the druid.

It had been his least favorite part of the class, especially since they weren't allowed to bring things that were considered useless for survival, like books.

Theo stood and shook out his tingling limbs, following Bria through the forest. He noted which plants she stopped at, realizing he'd left his notebook back at his camp. He would have to remember and draw them later.

She picked handfuls of berries off one bush, bright orange fruits squirting juice into the morning air.

Theo stepped forward, taking his own handfuls.

Bria moved around to the other side of the bush, putting more space between them.

"Oh no," she breathed, gazing downward. She dug into the center of the bush, shaking it so hard berries rained onto the ground.

"What are you doing?" Theo asked. Was this some tactic to put him off? Promise him food and then spoil it? Irritation flooded him.

She grunted, grasping something beneath the bush, then came back up with substantial effort, twigs and leaves and even a berry or two caught up in her hair.

A bird lay limp in her hands, its wings splayed out at strange angles, its chest rapidly moving up and down. It let out a distress call, thrashing until she could barely keep hold of it. She spoke to it softly, stroking its feathers.

Theo's irritation faded. "What's wrong with it?"

"Hunter's snare. I think it got free, though." She carefully turned the bird, as if looking for other injuries.

Theo swallowed. "You can't talk to animals? Find out what happened?"

Bria snorted. "No. I can talk to them, but I can't understand what they say back. Perhaps some druids could. I wasn't given that gift. I can tell he's in pain, though." Her eyes, normally so fiery and hard when looking at him, were tender and filled with sadness. She closed them, chanting something under her breath.

Theo clasped his hands together in front of him, feeling as if he were attending a funeral. He watched the bird's breath slow, the rise and fall of its chest becoming more gradual, and then Bria shifted its tiny body to one hand and drew runes in the air.

One of them meant death.

Theo opened his mouth to protest, then clamped it shut again. He wanted her to try harder to save the bird—surely a rune of healing would be more appropriate? But he suppressed the urge to challenge her and simply watched.

Maybe it was the time he'd spent meditating with her, trying to become one with the forest, but he found he wanted to learn from her. To do that, he would have to disregard his human instincts.

She blew on the amber-colored runes hovering in the air, and they shrank, vanishing into the little bird's chest.

It immediately stopped moving, stiffening as if dead for hours instead of literal moments.

A tear trailed down Bria's cheek. She knelt, carrying the bird's body with her, and waved her free hand over the earth. The soil sank, creating a hole large enough for the bird's body to be placed inside. The soil moved again, covering the bird from view.

Theo blinked, surprised at the tide of emotion rising inside him. He hadn't cried much in his life, mostly at particularly sad stories in books he'd read, and when his brothers' bullying had gotten to be too much as a young child.

But this image of the druid, her head bent low over a bird most would hardly consider worth the effort, choked him with genuine sadness.

A bird call sounded in the forest, then another. The rapid flapping of wings made Theo glance up, and his mouth dropped open in shock and awe.

Hundreds of birds gathered above, singing and chirping and trilling.

Bria glanced up, a beam of sunlight illuminating the brilliant smile spreading on her face.

She looked like a goddess.

Theo felt a pinch and yelped, beating at his clothes for the insect that had surely bitten him. He cursed it for ruining such an ethereal moment. A strange sort of pressure squeezed against his chest, and he froze, breath shuddering through him.

That was no insect.

She looked over at him, incredulous. "Are you all right?"

"Something bit me," he exclaimed, still looking for the bug, despite the growing feeling that something—or someone—less tangible had pinched him.

Could the real goddess of this forest have heard his blasphemous thoughts and made it known to him?

He shook himself, trying to rid his body of the unease making his skin crawl.

"Sorry," he said, feeling sheepish at his outburst during such a sacred moment.

Birds still flocked above, but were more subdued in their calls, and some were taking leave of their branches.

Bria stood, brushing off her skirts and hands. "Not sure what I expected from a human during a rite like that."

"Why did..." Theo cleared his throat, some emotion caught in it. "Why did you use your magic like that? Why not let it die naturally?"

She plucked a few berries off the bush, eating them thoughtfully. "It wasn't a natural injury. And as priestesses of Tala, we're given leave to relieve the suffering of trees and animals. Not every time. But when it's right, I feel it here," she pointed to her breastbone.

He'd had no idea that druids had that kind of power over life and death. If she could kill with her magic that way, what else could she do?

Bria moved on from the berry bush, and Theo grabbed a few more of the bright orange fruits, hurrying to follow her.

She took him to the river, where she bent down to drink, scooping water and bringing it to her bow-like lips.

Theo made his own way down the bank, admiring her expert balance on the rocks where her bare feet gripped, and the curve of her hips from behind.

When she turned around, he startled, flushing when he realized how long he'd been staring at her backside.

"Are you thirsty?"

Not for water, Theo thought to himself, hiding the flush of his cheeks as he turned away from her towards the river and crouched to get his own drink. That answered that question—he'd wondered if he would find himself attracted to the druid daughter, or if he would either have to admit defeat or force himself to perform despite low attraction. That would, fortunately, not be the case.

He'd noticed her wild, ethereal beauty the day he'd arrived, of course, but attraction, as he'd learned in class, was another thing entirely.

Was Bria attracted to him? Did she notice him the way he noticed her? Lips and thighs and neck and backside...or was she less visual, more intellectual or emotional? All women, druids and humans alike, had different attraction profiles.

Druids made it extra complicated by their hormones only surging during their three fertile periods, one in each decade from their twenties to their fifties. They would couple during other times—the reports Theo had read made that apparent enough—but the entries he'd read about coupling during fertile times, those were enough to really make him blush. Passionate embraces filled with wild abandon unlike any the men claimed to have experienced with a woman before, and most of them had a rather extensive history with other women.

Theo did not. Would it be to his detriment that he had yet to be with a woman? Or would the druid find it charming, possibly appealing? He'd taken a big risk remaining inexperienced in that area.

"I didn't intend for us to spend all day here," Bria said bluntly.

Theo splashed a bit of water on his face, his body buzzing all over after the explicit direction his thoughts had gone.

"Sorry," he murmured, standing up, and used his toes to grip the rock as he clumsily turned around, concentrating on his foot placement to get back to the bank without slipping in the mud that had formed at the river's edge with the sun thawing the frosted ground.

Bria gave a little yelp, and Theo whipped his head around, to find another man's arm around her neck. The man pressed a knife against the delicate skin at her throat. His threatening growl woke something dormant inside Theo—the desire to protect this woman he admired at all costs.

BRIA

B RIA BUCKED AGAINST THE man that held her, hoping to smash her skull into his nose and force him to break his grip, or at least move the knife further from her throat, but he tightened it instead.

"Careful, sweetheart. Don't want to slice that fair throat of yours," he growled, his beard scratching against her cheek.

She almost gagged on the whiff of rank, ale-laden breath that wafted into her nostrils.

"Release her," Theodore said, his voice dropping into a warning tone.

Bria resisted rolling her eyes. What was he going to do? She had little reason to believe his soft hands were capable of much more than wielding a pen on parchment. Besides, she was fairly certain he hadn't brought any weapons with him into the forest that morning.

No, it would be up to her to save them. Again. She reached for Tala's power. Unable to use her hands to create symbols of power, she relied on prayer, sending her heart out to the goddess and visualizing her intention. *Frighten him. Bind his legs with vines. Take the knife.*

Nothing happened, and Bria frowned. Tala had never ignored her when she was in trouble before.

"This is your chance to run, pretty boy. I have business with the druid," her captor snarled.

"What business could you have with her? She is a druid. They live non-violent lives, unless driven to it by a good cause," Theodore insisted, moving closer.

The man's dagger dug into Bria's skin, and she yelped. Theodore stopped moving, watching her with concern.

"She made the road swallow our merchant wagon!" The man bellowed, spit flying past Bria's face.

Her fingernails scrabbled against his arm as she tried to pull away from the knife so she could speak.

"I remember...you. Slave traders..." Bria managed to gasp out.

Theo's expression darkened. Faster than Bria could follow, he crouched and scooped something off the ground, whipping his arm around and shooting whatever it was straight at Bria's face.

The stone struck her captor square in the forehead, and he stumbled back, yelling.

Bria ran to get out of reach, then whirled around and formed symbols to awaken the earth. The man could face the same fate as the rest of his murderous, slave-trading partners.

"I missed you the first time. I won't miss now," Bria growled as the ground softened and the man sank, screaming, until his head was covered and the ground hardened again.

Theodore stood blinking rapidly and staring at the place where the man disappeared as if in shock. He glanced at Bria, who couldn't bear his gaze and stomped a few feet away, fully intending to leave him there.

Footsteps pounded behind her as he caught up. "You're going to leave him there to die? The man should be turned in, put to trial."

"He doesn't deserve a trial. You didn't see the state of the young girls they had chained inside that wagon. I'm not sure 'slave traders' is the right term for that man and his partners. They weren't trading anything, they were taking."

Theodore was silent for a long moment. "What happened to the girls?"

Bria swallowed past the lump in her throat. Her entire body shook with rage, and her stomach felt hollow. A few berries weren't enough for breakfast, though it wasn't long ago she could have gotten away with just a handful for hours. She needed bread, nuts, something heartier.

"I took them to the nearest village, made sure they found a healer, and promised to return to the village at the fall harvest to bless their land for next season," Bria replied stiffly. "Last I heard, the girls were divided among several households over multiple villages and being well cared for while letters were sent to their families."

Theodore grunted, and Bria glanced over his shoulder. His eyebrows were still knit together, his lips drawn into a thin line. Did he disagree with how she'd handled the situation?

He still didn't seem to realize that the Morwood was her domain, her stewardship. She was the last of her kind. In another time, a council might have convened. But she didn't have a council. She had no one but herself and her goddess, and if Tala hadn't approved of the punishment, she wouldn't have allowed it.

They walked in silence, which Bria appreciated. She didn't feel like speaking, especially not if she had to defend her decision to sentence the slave trader to death.

Instead, she turned her mind back to her earlier pleas going unanswered. Why had the goddess denied her at such a crucial moment?

"You don't have to be alone, you know," Theodore said, shattering the silence. He walked beside her now. When had he caught up to her?

Bria's throat tried to close again, and her hands flexed into fists. He still didn't understand. How could he ignore the reality of her fate?

"I will be alone until the day I die," Bria said, her voice coming out as more of an unhinged snarl than the fierce, strong tone she'd intended.

"You shouldn't have to be," Theodore said. "If you'd just let someone in—"

Bria turned on him. "I let someone in, I die. Is that what you want? You all parade through here, charming with your sweet words and empty promises. You want to be with me forever, you want to give me the world. But you can't! A few months, a few years, and then I fall pregnant and I die. I know you know this, so why pretend my life can be anything else?"

She wanted to run, to sprint through the forest and put miles of foliage between herself and this man who questioned her reality and tried to wedge himself into it. But her feet felt as if they'd grown roots, and all she could do was stare into his brown eyes, desperately trying to get him to understand so he'd leave.

His gaze softened to a sort of sympathy that Bria couldn't stand the strength of. He knew. He'd studied her kind, her situation, for years if her past experiences with suitors like him were anything to go by. He had more compassion in him than most. He had somehow sensed her desperation and wished better for her.

It's how her mother had been, according to her father. Filled with optimism and hope. She'd chosen Bria's father years before her next fertile cycle began, and they'd made the most of it.

It didn't seem like much of a life to Bria.

"I won't promise you anything I can't give you," Theodore said at last, spreading his arms slightly and shrugging his shoulders.

Bria glanced down, struggling to think of the words to say or to convince her feet to move away from this place, away from him.

Her gaze landed on his feet, bare and bleeding from numerous scrapes, covered in dirt and reddened from cold. Guilt flashed through her. She'd forced him to remove his boots, insisting he learn to hear the voice of the forest, as if he ever could.

"Your feet," she murmured.

Theodore glanced down and wiggled his toes. "I got used to the cold after a while. Don't worry, they weren't that pretty before today."

Bria reached out and grabbed his hand, pulling him behind her without a word. He protested but followed, stumbling as she led him the last part of the way through the forest to where the cottage waited.

Theodore hesitated at her threshold, pulling his hand out of hers. "What-what are you doing?"

Bria pointed at his feet. "That's my fault. I'm going to fix it. Come inside." Irritation slowly replaced guilt. If he was going to make things difficult, she would leave him to tend his own wounds.

"Are you certain? I can wait out here," he said, in some strange show of chivalry, as if he hadn't been planning to get inside since he'd arrived.

Bria marched inside and grabbed the door, gesturing sharply inside with her free hand.

"Come in or don't. It's your feet," she said.

Theodore hurried inside, and she slammed the door behind him, then stuck a finger in his face.

"Don't get any ideas," she warned.

Theodore held up his hands. "I won't." His gaze roamed around the cottage.

Bria tried not to feel nervous about what he thought. Having him there felt too intimate, like he could see her soul in the items on her shelves. At least she'd picked up her clothing from the night before.

"I don't have guests often," Bria said, stoking the fire and putting the kettle on to warm the water inside. Then she rummaged through a basket for an appropriate rag.

"I'm honored," Theodore said, and the bastard had the audacity to sound like he meant it.

Bria scowled. She didn't want to like him. She didn't want him to be here, in her space or in her life. She wouldn't have let him inside if she didn't feel terrible about the state of his feet, and the fact that she still hadn't thanked him for helping her get free of the man with the knife.

Why did water have to take so long to heat?

She went to her chopping board where the crusty end of a loaf of bread waited from a few days prior. She sliced it in two and held one out to Theodore without a word.

Theodore took it, inclining his head. "Thank you. You make this yourself?"

"I make all of my food," Bria said. It was mostly true. A few times a year, she received gifts of food on her doorstep from local villages outside the forest. Payment for services rendered, or gifts meant to placate her so she didn't bring the wrath of Tala upon them. Different peoples had different stories of the druids. Just as many wanted her out of the forest entirely, like most of those from the capital city Theodore hailed from.

Her piece was gone before she had really savored it, and her belly growled for more. She ignored the gnawing hunger, using a cloth to grab the kettle off the fire and bringing it to the small table.

"There's hot water and a rag. I've got some salve you can apply when you're done," she said, gesturing to a nearby chair.

Theodore stared at her for a moment, not seeming to comprehend.

Bria crossed her arms. If he thought she was going to clean and treat his feet, he had another thing coming. She didn't touch other people's feet. The thought made her shudder, and she felt like she needed to wash her hands even though she hadn't touched anything.

He got the message and limped over to the chair, pulling it away from the table so he could sit down. He set down the hunk of bread she'd given him, only half finished. How had she eaten hers so fast? Pouring some water from the kettle onto the rag, he picked his first foot up, resting it on his opposite knee. He dabbed at the wounds, cleaning away the dirt and streaks of blood.

She brought him the pot of herbal salve, a fresh one she'd made during the second season as the world turns, and he took it from her.

"Thank you," he murmured.

Bria turned away, busying herself at her pantry shelves. She'd gathered some eggs from a wild flock of turkeys the day before. Egg and leek soup, then. Or she could boil the eggs and spread them on some toasted bread.

Her stomach growled audibly, and she gripped it, embarrassed by the sound, then fled outside, breathing in the cool air. The sun had taken the frosty edge off, and everything had thawed.

She made her way to the suitor's camp and picked up his shoes and socks, scrunching her face in displeasure, but she didn't want him to undo the work he'd done on his feet by walking back across the clearing.

When she got back, Theodore had screwed the lid back on the salve, and was wiping his hands on the rag. He looked up as she came in, surprise forming on his face at the sight of his boots in her hand.

"I could have gotten those."

Bria snorted. "And cover your feet in dirt and leaves and who knows what else?"

He smiled. "You have a point there. Thank you, then." He took the boots from her, sliding the socks on and partially lacing his boots before he stood.

Bria nearly jumped backwards, his proximity far too close for comfort, but that rooted feeling came back to her feet, and she couldn't bring herself to move. She swallowed, glancing up at him.

"I, uh, should have thanked you for helping me earlier. If you hadn't gotten him with that rock...Well, good job."

"I meant what I said. And I don't mean that I think you're incapable," he said, voice softening to match the expression in his brown eyes. "You've proven you're so much more than that. I don't presume I can offer you anything, which is maybe why this is a mistake."

He moved around her, walking towards the door with a much stronger stride now.

Bria didn't reply. What could she say? He was right. He had nothing to offer her. Nothing she wanted, anyway, unless he knew how to break the druid curse for good.

Theodore opened the door, hesitating before he went out, then glanced over his shoulder. "Do you think, per-haps, we could be friends?"

"Friends?" Bria echoed. She wasn't sure she knew the true meaning of the word. She'd never had a friend. She knew what a friend was, in theory. The druid word meant "companion of the heart," according to her father. Her mother had taught him some of their language so he could teach her daughter. But Bria had never expe-rienced the concept for herself, and what little she'd picked up from her journals hadn't helped much.

She coughed, clasping her hands behind her back and rocking on her heels. "Why do I have a feeling that 'friends' is a way to trick someone into getting close to you so they'll let you share their bed?" Her tone was teasing, but she kept her expression serious.

"No, not like that," Theodore stammered, face flushing. "I like you. I mean, who wouldn't? I want to get to know you better, to do things with you."

"Things?" Bria said, raising her eyebrows. She crossed her arms, trying to look disapproving. She quite liked the way it made her feel to see him so flustered and caught off his guard.

"Not things like...things things," Theodore babbled, eyes darting to the bed on the other side of the one-room cottage. He sighed, adjusting his glasses and wiping a hand over his mouth. "Can I start over?"

Bria stifled a giggle and nodded.

Theodore steepled his fingers together and pointed them at her. "I like you. I admire your courage, your knowledge, and your strength. I would like to walk with you and have conversations and share food sometimes."

"Is that what friends do?" Bria asked, taken slightly aback by how genuine he sounded.

He nodded. "Yes," he said breathlessly.

"In that case, I accept," Bria said, giddiness rising in her chest again. She almost forgot her hunger as she stared at Theo.

"Dinner, then? Or I'll meet you sometime tomorrow?"

"Tomorrow," Bria asserted, a fluttery feeling taking over her stomach. She pressed against it as if she could make it go away, but the pressure had no effect.

Theodore bobbed his head. "Gooday, then."

"Gooday," Bria replied, feeling somewhat dazed, perhaps dizzy. As he shut the door behind him, she sat down and stared at the door. What had gotten into her? The strange lightheadedness persisted, and her stomach took several long moments to calm down. When it did, the hunger was there again, a vast hole yawning in her stomach.

Shaking herself from her stupor, she snacked on bread and nuts while she prepared her egg and leek soup, all the while thinking of the man who had, only a short time before, occupied the chair at her table and asked to be her friend.

THEO

T HEO HAD NEVER BEEN excited to see someone first thing in the morning. He wasn't a morning person, often sleeping in until long past when the rest of the castle was awake.

He didn't prefer the company of others, either. Fortunately, his early dedication to the path of the druid suitor and being the youngest of the three princes of Dunholm had stayed the queen's hand in setting him up with a bride, so he'd avoided most of the awkward state dinners where his brothers had met their wives.

He had a feeling that would change if his quest to win this druid woman's heart was unsuccessful, and he shuddered at the thought of returning home to not only military enrollment, but a woman intended as his wife, chosen by his mother.

Not that he knew Bria much better, but at least she was his choice, and he wouldn't have to live with her as his wife.

That thought sent a pang of guilt through him as he rummaged through his things, looking for the elusive brush he'd brought to tame his mane. He finally found it wrapped inside a dirty shirt from a prior day, untangled it, and set about getting ready for the morning he intended to spend with Bria.

It wasn't fair for him to feel relieved about her impending death. He'd expected it to be difficult to win her over. After all, she'd been through nearly a dozen suitors in only a few years. But he hadn't expected to grow so attached in such a short amount of time. Apparently, there was a bit of male competitiveness in him after all. Befriending her and getting to know her had turned out to be a challenge of the best kind, like when he was researching something, and the facts didn't line up and he had to hunt down the answers.

Something about Bria didn't line up. It made sense that she wasn't eager to throw herself into a relationship that could bring about a child and cause her death. But something about how on edge she was all the time, how reclusive and even violent she could be, made Theo's brain tick madly with theories.

She had a secret, and he would figure it out.

He tied his hair back with a bit of leather and, satisfied he looked decent for having slept in a tent for over a week, he exited into the frigid morning air.

He was surprised to find that Bria's chimney didn't emit smoke like it usually did at dawn. Had she already gone, or had she slept in for once? His boots crunched over the frost-tinged leaves as he wound his way down the slope and stopped in front of her door.

He wiped a gloved hand on his pants, as if that would do anything about the sweat forming on his palm. They hadn't explicitly agreed on breakfast, though that's how he'd interpreted their conversation the afternoon before.

He swung the canvas bag in his other hand, hoping he hadn't crushed the delicate pastries inside.

Finally, he took a deep breath for courage, and knocked.

A long moment passed. Perhaps she was asleep. But then the latch clicked, and the door creaked open. The crack revealed Bria, flaming curls far more askew than usual, as if she'd just rolled out of bed.

Her eyes, bleary and red-rimmed, widened at the sight of Theo.

He raised a hand and smiled at her. "I don't know if you recall, but we start our friendship today. Would you like to break your fast with me?"

Bria shook her head and cleared her throat in a rather unlady-like manner. "Can't," she croaked.

Theo frowned. "You're not well?"

Her hair swished back and forth as her head shook.

He might have thought it was a ploy to avoid him despite what she'd said about starting a friendship yesterday, but she did look properly miserable.

"That's all right. I could come in and help for a little while. Make you some tea? I'd do all the talking," Theo insisted, trying not to come across as too eager. He lifted the bag at his side. "I bought iced buns in one of the villages yesterday. Took a fair minute to get there, and I'd hate for them to go stale."

Bria shrank back into the shadows of the cottage, narrowing the gap in the door. She didn't have to speak for him to get the message.

Not today.

"I understand," he said, kicking at a leaf near his booted toe. "I don't like company when I'm ill, either. I'll check on you tomorrow."

She shut the door, none too gently. It felt as if she'd slammed it in his face.

Theo sighed and turned away from the door, failure tinging his mood. Everything that had seemed bright and full of possibility earlier now felt dull, damp, and miserable.

How could he have thought the gray, pre-sun morning was beautiful? He felt the cold now, biting his cheeks, stealing his breath as it clouded the air.

Underneath the dulling of the day, a whisper of excitement stirred. He rummaged through his mind for the information he sought, and stopped dead in his tracks when he realized where it came from.

Druid women tended to fall ill before their month-long fertility season started. Could it be a coincidence? He didn't think so, but then, druids were still something of a mystery to humankind, despite the copious records the suitors had kept. Theo couldn't be absolutely certain that Bria didn't have a simple cold, but the thought that this could be it, that her fertile period could be starting, made his heart burst into a gallop.

He would note the incident in his journal and check through the books and notes he'd brought with him for any mention of druid sickness. If nothing else, perhaps there was something in the records of Bria's past suitors that he could use to cheer her up, if not help her get better more quickly.

Newly invigorated by his purpose and the thought of spending the morning in research, Theo hurried back to his camp. He started a new fire in the pit outside his tent, then gathered his pens and books and settled on a log, using a boulder he'd dragged over as a table for his books. He longed for the oak desks of the castle records hall, where he could spread out as widely as he needed, but he'd make this work.

Theo set to studying, an iced bun stuffed into his mouth. He'd been over the past suitors' entries dozens of times and taken his own notes, but he hadn't been looking for something so specific. He had some of her likes and dislikes listed, but assuming he'd missed something, he combed back through. He turned the pages back to find the third suitor's report.

It was no surprise Bria had taken to Benton. He was a gentle soul, soft-spoken, and extremely skilled in the art of lovemaking. He'd taken a career in the Red Hall after his return, training others in the things he knew, never bragging about his conquest with the druid daughter, but bringing it up as a way to prove that he knew what he was doing.

Reading Benton's account now that Theo had become acquainted with Bria felt...uncomfortable. Before it had been a fun story, one he'd studied hoping to possibly emulate the charming man. He considered himself to be of a similar personality in some ways, though his gentleness was perhaps more a result of his desire to avoid people rather than set them at ease.

And he had none of the lovemaking skills Benton could claim. Now that he thought of it, what if Bria wanted a skilled lover?

Theo frowned through another bite of his breakfast. He had nothing to offer her there, especially compared with Benton's finesse. He knew theories only and had no experience. At this point, Bria would have to teach *him* a thing or two.

Master Graymont had emphasized that learning how to be intimate wasn't a requirement of the class, but a suggestion to be ignored at one's own peril. None of the other students had hesitated to get their time in at the Red Hall and become acquainted with adult pleasures. Theo, awkward at best through his adolescent years and reclusive and stand-offish through the start of his adult ones, had entered the Red Hall only a few times, not always willingly, and he'd never coupled with any of the ladies there.

The more he thought about it, the more depressed he became. He wouldn't change his experience, and if he went back now, it was unlikely he would take a different course. He'd had no desire to have intimate relations without personal connection.

Hence his approach to befriend the druid, hoping attraction would grow between them both, and by the time Bria entered her fertile phase, he would be able to move past the awkwardness he'd always felt at the thought of being with a woman.

It was a fallacy of thought if he'd ever had one. Theo snorted at his own blind optimism. Benton had come to the druid's door and, in his own words, had solicited her on their third encounter. She had accepted. Unless he'd blown his own success out of proportion, which didn't match the man Theo knew.

How had Benton gotten so close within moments, where Theo was met with what seemed to him an unreasonable amount of anger? Could Bria's past encounters with other suitors be to blame, or could the passage of time bringing her closer to her fertile time have made her more hesitant and afraid to let someone in?

Theo set down his journal and pen and stretched out his legs, putting his hands behind his head, considering. He supposed after Magnus, especially, she might be wary of whoever the queen sent. Over time, the suitors had gotten more desperate. The druid had coupled with two more, but only casually, almost as if she were experimenting, and both of them within her first two years of receiving suitors. The past three years, none of the suitors had had success getting into her bed, and she seemed to have given up letting them get close.

But why? Was she truly so frightened of death that she would risk the end of her kind? Did she assume she had more time, since she still had all three fertile periods before her? Or was she holding out for something to save her from the druid curse?

Theo leaned forward, gazing into the fire. He'd glimpsed the books in her cottage the day prior. When she'd left to go get his boots, he had almost hobbled over and chanced looking inside. He assumed they were druid records, and his mind itched to get a hold of the knowledge they contained. Perhaps he could convince her to allow him to read them.

Enough thinking. Theo adjusted his glasses and pulled open his notes one more time, scanning the list of likes and dislikes he'd noted from other suitors' records. His eyes landed on the line that read "White Thistlethorn tea." He'd even taken it upon himself to sketch an image of the plant from another book on herbal remedies. He could find it in these woods if he looked hard enough.

Raking out the fire with a stick so it would burn out faster, Theo took off into the forest. He stayed near the cottage, afraid if he went much farther into the deep woods he would meet more trees to offend. Without Bria leading the way, the forest seemed hostile, despite its beauty, and he moved quickly, leaving as little evidence of his passing as possible.

White Thistlethorn was a common plant that grew in abundance as a ground cover. It wouldn't have its tell-tale purple flowers this late in the season, and he honestly worried it would all be dead, and he'd have to start over finding something he could offer to Bria, but as the sun rose higher, creeping up towards its zenith, and as Theo's stomach clenched, reminding him it was nearly time for another meal, he found it.

Dark frost damage tinged its more delicate leaves, but the rest seemed all right. The white thorns along its dried stems were extra sharp. He picked several bunches, whispering his thanks to the plant out loud, as it seemed like something that might appease any nearby forest spirits.

He hurried back to his camp and, realizing his offering looked like a bunch of weeds, found a spare piece of clean leather he could use to tie the bundle together. Some of the stalks had wilted and it looked rather pathetic, but it smelled nice, and Bria would surely recognize his effort.

He marched back to the cottage, noting the lack of smoke coming from the chimney. He could offer to start a fire for her—surely she was chilled, and that wouldn't help her get better.

There was no answer when he knocked. He knocked again. Silence stretched. A third time. He waited extra-long, certain he was being impatient. She could be sleeping, but it still worried him that she wasn't well enough to start her own fire, much less answer.

He turned the latch and put his head through the doorway, eyes going to the bed first, where sure enough, Bria lay curled up, her face visible and at least three blankets covering her from head to toes.

Theo considered the sleeping woman. She wouldn't like him coming in here while she was so vulnerable, but the air in the cottage was nearly as cold as outside. She would be far more comfortable, and get well faster, if he stoked up a fire. He could find a hot water bottle or some stones he could heat to put near her feet as well.

Master Graymont had taught the boys many useful things. Theo didn't know enough to work as a medic, but he had some basic knowledge, mostly meant to be used if he ended up living in the forest for extended periods of time.

He busied himself with the fireplace. The fire had completely gone out. It took him a moment to replenish the woodpile inside, get the kindling to light, then slowly add logs until the fire ate at the wood and the cabin filled with a warm light.

Theo passed by Bria briefly, putting the inside of his wrist on her forehead. Definitely fevered.

He didn't know when she might wake, but he could prepare some sort of meal, something she could heat up.

A pot on the table needed to be cleaned of the previous meal's contents. He took it outside, scrubbing with a bundle of sticks and leaves until the stuck bits were gone. He returned and looked through the druid's larder.

Various wilting green leaves, several types of onion and mushroom, spices, and salt took up the shelves. What did the woman survive on?

He eventually found eggs as well, a few small speckly things, and he quickly planned out a simple meal he felt confident enough to make. First, he had to fetch more water from the river, as her supply had run low. Then, he chopped and tossed things in the pot and filled it with water, setting it on a grate over the fire.

Soon, the rich smell of the broth filled the cottage, and Bria moaned, stirring, but she didn't wake.

Theo stayed where he was seated at the table, resisting the urge to crack open her books. It nearly killed him to have so much knowledge he didn't know within reach. Why did he resist? After all, he might find something in them that could help her.

The pot of broth hissed in the firepit, the liquid boiling dangerously close to the top. Theo leapt to tend it, forgetting, for the moment, about the books.

He took the soggy vegetables out of the broth and scooped some into two mugs, including one for himself. In his opinion, it needed chicken. But he knew druids rarely ate meat, so he satisfied himself with vegetables and a runny yolk egg, then poured another mug and brought it to Bria's bedside.

"Bria," he said quietly, hoping not to startle her into turning him into a bush or something. His chest fluttered at the sight of her peaceful face, and the realization that he'd said her name for the first time out loud.

Watching her come out of sleep felt intimate, more so than he had imagined. Her eyelids peeled slowly open, eyelashes fluttering against her cheek before her irises appeared, stunning green and shining, though some of that shine was perhaps brought on by the fever.

She blinked several times, not moving, and Theo raised the mug between them.

"I made some broth. I'll leave you now, but there are also boiled eggs in a pot on your table, if you're feeling up to more. I'll come check on you again this evening." He set the mug down on the small shelf next to her bed and turned to go, not waiting for a response, as he assumed she might not be well enough to give one.

"Stay," Bria said in a rough whisper.

Surely he'd misheard her. "What was that?"

"Stay," she said again, a little clearer this time.

When he turned from the doorway, she had sat up in bed and was watching him, somehow looking wild as ever despite the illness.

"All right," he said gently and closed the door, crossing the room and grabbing a chair from near the table, bringing it closer to her bedside without crossing the invisible line of her comfort.

She watched his every move until he sat down, and seemingly satisfied, she picked up the mug and sipped at the broth. She seemed pleased with it, waiting until it had cooled enough for her to drink it, and then she set the mug down and wiped her mouth before laying back in her bed, pulling the covers up to her chin.

"Cold?" Theo asked, holding his arms crossed over his chest. Being in her cottage with her awake was far more disconcerting. Those green eyes remained fixed on him, as if she didn't trust him. Which, he supposed, she didn't. And he still didn't blame her, even if he had helped her when the man attacked her the day before and had made her soup. Neither of those things meant she owed him her trust.

Bria nodded in response to his question, and Theo stood. She shrank back as he did, eyes wide and alert.

Theo raised his hands. "I'm going to find some stones to warm. I'll put them under the covers with you, if you'll allow it."

She nodded after a moment, and Theo left the cottage, finding three rocks bigger than his hands. They would do nicely. He brought them in, wiped them clean, and set them in the coals at the edge of the fire to get warm.

Using rags, he pulled them out of the fire after a time, wrapped them, and carried them to the bed.

Bria, still alert, lifted the edges of the blankets for him, and he slid the rocks in under the covers, far enough from her that she wouldn't get burned. One on each side, and one at her feet.

When the covers were lowered again, Bria sighed and relaxed, eyelids growing heavy.

"Do you want tea?" Theo asked, thinking of the White Thistlethorn he'd picked earlier.

Bria shook her head. "Later," she said, her voice barely a whisper.

He crossed his arms over his chest and watched her fall asleep. As she'd drifted off, the books on the shelf near the fire caught his attention again.

Surely, she wouldn't mind him reading one or two pages.

BRIA

B RIA WALKED THE EDGE between dreaming and wakeful-
ness as long as she could manage, striving to stay
awake and keep her awareness on the man sitting in a
chair at her bedside. The fire crackled, and pages turned,
the sound and the warmth of the stones beneath her
blanket lulling her into a deep and dreamless sleep.

Dreamless, until her fever spiked, and she spiraled into
a vision from Tala.

The vision started the way they always did. A bright
green flare of light and the song that the forest sang to
itself along the networks of fungi that branched through
the soil—Tala's love song to all things living. Bria knew it
by heart, but her human voice couldn't create the right
tone, no matter how hard she'd tried.

The green light faded, leaving Bria walking through the deepest part of the forest, the part she rarely entered, as it tended itself and didn't need—or want—much outside intervention.

Being there felt like being deep underwater, the usual cheery bird chirps replaced with deep, low calls that might have been birds, or perhaps some greater leviathan that walked or flew through the trees. She had seen shadows moving there, in real life, between trees as tall as mountains, where she was a mere speck like an insect.

Somewhere, deep in those woods, she thought she might find Tala. She had tried, once, while looking for the sacred caves. She'd fallen asleep and woken back in her cottage clearing, a blanket of moss wrapped around her, and a dead rabbit at her feet. A gift, and a warning, from Tala.

Do not venture where you are not invited, daughter.

Bria hadn't been back since, but now, there she was, walking among the monstrous trees and feeling like nothing more than a borer beetle.

Had it always been so sweltering here? She wiped at her brow, and her hand came away wet. Every part of her was drenched and prickled with sweat. Her legs wobbled and she laid down on the soft forest floor, her body trembling between misery and longing. Waves of pleasure and pain swept through her, stopping at the root of her center and throbbing.

Bria cried out at the uncomfortable sensation. Clenching and tightening and releasing that she could not control. Her womb tightened, like a hard-shelled seed and seemed to strain, like it would crack open wide.

She resisted the sensation, clenching every muscle in her body, willing that seed to stay closed. Pain zinged along her limbs, her core aching, longing to be released.

Let go, Tala's daughter. You resist your very nature, a gentle, female voice said, permeating all of Bria's cells.

She arched her back, screaming soundlessly at a sharp burst of pain. She grabbed roots that appeared at the ground near her head, writhing with the strange sensations that moved through her. What was the purpose of this torture? What did it mean? Why would Tala bring her here and let her suffer? She would split open; she would die and become another tree in this ancient forest.

It is not yet your time.

Her body shuddered to a stop, heaviness filling her pelvis. Had she done it? Had she resisted the change?

Bria waited, breath held, feeling the sensations in her body, the aches and the pressure, still there but subdued. And then her womb cracked wide open, and essence poured out of her. It was vibrant, beautiful, inevitable, and she could not resist it. Light and warmth coursed through her, filling every crevice, even the darkest aspects of her soul.

A light unfolds in the darkness, beginning what will have no end. Tala's presence rumbled through her.

Bria wanted to cry out, to ask why Tala would subject her to the curse, but her voice would not respond. Darkness fell in the deepest part of the forest, and she lost sight of the leafy canopy so high above her it might have been the sky. A sky without stars.

She lay there, aware of herself and little else, waiting for roots to grow out of her body and make her one with the forest, but the roots did not come, and the seed inside of her did not crack more. Instead, a sensation of warmth pulsed within—hopeful, waiting.

Ready to kill her as soon as it bloomed.

THEO

TWO PAGES QUICKLY TURNED into more than a dozen as Theo read long into the night, the next day, and the next. Meanwhile, Bria fought against her sickness in a delirious, fevered state.

He sat hunched near the fire with two lanterns lit beside him, soaking up as much light as he could so he might translate page after page.

The writings were dated at the top of each page from over 150 years ago. Five, perhaps six generations back? The faded ink made the pages difficult to read. These books desperately needed to be transcribed to be preserved. The thought of them falling into oblivion was too much for him to bear.

It was painstaking, back-aching work to translate the scrawled druid script. He'd studied it extensively, even helped the realm's scholars discover new meanings for several words and phrases from the few intact druid texts they had available, but here he encountered constructions of the language he'd never seen before.

Occasionally, he got up to tend to Bria. He put a cool, damp cloth on her head and removed the stones to warm them in the fire, then replaced them in the bed once more. He trickled water and broth through her parted lips, watching as they eagerly closed around each mouthful.

The moon appeared on the ground outside, shadows moving as it passed through the night.

Sometime after midnight on the second day, after stoking the fire to build up the flame again and create more light, Theo's finger trailed underneath a paragraph one word at a time, bringing the wise druid's words out of obscurity.

This curse that fell on my ancient druid sisters and devastated our nation has a cure, or so I've been told. I'm not certain what is true and what is lore now, as many decades have passed since the first cursed druids became one with the forest and left us with only their texts. But we've lost the ability to read their words. They differ from our own too much. The language has changed. My father did not know more than the few words he'd learned from my mother, and I am no scholar.

Theo's head shot up, and he stared at Bria's blanket-laden form for a long moment. If her great-something grandmother could not read the oldest records, was it possible that Bria could not read this record? Generations of druids had been raised by human men who did not have sufficient knowledge of druid culture, writing, and language to pass it down to their children after the druid women died.

No wonder Bria was angry. She had lost so much before she was even born. More than her mother. Her entire culture. It was amazing she had maintained her connection to her power and nature. That, too, would eventually be lost if the last druid died.

Theo shuddered and returned to the text. He wanted to know more about this cure.

I've poured over the ancient texts, praying Tala would reveal their meaning to me, but the lines and swirls float before my eyes and blur together, never gaining any form I could understand. I have one phrase that our human fathers have passed on from our druid mothers. Perhaps it contains the secret that will unlock the cure, but I have not yet figured it out. Perhaps you will, Tala's daughter.

A light unfolds in the darkness, beginning what will have no end.

A light in the darkness? Had he translated that correctly? Theo went over that page, and several pages after it, three times before his eyes ached so terribly he was forced to close the book. The druid had a few theories, and mentioned something about a cave, a cave that no one had found since the last druid war with the humans. He'd had to skip lines in that part that he couldn't decipher. Yet. He had all the tools and knowledge, what he needed was time.

Time, and perhaps Bria's permission. He hadn't waited to ask permission as he should have. Knowing what these books contained, he had a feeling Bria would forgive him once she knew what he'd discovered.

But if they found the cave together and somehow ended the curse, he would be helping to end the druid's reliance on mankind. Bria would never be with him then. He would lose his library, his freedom. And in a few generations, druids would repopulate the forest.

Would they war with the humans again? Would his mother banish him from her court? She certainly wouldn't be pleased to lose control over the sole remaining guardian and steward of the forest, especially not since she aimed to put a druid daughter on the throne.

His druid daughter.

That reality settled onto his heart like a heavy weight. Here he sat, in the druid's home while she lay ill, literally considering her demise and holding the future of her people in his hands.

She would hate him if she knew. Loathe him, even, far more than she already did. Though he'd made some headway there. She was starting to trust him. Would he lose it all if he told her he'd read the books? And yet, if he kept it from her, could he live with the knowledge and raise their child without ever telling her that he knew something that could have saved her mother and restored the druids?

He put the book back on the shelf and sank his aching head into his hands. He rubbed his temples, but it did no good. He was thinking in circles. When he got like this at home, his friend Rhae would tell him he was too much in his head, and she would take him out drinking or dancing or make him spar with her, even though he wasn't any good at any of those things.

She would tolerate no discussion of the thing he was pondering, insisting that "that big head of yours will sort it out eventually," and she wouldn't let him go home until he was too drunk to hold a book steady, much less read.

But when he needed to talk about his mother, Rhae was always there, ready with a quick insult for the cold-hearted queen's treatment of her son and a bit of advice that made Theo feel better, even if he rarely took it.

What would Rhae think of Bria? Theo snorted, glancing at the sleeping druid's form. They would be quick friends, no doubt. Rhae was liable to call him some terrible names for even thinking of withholding this knowledge from Bria, but he needed to hear it from her. Maybe that would prick his conscience enough that he would know the right thing to do.

He stood and walked across the room before he could think his way out of it. He needed to talk to someone, to get out of his head, before he confronted Bria again. She would be all right until he returned, he was sure, but he could let someone in the village at the edge of the forest know to check in on her in a few days if he didn't return.

Because if his mother found him back in her castle without confirmation that he'd impregnated the druid according to their promise, she would be livid. Never mind that he still had six weeks left in their bargain.

That gave him pause. He had made it past the point where Bria typically chased her suitors off. Perhaps she hadn't because she was ill, but a surge of confidence went through him, nonetheless.

Theo double-checked his camp and gathered a few items he wanted for the trip. He didn't want to leave Bria alone for long. If she remained ill, she wouldn't be able to care for herself.

He rushed through the damp forest to the village, tipping the hand at the stable where he kept his horse and requesting that someone be sent to look in on Bria if he didn't return the next day. The boarder agreed far more readily than Theo expected, even looking concerned at the mention of the druid's illness. Perhaps this close to the forest, the people were more fond of the druid than afraid.

Settling into the saddle and taking the reins, Theo urged his horse forward, moving as quickly as he dared in the muddy conditions.

It was past nightfall when he arrived, his cloak soaked through, feeling hungrier than he had in a while. He paid a courier in town to get an urgent message to Lady Rhaessa Goldenvane, and settled into a quiet corner at the Cloak and Stagger to wait.

Rhae slid into the seat across from him so suddenly, Theo nearly choked on his meat pie. He wiped his mouth and took a gulp of the weak ale he'd paid far too much for before grinning at her.

"What do you need now, you great useless lump of a half-cousin?" Rhae asked, crossing her arms but grinning back with a friendly-enough expression. She still wore her plate armor; she must have just gotten off a guard rotation in the palace.

"Can't I just want to visit with one of my favorite people in Dunholm?" Theo asked innocently, playing the game they always played.

"Aren't you supposed to be bedding a druid right now?" Rhae replied, leaning forward.

He wished she'd lowered her voice more.

Theo tugged the damp hood of his cloak up to cover more of his face. "As if. We're barely past the 'please don't murder me with your magic trees while I sleep' stage of our relationship. But since you mentioned it, that's exactly what I need to talk to you about."

Rhae clapped her hands together, rubbing them vigorously and giving him a lecherous grin. "Finally! Do you know how long I've waited for the day you asked me how to please a woman? Ever since you turned *me* down, I've wondered if you were...you know...*cut out* for your chosen career as a druid suitor."

Theo wiped a hand down his face and sighed. "I turned you down because I didn't have romantic feelings for you, Rhae, not because I'm not attracted to women."

"Really? Because you could have fooled...well, everyone," Rhae said, leaning back into her chair, enthusiasm draining from her expression. "And I'm guessing you didn't actually come to get all the best tips from someone who is clearly an expert?" She raised her eyebrows.

Theo snorted. "No, I think I've gotten plenty of 'tips' over the years, thank you. As you said, it's literally my job to woo the druid, and despite not having any actual experience, I'm confident I can—"

A figure moved across the room towards a table, making Theo duck his head down towards the table.

"What is it? Who is it? Theo, are you in trouble?"

"Magnus. If he sees me, he'll tell my mother and she'll, well, you know..."

"Take away your books again?" Rhae asked dryly. "You're not supposed to be here, but I doubt she'll do anything drastic."

"You mean put me in military training and marry me to the highest bidder if she gets any hint that I've failed? No, definitely not that," Theo said, putting his hand up next to his head.

Magnus had grown closer to his mother, was perhaps even her lover based on what Theo had witnessed before he left the castle. And he hated Theo. He wouldn't hesitate to sell him out.

"Old bag finally gave you an ultimatum, huh? You know I don't like her, but I agree that you need to broaden your horizons. Anything to get you out of that dusty atheneum—"

"Rhae!" Theo hissed. "I need your advice, not your criticism. Listen, I don't know if I can do this. Not the sex thing." He gritted his teeth. This was turning out to be far more stressful than he'd imagined. Nothing was going the way he'd expected.

Rhae tilted her head, her expression softening. "I'm listening."

Theo took a deep, calming breath. "She's starting to trust me. Tried to teach me to listen to the trees. It was...nice, actually. Strange but nice. And we were supposed to have breakfast together a few days ago, but she got sick. She let me take care of her and I found some books—"

"I should have known this was about books," Rhae muttered, rolling her eyes.

Theo glared, and Rhae clamped her mouth shut, doing a "go on" motion with her hands.

"I translated a few pages in one and found out some information that could restore the druid people...but I don't know if I should tell her. We could start a war. Not to mention, I might break her trust by telling her I read her books and..." Theo halted, blinking at the expression on Rhae's face. She looked about to explode with laughter. "What now?"

Rhae took a calming breath, fanning her face. "Not everyone cares about their books the way you do, Theo! What you consider a grave crime—borrowing a book without permission—most people would barely blink at."

"But I invaded her privacy."

"It's not her personal journal, for crying out loud. And if you tell her something she didn't know before, maybe something she's been looking for her whole life, she's probably going to—" Rhae described an action that Theo heard women do to men in the Red Hall, and his ears burned. He couldn't help but imagine Bria doing it, even for a moment. Thinking about that in the middle of a crowded tavern with an enemy seated a few tables away and his cousin sitting across from him was too much.

"Rhae," he clasped his hands together and pressed them to his lips. "Could you not?"

Rhae smirked. "As you wish. But she'll be pleased, Theo. Grateful, at least. And this war you're talking about is ages off. A few decades. Populations don't recover from total decimation that quickly. Your dear mum will be tossing in her grave before then."

"She wants to put our child on the throne. My child. The druid's child." He hadn't planned to tell her, but he needed someone to know, and it seemed important.

Rhae looked stunned. "What? A druid has never sat on the throne."

"My mother hasn't been able to have a female. And all of the last druids have had girls."

"What if you have a boy?" Rhae challenged.

"That won't happen. Or at least, it's not likely." Theo sighed. "That's not all, Rhae. I-I'm starting to wonder if I can do this. Not only because of my mother. Bria doesn't want this. She doesn't want to die, and I don't blame her. I think she might be considering ending it."

"Killing herself?"

"No, not that. But I think she's planning to let the druid line die. With her."

"Is she in her fertile period?" Rhae asked, her voice dropping so low Theo almost couldn't hear it. Her gaze intensified.

"I-I think it's starting, yes. Sickness like this is the first sign. I've never read or heard about a druid getting sick otherwise," Theo said.

"I understand why you hesitate—you have a heart bigger than any man I've ever met. But your mother won't give up if you aren't successful. Nor will the queen after her. The druid has two more fertile periods to get through after this one. The queen will keep sending men until one is successful, and she gets her druid heir. Do you *want* the druid to be with someone else?"

The thought of another man in Bria's cottage—sitting where he had sat, tending to her, making her laugh—he hated it.

"No," he said, heart thudding.

"Then your dilemma is solved. Be with her. Enjoy the time you get. Treat her like the queen she is and rest easy knowing she had a good life. Besides, there's nothing that says you couldn't enjoy the next twenty years together, right? Some suitors have waited in the past," Rhae said.

Theo scoffed and reached for his mug, rubbing a finger through the beaded condensation on the side.

"Unfortunately, my mother isn't that patient. She's given me three months, and that's half over."

Rhae clenched her hands into fists. "The queen would do well to learn some patience."

"And you would do well to learn your place." Magnus's voice came out of thin air, making Theo jump.

Theo ducked his head further, facing the wall. Magnus might not have seen; he might not know.

"Who's your friend, Rhae?"

Theo could hear the sneer in Magnus's voice.

"Merely a lover wishing to hide their identity. You can understand that, can't you?"

Theo gritted his teeth. He had to stop himself from spinning around and telling Magnus off himself, but Rhae was trying to protect him. He could set his pride aside and let her. He was used to it at this point in his life.

Rhae continued, "What's got an Ironcrest crawling through the underbelly of the capitol, anyway?"

Magnus snorted. "You think I believe that? Looked like you were arguing."

"What's it to you?"

"I want to make sure no one is disrespecting one of the Queen's Own."

Rhae said something about the male parts of a bull, and Theo cringed, but couldn't help smiling at her tenacity. "Go mind someone else's business, Magnus. We're done here."

"I want to know the identity of your friend before I go," Magnus said, a hand landing on Theo's shoulder.

Rhae stood, her chair crashing to the floor behind her, and she launched herself at Magnus.

Theo darted from his seat and ran for the door, holding his cloak over the bottom half of his face. He untied his horse from its post outside and mounted, squeezing his horse's side to bring it to a gallop.

He didn't dare look back, not even to see how Rhae fared in the fight. He could only move forward, towards the forest and the druid slowly stealing his heart, and hope that his mother's lover hadn't seen his face.

BRIA

EVENING HAD FALLEN WHEN Bria stirred again. Sleepily, she lifted her head from the pillow, blanket falling to her waist as she sat up.

A cough alerted her to the other presence in the room. He sat in a chair near the fireplace, head turned away from her as if shy of her appearance.

Bria glanced down. She wore nothing but her woolen shift, stiff with dried sweat. It wasn't entirely immodest; all of the important bits were covered. She wasn't one to feel shy of her body, regardless. She belonged to the forest. What did it matter if a man admired her or not?

She found the fact that he'd averted his eyes admirable. Far better than the lecherous gaze of one Magnus Ironcrest and a number of suitors who'd come before.

Bria grasped the blanket and brought it up higher, then cleared her throat. "Hardly the best way to earn my trust, staring at me while I sleep."

Theodore turned back around. "I assure you, I have done nothing more than watch over the fire since arriving."

"I recall your hand on my forehead," Bria replied, the accusation barely reaching her voice. He'd been tender, his soft gaze and touch the only things she remembered through the haze of sickness.

"Only to assess your condition," Theodore said.

"The soup did give me some strength," Bria admitted. "Where did a pretty city boy like you learn to cook?"

"Survival camp," Theodore said somberly.

Bria laughed. "The one where they toss you into the woods and tell you to make do for a few days?"

He nodded, flushing. Like her comment had pricked his pride. She hadn't thought he had any—he didn't match her typical male experience. Then again, maybe that was his angle. Make her comfortable with him, get her guard down, and seduce her when she couldn't refuse.

If her dreams were any indication, that time was far nearer than she cared for. She only had a vague sense of what she'd dreamed about. Strange urges had filled her body, and she remembered something about laying in the womb of the forest...or did it all symbolize her own womb? She shook her head violently and rubbed at her arms, trying to rid herself of the uncomfortable prickling on her skin.

"Are you cold? I can heat up the stones again." Theodore leapt to his feet, moving towards her.

"No! No. I'm fine. I could use a cup of tea." Give him something to do, something to get his attention off of her while she figured out what was wrong and if anything had changed.

She had gotten sick—that had changed. She had never been sick in her life. Tala didn't allow it. But it was one of the signs she'd been told to watch for.

A sign of her first fertile cycle beginning.

She didn't want to think about it. If she knew, then Theodore likely knew as well. She needed to distract him, make him forget what he'd come to her forest for.

"Watching those survival outings served as great entertainment from time to time," she said, forcing a note of teasing into her voice.

"You...watched us?" Theodore asked, adjusting the pot of water on the fire. He grabbed a bunch of dried leaves from the rafter where they hung. White Thistlethorn. She had run out before she'd gotten sick, she was sure of it. Had he gathered some for her?

Bria nodded. "Nothing happens in my forest that I don't know about. Besides, who could miss it? A bunch of awkward boys pretending at forest survival. Mostly scaring the local wildlife and cutting into my trees." She scowled at that.

"In any case, I'm glad you seem to have perked up," Theodore said, changing the subject.

Was that...guilt in his expression?

"Are you hungry?" he asked.

"A bit," Bria admitted. "Is there more soup?"

"No, but I can make some." He took the pot from the fire and poured some of the water into a mug where he'd placed the leaves, then immediately put it back on the heat. He seemed particularly at ease doing the cooking. It surprised her, though she wasn't sure why.

Everyone had to eat to live. Except he was a coddled city boy, most likely noble from the apparent softness of his hands and his affinity for reading. When had he learned to enjoy cooking?

She watched with fascination as he chopped mushrooms—again, surprisingly edible, as she'd been out of mushrooms when she'd fallen ill—and fragrant herbs and leeks. He slid it all into the pot of boiling water.

Bria whistled. "You were paying attention in class."

He ducked his head, cracking tiny quail eggs into a pot. "I just don't like starving." He glanced her way. "Where do you get your bread and butter? You don't grind grains yourself?"

"I trade with the villagers. Sometimes they leave offerings at the edge of the forest. Sometimes I leave offerings back."

Theodore chuckled. "I wonder what they think of that?"

"Honestly? I think they're too scared to reject what I leave. They don't see me as a mortal like them."

"You're not like them," Theodore said, pausing his preparations and staring at her intently. "You're not like me."

"That's the kind of thinking that made my people extinct," Bria snapped. "I might have magic, but so do some of your kind. Otherwise, I just live in the forest and have a slightly different biology."

Theodore rubbed his chin. "When you put it that way, I suppose you're right. Sort of. You have a longer lifespan, and all of your people could use magic, not a select few."

"Emphasis on used to," Bria said. Her arms grew tired of holding the blanket up, and her legs itched for a walk around the cabin. Not to mention other bodily needs that were screaming for her attention. "Erm...is the soup nearly done?"

"Oh, yeah," Theodore said, spinning around to the pot that was nearly boiling over. "And your tea is done. I can leave them here for you, unless you'd like to take them in bed?"

Bria rolled her eyes at his fumbling, but her chest warmed. His sincerity was infuriatingly endearing.

"Leave it there. I can manage."

"I'll go, then." Theodore straightened his vest and gathered a few items he seemed to have brought with him—parchment and quill and a book with an intriguing title. "Druid Time and Lore" it read.

"Is that by Lorenzo Graymont?" Bria asked.

"What? Oh, the book? This book?" Theodore stammered, taking the book out from his arm and staring at it. "It is, yes. I suppose...I suppose he is your grandfather?"

"Indeed," Bria said, wrapping her arms around her blanketed legs.

"Did you ever meet him?" Theodore asked.

Bria nodded. "A few times. He didn't agree with the way my father was raising me. Too wild, he said. The last time I saw him they argued. I was twelve years old."

"Master Graymont has many...interesting opinions on druids."

Bria glanced down, then back up again. "And you? What is your opinion of druids?"

"That they're unbelievably powerful and impossible to get close to," Theodore replied, a wry smile on his face.

"Good," Bria said, amused.

A long pause filled the room between them, and then Theodore moved towards the door again. "Well, I'll see you—"

"Tonight. Would you come back tonight?" Bria asked breathlessly.

Theodore gave a small bow, and the smile he gave her when he lifted his head made her heart flip-flop.

****

Theo's knock came at the door the moment Bria reached the end of her braid. She tied it off and straightened the covers over her legs. She felt much improved from that morning, but fatigue and uncertainty clung to her like tree sap.

"Come in," Bria called.

Theodore ducked inside, another bundle of books and papers tucked under his arm.

"Do you plan to study?" Bria asked, feeling a touch of disappointment that he might be distracted from their conversation.

Theodore grinned sheepishly. "Force of habit, I'm afraid. But I noticed your collection," he gestured to the journals lining the one shelf next to the fireplace. "And I thought we might be able to share some information."

Anger rose up inside Bria, reflexive and hot as red-orange coals. She gripped the blanket in her hands, feeling the power of Tala building within her reach.

But no, she was meant to be befriending this human suitor. The one who tried. She couldn't entirely convince herself that he didn't mean to glean all of her secrets and betray her the moment he got the chance, but she had invited him here.

Let go, daughter of Tala. The voice, echoing from her fever dream, brought Bria out of her angry stupor. She recognized the voice of the One who Made the Forest, even if she didn't agree with it. She blinked, relaxing her fingers, and forced a smile at Theo.

"That's kind of you."

Theodore set his books down on the table and started rolling up his shirt sleeves. "How are you feeling?"

Bria blinked a few times. Who knew forearms could be so distracting? "Feeling? Good. I'm good. Hungry."

She sounded like a fool. The thought made her cross, but curiosity was winning. She followed his movements, watching as he turned to the pots still dirty from the earlier meal.

"Ah, yes. Dishes. Where do you wash them?" he asked.

"There's a basin outside that collects rain. I clean them there," Bria said, feeling dazed.

Not once in all her years of being pursued had a man offered to do her *dishes.*

He stacked the dishes and left the cabin, leaving Bria with her thoughts. Very confused thoughts.

Are you in support of this human, Tala? Do you wish me to make him my lover? To bear a child with him? Are you ready for me to die? The tone in her head didn't contain near enough respect to be considered a prayer. No, this was a childish rebellion. Hardly befitting a priestess of the forest.

It is not yet your time. The voice came again with an edge to it Bria hadn't heard the first time those words had been said to her. A harsh edge, like lightning splitting a tree down the middle.

Show me where the cave is. Save your daughter and your people! Bria pleaded, hoping without hope that the goddess was near and cared to answer her plea.

The opening of the cottage door disrupted Bria's entreaty to her goddess.

"Wind's got a bit of a nip in it tonight. I'd best get some more firewood in here before I leave. Are you getting tired of soup? I'd make something else, but most of them contain meat, which I know you don't care for," Theodore said, carrying in the pile of now-clean dishes.

"Only in the midst of the Sleeping when plants are scarce," Bria affirmed. She glanced out the window at the leaves being blown from the trees. It was nearly dark. So early? It seemed like yesterday she'd seen the first hints of the Gathering time. Now the Sleeping was upon them.

"I've always been impressed with the druid terms for the seasons. They're so much more comforting than the human ones. Are you aware?" Theodore asked, clattering dishes together as he returned them to their places on her shelves.

"Of the human terms? No," Bria said, though it was only partly true. She wanted to hear him talk some more.

Theo's face lit up. "So there's the first season as the world turns, you call it the Quickening where we say the Greening. That one isn't too terrible, but then the second season is the druid Warming versus the Long Days. Right now, humans are in the Fading, which is straight up depressing, while you celebrate the Gathering. Soon you'll be embracing the Sleeping while humans endure the Darkening." He paused, glancing her way. "The Darkening—the Sleeping, rather—is my favorite. It's so cozy and comforting, and possibly the most beautiful. Plus, no one expects me to go outside or socialize much."

It surprised Bria that he expressed disinterest in socializing. He was so friendly and talkative with her, but perhaps that was simply because she'd been alone for too long. Among his own kind, she could see how he might be considered reclusive, with his preference for books and lack of interest in things most of the men she'd met seemed to enjoy.

"Do you eat cheese? I brought some dak cheese from home." Theodore interrupted her thoughts, holding up a waxen cloth-wrapped package.

Bria's mouth watered. Dak cheese would taste far better than the goat cheese she usually ate.

She nodded, not trusting herself to not drool.

"I noticed you're out of bread as well. I don't know how to make that. But you can teach me. I'm a good pupil." His earnest, brown-eyed gaze caught Bria off guard as he looked up from the vegetables he chopped.

"I, er, suppose that would be all right. Except I don't have any grain right now," Bria said, thinking over what she had in her stores. It was prime harvest time, and she'd spent the first few days of it sick.

Theo's expression deflated, and his shoulders slumped.

"I could teach you how to make my seed bread. It's much denser than what you're used to, but I think it's delicious," Bria said.

His face brightened again. "That sounds perfectly agreeable. When do we start?"

"Dawn, of course," Bria said. "Best to not waste daylight."

Theodore groaned. "I should have guessed you'd be the early morning type. You know it's a crime to neglect sleep so much?"

"I am always well-rested. I don't stay up reading by firelight until all hours," Bria said. She clamped her mouth shut. Had she just...*teased* him?

She thought she caught a grin on the human's face as he focused on the chopping block. She crossed her arms. No doubt he thought his overtures had been successful. She could watch him prepare food for her all day. That didn't mean she wanted to share a bed with him.

He glanced up and caught her glare, a look of confusion crossing his face. "Did I offend you?"

"No," Bria replied, not offering any explanation. She was acting childish, but did he know what was at stake? She wouldn't be swayed by a man who did chores and made her soup.

Silence filled the cabin. It creaked, the wind outside whispering of a storm coming. Tomorrow would be a good day for gathering nuts.

"Might get a storm blowing in," Theodore said.

Bria rolled her eyes. Humans had no senses. They were deaf, mute, and blind compared with her goddess-blessed abilities. Why would Tala want her to mate with one?

She slouched down under the covers, feeling somewhat chilled and quite irritable. Why had she invited him to come back?

Because it feels nice to be looked after. To not be alone, she thought, some of her stubbornness melting away.

Once everything had gone into the pot and the area had been cleaned, she expected Theodore to start asking her questions, but instead he pulled a chair up to the table, laid out his parchment, ink, and quill, and opened a book. He didn't speak, didn't even glance her way.

As the moments passed, Bria found herself even more irritated than before. The bed felt too hot, but she didn't want to remove the blankets that acted as a protective barrier between herself and the man at the table.

And no matter how uncomfortable the silence got, she wouldn't be the first to break it.

Bria resigned herself to studying him. Her gaze trailed up his legs and torso, then down his arms. She spent the most time on his face, watching the expressions shift ever-so-slightly or the way he bit his lip as he scratched out an error on his parchment. She became so engrossed with examining him, when he looked up from his work and met her eyes she yelped.

Covering her mouth, Bria coughed. "Something in my throat."

Theodore got up and went to the fire, where he had a pot and a kettle both going. He stirred the contents of the pot, removed the kettle, and filled a cup with tea.

She smelled the pine and citrus scent of whitethorn before he finished drizzling the honey in.

"Careful, it's hot," he said, handing her the stoneware mug.

Bria clasped the handle, her fingers brushing his. She tried not to have any reaction at all, but his protective admonition—something anyone might say anytime they handed someone a hot drink—combined with his soft gaze and the slightest touch, sent tingles up her spine, and warmth sprouted in her belly.

"I-I-thank you," Bria stammered.

He bowed to her—*bowed*—and then returned to his seat, hunching over his notes.

She longed to know what he was reading and his thoughts on it. She had a feeling he could make any subject interesting. But her stubbornness was like a moss-laden boulder—not going anywhere anytime soon.

Theodore did not give her any reprieve from her growing boredom. He continued reading and checking the soup until at long last he sighed, stretched, and corked his ink bottle. He filled a bowl with a hearty combination of parsnips, pine nuts, leeks, and tubers, with a blob of butter floating on top.

Bria dipped her spoon in and took a sip. Flavor burst in her mouth, and she took another bite, and another, until she drank the dregs, emptying the bowl.

She had rarely eaten anything other than her father's or her own cooking. She enjoyed the food she made for herself, but this...this was something else entirely.

"An empty bowl is a compliment in itself," Theodore said, retrieving her dish.

"Thank you," Bria replied, leaning back in bed. Despite her best intentions, the walls she'd built over the years were dropping fast.

She almost couldn't help it. Ease seemed to follow Theo. He demanded nothing of her—no further conversation, no expectations. Her first impression of him had been based on recent interactions with suitors from Dunholm. Theodore was in an entirely different class, and neither her brain nor her heart knew what to do with him.

He disappeared for a while, returning with freshly washed dishes, and once everything had been cleaned up, he gathered his things and faced her.

"If there's nothing else, I'll take my leave and bid you a good night."

So formal. So *attractive.* Bria shook her head. She couldn't let her guard down because the man treated her with respect. He still had her trust to earn.

"Goodnight, then," Bria said.

He bowed again, and the gesture made Bria's heart flutter. She watched him walk out the door, biting her tongue to avoid inviting him to join her foraging in the morning.

After all, he'd probably invite himself along. If there was one thing she could count on, it was suitors and their relentless pursuit of her.

BRIA

S OMETHING WAS WRONG WITH the suitor.

Bria waited in her cottage an excessively long time the next morning, expecting him to knock on the door and ask if he could join her. She'd already planned to pretend to hesitate, to let him persuade and pursue her until, reluctantly, she agreed.

But Theodore still hadn't emerged from his tent when she finished her breakfast, so she stuck close to the clearing for her morning meditation. Every creak of the trees interrupted her communion with Tala, and the goddess didn't seem to be in an answering mood anyway, so Bria finished early. Finding the human's fire still cold, she gathered wood until her stomach rumbled.

The rest of the day passed much the same, and she went to bed confused. Why hadn't Theodore made an appearance? She'd seen him every day since he'd arrived, regardless of the fact that she'd made it clear she wanted nothing to do with him. He'd cared for her so respectfully during her sickness, it didn't make sense that he'd avoid her on purpose.

Troubled, she tossed and turned in her sleep, dreaming senseless dreams of a forest as dark and deep as an ocean, with massive creatures roaming between the trees, and a tiny seed planted in the mossy earth that glowed and pulsed with the rhythm of a goddess's heartbeat.

Three more days passed this way, and though Bria loathed to admit it, she was afraid he'd caught her illness. What if he lay so sick he couldn't even call out for help? The nights had grown colder, and he hadn't set a fire in four days as far as she could tell.

Bria paced her floor in her nightgown, glancing out the window every so often. Not even a lantern glow came from the suitor's tent at the edge of her clearing.

What if he had decided he wouldn't pursue her anymore? That was good, wasn't it? But then, why stay? It didn't make sense.

Her pacing intensified. She'd wear a groove in the floor if this continued all night, but she couldn't imagine going to sleep without finding out if the human was ill or simply playing some game.

If he was playing games with her heart, he would rue the day he tried to fool her. She would send the birds of the forest to shred his tent and chase him from the forest.

Bria couldn't give him the satisfaction of preying on her kindness. She needed a reason to see him, in the case that he hadn't taken ill.

She wracked her brain for an excuse to speak with him, rejecting them one after the other. Borrowing the book on druids by his mentor—her grandfather—made the most sense. But then he might want to borrow one of her books in return, and she wasn't ready to share them. She couldn't even read the majority of them herself. Could he read the ancient druid language? Should she ask him?

Bria shook her head, then swiped impatiently at the hair that strayed into her mouth. The excuse she made couldn't be anything that would make her beholden. She was beholden enough after he'd taken care of her. He'd even done the dishes. She glanced around the cottage sheepishly—she hadn't done her own dishes since he'd left. They sat as silent, chastising reminders that she was letting herself get distracted.

What day was it? She'd lost all track of time. She often did, but the first full moon of the Gathering season was when the nearby villages often held their harvest festivals, and she liked to attend several if she could manage. The locals considered it good luck to have the last druid eat and drink and dance with them.

Rumors abounded about increased fertility for their herds and humans alike, not to mention the blessing of Tala promising safety from the forest. Bria didn't do anything but show up most years.

What if she invited Theodore to one?

It was the perfect chance to talk to him. She could repay him for his kindness in caring for her, and she didn't have to be in close quarters with him.

Excitement surged through her, and she had thrown on a shawl and opened the door before she could restrain herself. The sun had gone down hours ago. It was unlikely the suitor was even awake. Should she wait until morning?

Wind rushed through the tree boughs, and a nightbird called out, the sound pricking Bria's heart and sending it soaring. She felt so much hope she could hardly sleep, especially with the wind on her face and the cool dirt under her toes.

Using moonlight to guide her way, Bria approached Theo's camp. His tent stood silent and dark, and she questioned again whether she ought to wait until morning, but she couldn't bear the thought of him passing another night ill and unattended, if he was indeed ill.

"Theodore?" Bria called.

Silence. An owl hooted, and Bria sensed it taking flight through the brisk air above her head, seeking its next meal.

"Theodore!" she tried again, a little louder.

He was likely sleeping. If he didn't answer, should she enter his tent uninvited? What would he think of her then?

A hiss accompanied a flare of light inside the tent, and the sound of rummaging startled Bria to attention.

The suitor appeared holding a candle and tucking a billowy white shirt into the top of his breeches with his free hand. He gave her a perplexed smile, brushing an unbound strand of long, brown hair from his face, and she realized he didn't have his glasses on.

She wasn't prepared for the vulnerability of catching him straight from his bed, nor how much his features stood out to her now. Her eyes traced the shape of his jaw and cheek bones and the slightly concerned smile he wore.

"Bria? What can I do for you?"

"It's-I just—" All words fled Bria's mind. She'd wanted to be sure he wasn't ill, and here he was, hale and healthy as could be. So why hadn't he called on her? And why had she come, again?

"I-I wanted to thank you for caring for me while I was ill," she said, finding her tongue at last. She adjusted her grip on her shawl and tried to change the grimace on her face to something more neutral, if not pleasant.

"You seem to have recovered well," he replied.

"Yes, I have," Bria said.

"Ah. Good, then." Theodore straightened, wiping his hands on his breeches. He raised his eyebrows expectantly.

Bria spoke in a rush, making her words blend together. "Come to the Gathering festival in Greenflower with me tomorrow?" Her pulse pounded in her ears, and her blood rushed traitorously to her face. Thank goodness it was dark.

"A festival? I don't think I've ever attended any outside of the palace."

Of course he hadn't, the precious princeling. Bria stopped herself from rolling her eyes and shrugged instead.

"Oh, well, if you don't want to come..." She turned as if to go back to her cabin, swallowing hard over the lump in her throat.

"No. No! Your invitation surprised me, is all," Theodore said. "I do want to come."

Bria turned back, a smile coming unbidden to her face. "You do?"

"I do. My tent has gotten rather stuffy as of late. Getting out will be a fine reprieve."

She wanted to ask why he'd stayed in his tent rather than chase after her like any sensible suitor, but that seemed too pretentious, even for a standoffish druid.

"I'm glad. Meet me in the clearing when the sun touches the tallest pine." She pointed across the clearing at one of the great-grandfathers of the forest, an ancient white pine she loved to climb.

Theodore squinted at the tree, then nodded. "I'll be there." He bowed slightly. "Thank you for the invitation."

Her heart fluttered. No, no feelings. Keeping him around was an advantage only if she didn't fall in love with him. He was nice, but nice wasn't worth dying for.

She turned on her heel and started down the rocky dirt path towards her cottage.

"Oh, Bria?" Theodore called.

Bria stubbed her toe and nearly fell face-forward down the path at the sound of her name. She faced him, trying not to reveal her surprise or the pain in her foot.

"Only my mother calls me Theodore. And she's pretty much a witch. It's Theo."

"Theo," Bria repeated.

Theo smiled again and disappeared back inside his tent.

Bria descended on the path again, feeling dazed. What had just happened? And why did she have this fool's grin plastered to her face?

****

The sun shone in pure golden tones as it cast its reaching beams through half-bare trees on what had to be the most gorgeous Gathering day Bria had ever lived to witness. She stood outside her cottage, tucking the last edge of her braid in a twisted crown on her head and rubbing her feet in the cool dirt, swishing her skirts like a young girl in a new gown.

The dress wasn't new, but it was her best—bright royal blue with a silver gilt belt draped across her hips. She loved the way its calf-length skirt flared out when she spun it, tiny silver charms winking at her from the decorative hem. Not to mention the pockets, so deep her hands disappeared nearly up to her elbows.

It was in this frock-drunk state that the suitor came upon her, so quietly that Bria wouldn't have noticed except he cleared his throat.

She nearly jumped out of her skin, like a young deer on its first forage out in the woods.

"You shouldn't be so quiet," she stammered.

"No? It's you who taught me to not 'tramp about in the woods,'" Theo replied, clasping his hands behind his back and rocking.

Bria appraised his mood. He seemed...anxious? In an eager and not at all overwhelming way. She let her sense of the forest wash over her, bringing stillness to her own fast-beating heart.

"Which way...Greenflower...was it?" Theo asked, adjusting the strap of his pack.

What did he have inside it, anyway? Probably a book.

"Follow me," Bria said, a grin tugging at the edge of her mouth. She forced it away and took off down the path, not waiting for the suitor, but not actively trying to lose him, either. She took the easier route, going around obstacles she thought might make travel difficult for her less coordinated companion.

She was as aware of him behind her as she was of the sun on her face. The trees seemed to whisper as they passed. Bria imagined them as the gossipy groups of ladies she'd seen in villages she had visited, their sparse crowns bending towards each other with the breeze, their branches clacking together like little gasps of astonishment at the young and handsome couple that moved among them.

A scent wafted by, sweetness and spice, a gift and a message from the goddess she served.

Don't get your hopes up. I'm simply repaying him for his kindness. Bria sent the thought as far as she could into the forest, stepping onto the root of a great oak as she did, hoping the tree would pass the message and that the goddess of the land would behave.

Bria didn't need copulating animals to decorate their path today.

She paused at a rise in the path and turned back to watch Theo climb. A fine sheen of sweat glistened on his forehead, and he gripped the straps of his pack like it was a lifeline.

"Is it much farther?"

Bria tugged the leather strap that carried her water sack over her head and handed it towards him. He waved it off, leaning against the tree across the path from her and taking off his pack. A metal canteen emerged from its depths—right next to not one, but *two* books.

Bria smirked. "What do you think you'll do with those at a festival?"

Theo took a big swallow from the canteen, then replaced the cap. "I do not go anywhere without a book. Ask my brothers sometime."

"You have brothers? How many?" she asked.

"Two. Both older. Married. You'd think them dull." He shrugged back into the pack and gestured for her to continue.

Bria moved forward, but restricted her pace so she could continue their conversation. She wasn't sure why she cared about Theo's family. He wouldn't be around long, only until she found the caves and broke the curse, but it couldn't hurt to participate in small talk.

"Dull? Why?"

"One is a warlord; one is a politician. Neither cares much for nature or the like. Or me," Theo added. "In fact, they'd probably be relieved if their odd-ball baby brother got eaten by wolves or buried by angry trees or something."

He tossed a grin her way, but Bria didn't return it. Her forehead wrinkled.

"You don't like your family?" If she had a family, she would cherish them. She had only ever fought with her father once—the day he left. He hadn't prepared her for the fact that he was required to leave the forest and never see her again the day she came of marrying age. She still shuddered to think of their last interaction, of her sorrow making the trees move so close together, they almost closed the path out of the forest entirely.

Only Tala had prevented her from doing something she would regret that day to keep her father near. What she wouldn't give to see him again.

"Er, Bria? Did you hear me? You look...preoccupied."

"I'm sorry, I did get lost in my thoughts. Memories. I do want to know what you were saying." She forced herself to watch his face and pay attention. She might not *like* him, but she didn't have to be rude.

"Oh, well, I don't hate my family. They're just...difficult to get close to. My brothers have different fathers, and they're both quite a bit older than me. I don't like politics, and they think history is useless. My mother openly dislikes me, so anyone who spends time with me gets rejected by anyone wanting to find favor with her, which is everyone. Really limits the pool of people who are willing to talk to me."

Why did it surprise her that he didn't have many friends? He was respectable and kind, apparently smart and even showed a sense of humor. He was surrounded by people, and yet, he seemed just as lonely as her. Perhaps lonelier, because he didn't belong in the place he was from.

"Perhaps you haven't found your place yet," Bria said out loud.

"A prince of the realm has limited options when it comes to finding their place," Theo said, gazing solemnly at her.

"Prince of the..." Bria trailed off. Of *course*. He'd said it before without saying it. Everyone wanted to have favor with his mother? His brothers enjoyed politics?

Queen Runa had played the biggest card in her hand, sending her youngest son to woo the last druid. Only...it seemed as if Theo had come more of his own accord, and unless he was a master manipulator and hid his true intentions, he didn't seem much like his mother at all.

It intrigued her that he hadn't led with the fact that he was a prince. Most men would have made sure to mention it the first day. Certainly within the first week. Status seemed to be everything with most humans. But not this one.

"I would have told you sooner," Theo explained. "I was looking for the right moment."

"It's evidence of your merit that you didn't bring it up," Bria said, truly meaning the compliment. "You're far more humble than I would expect from someone of your station."

"Thank you," Theo said, dipping his head. "Does...does it bother you that I'm a prince?"

"I would worry if you had shown yourself to be a different kind of person," Bria replied honestly. "But you seem entirely normal, not some puppet of the queen."

He hesitated, mouth opening and closing a few times as if unsure what to say to that.

"Queen Runa isn't known for her generosity or kindness. My father hated her," she added, by way of explanation.

Theo snorted. "It sounds as if I would get along with your father. Where is he now?"

Bria kicked at fallen leaves scattered across the path, twisting her hands behind her back. "I don't know. Letters stopped coming a year ago."

"I can inquire about him for you. Maybe someone at the castle knows where he is."

Bria shook her head. "He always wanted to travel. Perhaps he's simply gone too far for the letters to reach me."

Silence graced the air between them, except for the faintest hint of folk music wafting among the trees and their falling, dancing leaves.

"Hear that?" Bria asked, shaking off the worry for her father and letting the excitement build in her. She loved festival days. Her tasks as Tala's sole remaining daughter tied her to the forest, but she loved when she got to go out among people who didn't mind that she wasn't human.

Theo's head picked up and he glanced at her, wide-eyed. "Is that...music? Are we close?"

"Come on!" She picked up her skirts and leapt forward, the wind rushing against her back as the energy of the forest urged her forward. Theo's heavy footsteps followed, and he kept pace with her until they broke through the tree line, bursting onto the merry festival scene of the village of Greenflower.

Tents filled with vendors selling wares dotted the fields leading into town. Games were well underway, and squealing children darted between tables and tents, holding sweets in both hands.

"All the food on those tables is free. They share their bounty as a gift to Tala," Bria explained, pointing at several long tables loaded with food. "That chair at the end is for Tala herself. They will fill her plate several times throughout the day, so that everyone's offering is received."

"Fascinating," Theo muttered, adjusting his glasses and twisting to rummage in his pack without taking it off. He tugged out a small book filled with paper and dug around further until he took out a bit of charcoal. He scrawled in the book, hunching over and glancing up at the scene every so often.

Bria stood on tiptoes, trying to see what he was writing.

Theo tilted the book towards her. "A hobby of mine," he said, like someone might say of embroidery or whittling.

Bria hadn't expected to see a sketch of such incredible detail it nearly took her breath away. He'd somehow made the whole scene come to life in a matter of moments with only parchment and charcoal.

"How?" she breathed, glancing from the paper to him and back again. "I thought you were a scholar!"

Theo shrugged. "I am. But there was a time when I wanted to be an artist. Mother forbade it. She has no use for drawings."

"Your mother *is* a witch," Bria said, borrowing his word from earlier.

"Now that we can agree on," Theo said. He didn't put the book away but tucked it into the pocket of his pants with the charcoal, then rubbed his hands together. "What should we do first?"

Bria pointed at a burly man standing in front of a thick rope, bellowing at two lines of people who pulled in opposite directions.

"I challenge you to a tug!"

Theo adjusted his glasses again. "Don't you need a lot more people for that? I don't know—"

Bria bolted forward as one side of the rope managed to pull the other side over the line. She put her hands on her hips and shouted as loudly as she could.

"The last druid challenges the third-born prince of Dunholm to a tug-of-war!"

17

THEO

ALL CHATTER IN THEIR part of the festival died. The music continued in the background.

Theo wanted to crawl into a hole in the ground and disappear. Everyone turned their heads to look at Bria, and they craned their necks to find the prince she challenged. Him.

"Who will side with the forest?" Bria called again. The crowds surged forward, some approaching her with smiles and taking up the rope on her side, others making a circle. Bria stood on her tiptoes to see him as the circle closed, and she raised a hand, gesturing for him to join her.

It's just a game. A bit of fun. No harm in that, Theo thought as he made his way forward. She seemed to have taken the news of his title extremely well. Perhaps too well.

"Who will side with Dunholm?" Bria shouted, pointing to the opposite side.

Another cheer went up, a mix of supportive and jeering, as one might expect. Not nearly so many came forward to stand behind Theo as he took his place at the rope.

The large-bellied man judging the contest held a bit of cloth tied at the center of the rope and nodded to both Theo and Bria.

"The leader who crosses the line first loses," he said, pointing at the white chalk line marked on the grass. Are you both ready?"

Bria took up the rope and nodded, her face as fierce and wild as the day Theo had first laid eyes on her.

He licked his lips and breathed in, steadying his nerves. He was a prince—this sort of thing wasn't done at the palace. But he knew the principle. Dig in, stand your ground, don't back down. Don't let the beautiful woman distract you.

"On three," the man said.

Bria's eyes flashed and her eyebrows raised. "Ready, forest?" she called. Cheers erupted behind her.

He should say something too. "For Dunholm!" he managed, though somewhat weaker than he would have liked. A few supportive hurrahs went up, and confidence surged through him. Someone was on his side, even if their numbers were fewer.

It was all happening too fast, he hadn't had time to prepare, and had the man just said two? He couldn't hear above the crowd.

The man dropped the center of the rope and stepped back. The strength of the first pull caught Theo off guard, and he was nearly yanked off his feet. He grunted and dug his toes in before the line, heaving backward with all his strength and regaining some of the lost ground.

He couldn't bring himself to look away from Bria and the laughter in her eyes. She hardly looked troubled, pulling on the rope without a grimace on her face, shouting encouragement to her followers.

Theo's heart slipped along with his feet. So slowly at first, he almost didn't notice, until all the ground he'd gained was gone and he toed that line once again, hovering for a split moment, and then toppling forward, his momentum taking him to the ground.

No, not the ground. He blinked into the green eyes of Bria Glenraven, the last druid and the most beautiful woman he knew in both heart and soul.

She locked eyes with him for a moment, then grimaced and shoved at him. He replaced his glasses, which had been knocked askew, then scrambled up and extended a hand to help her off the ground. To his surprise, she took it, even if she did yank her hand back the moment she was upright.

Bria turned back to her rope-tuggers and raised her arms in victory.

Hands clapped Theo's shoulders as men and women he didn't know consoled him on his loss. It didn't feel like a loss.

He glanced at his hand, still warm and red from the rope, and imagined her hand clasped in it.

A young woman ran up to Bria and placed a flower crown on her head, then brought one, shyly, to Theo. He ducked, cheeks flushing, to allow her to place it, the stems tickling his scalp.

All of a sudden, it was as if he were a new man. Theodore Blackwin faded, and Theo, just Theo, surged to the surface.

He could be himself, here. There were no spies, no political games, no mother to placate.

A full, true grin widened on his face, and all of his courage caught up to him. He walked up to Bria, facing her with his hands on his hips.

"I think we ought to find a game I can beat you at," he said.

"Good luck," Bria said, returning his grin. "I've been playing all of these since I was a child. By the looks of things, this is your first time." Her tone was definitely teasing. As if the druid had left something of her own protective walls back in the forest and allowed herself to be more vulnerable today.

"It may be my first time, but that doesn't mean I don't have something to offer," Theo said, raising his eyebrows.

Her hand found his, cool and soft. He let her tug him to the next game—darts—which he failed at spectacularly, blaming the sun's glint off his glasses. He thought he might best her at the climbing wall due to her dress and his longer legs, but she hiked her skirts forward and up and was sitting at the top, laughing, while he wheezed his way to the finish to keep his dignity intact.

She bested him at knife throwing and archery, which didn't surprise him in the slightest. He had passable skills in all fighting arenas, where Bria had to use those skills every day in her life in the forest.

Tugging on his shirt to pull some of the cool air in to dry his sweat-soaked skin, Theo followed Bria, listening to her mock his manhood yet again as they walked away from the foot racing area. Coming from her, it didn't hurt nearly as much as it had coming from his peers back home. Perhaps because Bria didn't mean an ounce of it, and her eyes sparkled like the finest emeralds as she chatted on. He could have done it for hours to keep hearing her laugh.

It made the past several days of keeping away from her entirely worth it.

They neared a large tent, where mostly men gathered at a table, wiping their mouths. Theo nearly passed by thinking they were simply feasting together, when he noticed a woman writing scores on a large board at the back of the tent.

"What's this then?" Theo asked, stopping.

"Eating contest. Meat pies, I think," Bria said, glancing from him to the men at the tables.

Theo clapped his hands together. This, he could win. "Let's do it."

Bria wrinkled her nose. "What? No, anyone can stuff their face. It's not really a game, is it?"

"Bria Glenraven, you're not scared you'll lose, are you?" He crossed his arms and gave her a playful stare.

Bria crossed her arms. "No, I'm not scared. It's just stupid."

"I've played every one of your little games, no matter how foolish it seemed. It seems only fair you allow me one indulgence. After all, it is my first time," he emphasized.

She rolled her eyes but didn't give.

Theo swept his arms out wide. "I, Theodore Blackwin, third prince of Dunholm, challenge the Last Druid Bria Glenraven to an eating competition!"

Bria uttered a very unladylike groan, dropping her arms like dead weights to her sides, but put on a grin for the folks who gathered to see the druid beat the prince yet again.

Only this time, he would win. Theo smiled to himself. He'd always been a fast eater, wanting to get out of political and family dinners he'd been forced to attend. His mother always complained about how quickly he finished meals. He'd never known it could be considered a useful skill, until now.

He took a seat under the shaded canopy, grateful for a reprieve from the sun. Despite the cool day, he'd gotten overheated running around after Bria.

Bria sat across from him, some of the hardness returning to her gaze. One thing he'd learned today, she was extremely competitive. She would hate anything that put her at a disadvantage. He wasn't doing himself any favors in the wooing department by challenging her to a contest she didn't like, but this wasn't for her. This was for him and his wounded pride.

A burly woman brought out a tray of hand pies and set them on the edge of the table.

"Four pies each and one pint of ale. Whoever cleans the plate and drains the mug first wins. You can start when I drop the cloth."

Theo readied himself, licking his lips and tensing his muscles to spring at the pies the moment the woman gave the sign.

People crowded at the tent entrance, eagerly cheering and chatting and even betting as coins exchanged hands.

Bria placed her palms down flat on the table, looking as still as a stone.

The woman set the plates down in front of each of them, then dropped her cloth on the table.

Theo dove into the pies with two hands, dunking them one at a time in the ale, giving them each a moment to get a bit soggy. He shoved the first one in his mouth. It wasn't the most genteel way to eat, to be sure, but this wasn't fine dining—it was war.

The second one followed quickly, the minced meat and potato filling going down easily without much chewing. He took a swig of the ale to wash the two pies down and grabbed the last two, dunking them as he glanced at his competition.

She was halfway through her first pie and frozen on her next bite, watching him with eyes as round as saucers.

Theo finished off the third and fourth pies and chugged the rest of his ale by the time she finished her first pie, raising his arms and standing to receive the cries of the people. His people this time.

Hands clapped his back, congratulations washed over him, and he basked in the attention. The third son of a queen who wanted a daughter had never had so much attention in his life.

Bria, he noticed, thanked the woman in the tent, pressing something into her hand. A token of the forest, perhaps? He'd ask her later. For now, he would enjoy his moment of glory.

The glory lasted all of a few moments, until the people grew bored and moved on to the next thing to enjoy. And Theo was grateful when they left, for his stomach had rejected what he'd put inside.

He'd always eaten fast, but he'd never eaten so much at once. He put a hand to his mouth as Bria approached. No, he didn't want her to see him like this.

His stomach heaved and he forced it back down painfully.

"Er," he swallowed before continuing. "Where does one...relieve oneself here?"

"There's a tent across that way," Bria said, gesturing.

The distance swam in Theo's vision. He wouldn't make it. He would—

"Are you all righ—" Bria's sentence clipped short as Theo retched, turning just in time to avoid getting any on her.

It wasn't a pretty sight, but as soon as the heaving stopped, he felt loads better.

He wiped his mouth, steadied himself, trying to recover some of his dignity before he turned around to face her again.

Arms crossed, eyebrow raised, Bria had a look of smug satisfaction on her face.

"Sorry about that," Theo said, wiping his hands on his breeches.

"Oh, no need. If you're keeping score, that's another win for me, by the way," she said, sauntering past him.

Theo sputtered, staggering after her. "A win for you? I ate four pies in the time you ate one!"

"But I kept mine down and you didn't," Bria said. "Common sense would side with me, I think, but we can ask the people if you want."

"No, no, that's all right," Theo said. The last thing he needed was for word to get back to the capital that he couldn't hold his own against this insanely talented, witty, incredible woman. He would have kissed her right then and there if his mouth didn't still taste like bile and his hands weren't sweating up a storm.

"Some ground apricot wine will get that taste out of your mouth, I'll bet. Come on," Bria said.

Theo followed her to the feast table, somehow still laden with goods, though sparser than before. Lit torches danced all around, and he realized the sun had nearly touched the horizon. Where had the day gone? He hadn't felt this sort of feeling since the last time he'd read a book he couldn't put down.

A man approached Bria, looking nervous. She replied with a gentle smile and a nod, hand going to her pocket and pulling another item out, pressing it into the man's palm.

Theo squinted but couldn't see what she'd given the man.

The man stood in front of the table, spread his arms, and raised his voice. "Greenflower has been graced by the presence of Tala herself tonight, and her priestess has a blessing to offer us."

Theo stared at Bria, who seemed a bit embarrassed as she approached holding two wooden cups with a dark liquid inside.

"Hold mine?" she asked, pressing it towards him.

He took both without hesitation, eyes following her as she stepped forward, spreading her arms.

"People of Greenflower," she said, projecting her voice over a quickly growing crowd. "Thank you for welcoming me and my companion among you today. You have shown great faith in Tala this season, and she is pleased. I bless your soil, that it may be enriched, and your water, that it will be plentiful, your flocks and your women," her voice faltered, and her eyes sparkled with what must be tears. Bria cleared her throat and continued. "And your women, that their wombs will ripen and bring forth strong children, that all generations will be blessed through the power of She Who Gives All."

Bria put a hand to her chest and sank low in a sort of bow, her other hand drawing something—a druidic rune, Theo realized—in the air. It glowed with a green fire, then dispersed, and as the last light of the sun faded, tiny pink lights rose from the grass around them, darting to and fro, eliciting delighted cries at the enchanting display.

Bria straightened and approached Theo, taking her cup from him and sipping from it.

"What are they?" he asked in wonder, watching children and adults alike cup their hands and chase the little beings.

"Glow flies. They hatch every dozen years or so. I only woke them up a year early," Bria replied.

Dusk had faded into nightfall, and the expression on her face grew harder to read in the dim torchlight.

"It was nice of you to say those things. Does Tala...will she truly grant them? Or is it just something you say to..." Theo trailed off. As he said it, it felt wrong. To question someone's culture, someone's religion in such a blatant way.

"To appease them?" Bria finished for him. He thought she might not answer as she glanced back at the crowd, dispersing now as the glow flies scattered and woke in other parts of the field.

Theo also made out the light and smoke of a bonfire several tents over, the final part of a day filled with richness and laughter. He could imagine the warmth, the orange light on every face, the stories that would be told. To be part of something like this village, however, was too foreign for him coming from a world of cold and stone with nearly no one but his books for comfort.

"I do it for myself, I think. To remember that it's not just about me, or even the trees and the animals. Humans are Tala's creation, too. We all are. They need as much protecting and nurturing as every seedling in the forest. If I forget that...I might as well let the curse take me, and let Tala find a new people to be her stewards."

Time seemed to take a breath as Theo gazed at Bria. He'd thought she hated humans, hated him, but he'd been proven wrong. Underneath her mask of brazen confidence, she had insecurities and doubts and fears just like him.

"Well, I think Tala is fortunate to have you."

Bria shook her head, taking another drink. "Truly?"

"Truly. I have never heard of a druid more faithful in all my reading."

She ducked her head and wiped at her eyes. "It's the smoke," she said, sniffling. "From the torches."

"Ah," Theo replied, not digging any further than she was willing to share. "Do you want to avoid the bonfire, then? Or are we going to join them?"

Bria shook her head. "I think it's time we headed back."

"Lead the way, then," Theo said, inclining his head. In truth, he was disappointed.

The day had been fun—aside from the retching—and he didn't want it to end. This vulnerable side of Bria might vanish the moment they entered the forest, and he didn't want to lose it.

Nor did he want this confidence to fade. He felt the genuineness of his own self, all pretense stripped away by the drastic difference between this place and where he'd come from. Or maybe that was the wine.

He set his empty cup on the table next to Bria's and offered her his arm. To his shock, she took it, sliding her arm through his and leaning in a little. They walked together to the place he'd left his pack. He hadn't thought of reading his books once the entire time they'd been there.

He pulled it on and offered his arm again, but Bria ignored the gesture, staring at the forest edge before them, as if her mask was already falling back into place.

"Thank you for bringing me here," Theo said, desperately clinging to the feeling of the day, though it had already slipped from his grasp, fleeting as any memory.

"It was the least I could do," Bria said, giving him the faintest smile.

She moved forward, not running as she had that morning, but walking and trailing her hand along the plants that lined the path.

Theo followed her into the forest, the shadows of the nearly bare trees falling over them and feeling far more oppressive than usual. He hadn't felt so unsettled in the forest since his first week there. The trees had come to accept him, maybe even approve of him a little bit as he attempted to commune with them the way Bria did. Now they clustered around him, shadowy sentinels guarding the secrets of the forest.

Did they guard the secret to breaking the druid curse? And if the forest held the secret, why would Tala not reveal it to Bria and save the druids? What kind of goddess hid that kind of knowledge?

Theo bit his tongue, wanting to talk to Bria about what he'd been studying the last four days. He'd combed over every book, every note he had with him, dredged up every bit of information in his mind about the druid curse and how it had started and the prophecy he'd read about in Bria's book.

None of his resources mentioned anything about a prophecy. Not even Master Graymont's book. Not a hint. If he could translate more of her texts, surely she would want to know what her ancestors had written, and she'd willingly lend him the volumes if it meant he could translate them for her. But that meant revealing he'd read them before. Or, if he didn't mention the prophecy specifically, he'd have to give some reason for wanting to read the books, and that meant coming up with a lie, and a lie didn't sit well with him. He couldn't taint what they had with a falsehood.

Which meant one thing—if he wanted a chance to read the texts, he had to tell her the truth. Even if it would cost him the atheneum his mother had promised to build if he succeeded in winning the druid's heart. His library and his freedom for Bria's life.

When he thought of it that way, it wasn't such a terrible exchange.

"Bria," he said, stopping his progress along the path.

"Hmm?" Bria replied, pausing to turn back and look at him.

He took a deep breath in, glancing up at the stars peering through the trees at them. He couldn't see much of Bria's face, even with the full moon's light.

"I-I have something to confess," he said. No backing down now.

Bria cocked her head and waited for him to speak.

"I read one of your books. In your cottage. While you were sick." He closed his eyes, then forced them open, forced himself to look at her.

Her mouth dropped open. "You-you *read* one? As in, you understand the words?"

Theo nodded, gripping the strap of his bag so tightly it dug into his palm. "Yes. I can read much of the ancient language. Well, some iterations of it. And there are words I don't understand, and—"

Bria raced back down the path and put her hands on his shoulders. "Did you read anything about caves? About the curse? Anything?" Her eyes, dark as pools of emerald ink, searched his with a desperation he could not know or understand.

"Yes. Yes! There's a prophecy—I thought you'd be angry—I wrote it all down, and there's so much more, but I didn't have time—"

Bria grabbed his hand and dragged him down the path. "I want you to read it to me. All of it."

It wasn't the way he'd imagined getting invited into her cottage, but he would take it. But as he raced beside her through the night-ridden forest, leaves crunching beneath his hurried footsteps, the frosty air cutting into his lungs, Theo realized that what he was about to do wasn't as simple as reading a long-forgotten text to a woman he was fond of.

No, to translate the ancient druid records that might contain the end of the curse was an act of rebellion against all of Dunholm. One that, if discovered, would get him banished or worse. Because if the druid curse was broken, his mother wouldn't get a druid granddaughter to put on the throne, and she would punish him as the one who ruined all of her plans.

BRIA

B RIA TREMBLED LIKE THE leaves that still clung to their branches overhead as she rushed back to the cabin with Theo in tow behind her. She hardly noticed that she still held his hand clutched in hers, so desperate was she to know what the journals of her foremothers said.

She'd always wondered if one of them held the answer, and if Theo could translate, she would finally know. Keeping him around had been worth it after all.

Bria's feet knew the pathway, had it memorized by the texture of the ground and the bends that twisted and wove through the forest. She flew along, feet barely skimming the ground, until they reached her cottage clearing and she burst through the door.

"The fire's low. Let me stoke it," Theo said, and footsteps indicated he had turned around and headed for the wood pile outside.

"No! I'll do it. Just start reading," Bria said, darting past him and piling wood into her arms, whispering warnings to the critters that hid among the logs so they wouldn't end up perishing in the flames.

When she returned to the cabin, she found Theo obediently sitting at the table, a stack of her ancestor's journals at his side, and one open in his arms.

He studied her through spectacled brown eyes. "Are you certain you're not upset that I read this without your permission?"

"Theo," she said, very carefully and seriously, "If you can translate this, I might very well kiss you."

He adjusted his glasses, licking his lips and looking flustered. "That won't be necessary, I'll gladly—"

"Read!" Bria insisted, dropping the wood on the floor and kneeling at the hearth. She needed something physical to do so she didn't pace or stare at Theo like a fool. She had already made a fool of herself with that comment about kissing him. Why had she said that?

Theo cleared his throat and read, pausing every few words or lines. Bria sat back on her heels and closed her eyes, imagining the voice of her own druid ancestor, some six generations back, the words echoing the pain in her own heart.

But we've lost the ability to read their words. They differ from our own too much. The language has changed. My father did not know more than the few words he'd learned from my mother, and I am no scholar.

"A light unfolds in the darkness, beginning what will have no end," Theo said. "Do you know what it means?"

Bria couldn't see the flames that had grown as they fed hungrily on the logs she had added. Her eyes had filled with water, brimming to the point of spilling over and trailing down her cheeks.

"I've never heard that before," Bria admitted, turning to face him. She wiped her eyes. "A light? Like the sun, or the moon? Or fire?" she gestured at the fireplace.

"Darkness could have many meanings too. Nighttime. Wintertime. A shadow. A cave. Or it might not be literal at all."

"Wait, what did you say? A cave?" Bria pushed to her feet and started pacing.

"She does mention a cave, but I had to stop after that part. I only read a few pages."

"Then you need to read more," Bria said. "I'll make tea."

⚜

The night passed like a fever dream. Exhaustion hovered out of reach, kept at bay by her need to know. She couldn't let this chance pass her by. Perhaps Tala had heard her prayers after all and had sent this human suitor who held so much knowledge of her people and was tolerable enough.

Tolerable? Who was she kidding? She *liked* Theo.

Eventually, her nervous energy calmed, and she sat across from Theo, cradling a cooling mug of tea, listening to the lilt of his voice as he pronounced the language of her ancient people, then repeated it in the modern common tongue they shared.

"She talks of three possible locations here," Theo said after a long silence.

Bria lifted her head off her arms, wiping at a drop of drool that lingered in the corner of her mouth. Sleep had nearly gotten her that time.

"What do you mean?"

"Well, it's hard to say. I don't know these woods the way you do, and this phrase has me confused." He repeated a string of words in the druidic tongue. "It would translate as 'deep water trees,' but that doesn't make sense. Is there a place where trees grow in deep water? Like a swamp?" He glanced up at her, his expression so tired and so perplexed that Bria nearly burst out laughing.

Perhaps she was more exhausted than she thought. She rubbed a hand down her face.

"Lands above, you look tired. Maybe we should call it quits here and get some rest," Theo suggested.

"No!" Bria said, her hand flying out and landing on his arm.

He looked down at where she touched him in surprise.

Bria jerked her hand away. "No, we can't stop. I've waited so long to find a hint of where to look. A place where trees grow in water..." her brow furrowed and she muttered to herself. "Not *in* water, *like* water. Where trees are like deep water."

"That's it!" Theo said, snapping his fingers. "This word must be 'like' or 'as.' I've got to write that down."

While he scratched the note down in his book of parchment, Bria sank further into her chair, her heart sinking with her.

The southern part of the forest, where the trees gradually became true giants, and regular forest creatures turned into something akin to monsters of old, where no mortal person could tread without fear—even the last remaining druid priestess herself.

Bria pressed her hands to her face, fingertips putting pressure on her eyes to stop them from crying, and failing.

"What's wrong?" Theo asked, his voice so tender it drew out the sobs locked in Bria's chest.

She clamped down on them and drew in a deep breath. Now wasn't the time to fall apart. She dropped her hands and rubbed them down her skirts.

"It's the southern part of the Morwood. Surely your people have tales of it?"

Theo's brow furrowed. "All the old books talk of a place where the trees touch the sky, and monsters lurk. I always assumed they were children's tales. Your forest here is frightful enough." He smiled good-heartedly, but Bria couldn't bring herself to return it.

"There are places even I'm afraid to go. I had a sense that the cave I had heard of and sought all my life might be in there. It's an hour's walk from here. But it's so dark and feels foreign. Like the trees don't speak my language."

"Perhaps their language was lost with your ancestors," Theo said, and he sounded truly sorrowful at the thought. He glanced over the other volumes. "One of these might have more, but translating is painstaking work. The work of days and weeks, not hours."

Bria nodded. She understood. And she had work to do to prepare for winter. She couldn't afford to stay up night after night, wasting precious time and resources. There were saplings in the north forest that had come up far too late in the season, they needed their bark hardened if they would make it through the howling ice storms. And the wild goats did better when she walked with them to the southwest valley to winter over.

Not to mention the trading and patching she had yet to do for her own sake.

She sighed. "Thank you for humoring me. Tomorrow, I have work to do. Please, feel free to use my cottage for your studies. We can share our evening meal and discuss what you find, if that's agreeable to you."

Her words came out stilted and formal. She hoped he wouldn't take them as her feeling angry.

He closed the books and stacked them neatly next to his notebook and inking supplies.

"Thank you. I'd be honored to continue translating." He stood and bowed more deeply, then left.

Bria stared at the door for a long moment, the fire popping and her belly rumbling. She added "make bread" to her growing list of chores for the morning, then tidied up, undressed, and collapsed into bed. She was unconscious the moment her head hit her pillow.

A moment later, she woke. Except the sun shone through her windows, and the fire was nothing but dusty white coals, and her feet were chilled where they stuck out of her blankets.

She pulled them back in and let them warm up a moment before she forced herself to emerge. Judging by the sun's position, it was far later than she usually slept, and nightfall would come sooner than ever.

Every day that passed brought less sunlight, more cold, and winter closer. Bria filled her day with prayer and preparation, turning her mind towards Tala more and more as each day she returned after sundown to her cottage and found Theo waiting, tea poured and a meal prepared, ready to tell her what he'd translated that day.

Mostly mundane, day-to-day type thoughts and happenings. Bria soaked in each word, starting to feel like she understood her sixth-great grandmother Aethena but coming no closer to understanding the prophecy, or discovering the location of the caves.

A week passed, then two. Even the ever-patient Theo grew agitated. He took up pacing, running his hands through his hair until the front stuck up. He became disheveled, and Bria had to remind him more than once to take care of his own needs. The translation could wait—they had time. All winter if need be.

Only, they didn't have time. *She* didn't have time. Every day her hunger grew, both hunger for food and the hunger to be near *him.*

On the eighteenth day of translating, Bria came in from foraging, and Theo's head rose from his books. He smiled at her in his tender way and rumbled a low, "How was your day?" in a voice raspy from disuse.

The sudden desire to fling herself into his arms and sink into his warmth took her completely off guard, frightening her so much she turned right back around and tromped through the woods for another hour in the dark until her body shivered with cold instead of desire.

Would it hurt to invite him into her bed for just one night? To ask him to stay instead of returning to his tent?

"Bria, did you hear me?" Theo asked, waving a free hand in front of her face.

"Mmm?" Bria asked, startling out of a rather vivid daydream that had nothing to do with caves or prophecies, and everything to do with what Theo looked like with less clothing on. She flushed head-to-toe with the realization that he'd caught her daydreaming, even though he didn't have any idea what she'd been daydreaming about.

Her skin tingled pleasantly, and she rubbed at her arms to rid herself of the feeling. "Chilly in here, don't you think?" She stood and crossed to the fire, poking at it. "I'm going to put another kettle on. Do you want some?"

"You didn't hear a word I said just now. I know you didn't," Theo said, adjusting his glasses.

"How can you be so sure?" Bria said, still trying to force away the image of Theo pulling her in for a kiss and dragging her to bed out of her mind. The thought hung on stubbornly, persistently. She wouldn't look at him until it was gone.

"I have found several items of interest."

She glanced down at the book he sat in front of. One of the oldest in her collection, the cover long-gone, pages threatening to crumble with every turn of the page. Theo wore gloves, of all things, and looked at the book with an awed sort of reverence.

"What is it?" She sat at the table across from him, the thought of kissing gone, for the moment.

"This passage here. I always wondered why Tala would curse your people, when they were the ones defending themselves against the humans. But listen here,"

"Oh, that our mothers and fathers had withheld their anger and waited for Tala's blessing before attacking the humans. Then she might have withheld her fury from us."

Theo glanced up from the text. "There's more, but that's the most important bit."

Bria blinked rapidly, gazing at Theo. "I always thought...I was told the humans brought the war to the druids."

"I believe they did—at least, they did so much harm, perhaps a little at a time, that the druids ultimately believed they were acting for good when they attacked, and the humans returned their violence in kind. It only takes a small spark to start a fire." He cleared his throat. "This text is a much older form of your ancestor's language, and it's harder to translate, but I'll keep working at it if you'd like to understand more."

"Yes, I'd like that," Bria muttered, unsteady emotion swirling inside her.

"There is good news as well," Theo said, perking up. He slid the gloves off his hands, setting them beside the crumbling book.

She gestured for him to continue, struggling to find her voice after the revelation that her ancestors may have been just as responsible for the erasure of her people as the humans. No wonder Tala had cursed them.

"I've cross-referenced several locations that have been repeated in multiple journals that seem to have significance to your ancestors and stand out as possible sites for the caves. I think we should go out tomorrow and look for them."

Ignoring her earlier conviction, Bria jumped to her feet and met Theo's eyes. "Really? You're certain?"

Theo stood, stretching his arms up and behind him. "If it's not one of these, then we've completely wasted our time, which would be a bit of a letdown. But I'd bet my books that one of them is it. I'm leaning towards the waterfall grotto."

Excitement overcame her and she rushed forward, wrapping her arms around his midsection. The thrill lasted for a blissful moment, but the moment his hands hesitantly touched her back.

Her cheeks burned, and she sprung away, looking every-where but at him.

"Bria," he said, voice soft, like she was a wild animal he didn't want to spook.

She closed her eyes. She *was* a wild animal. And she'd been alone for far too long. Her father had warned her about this, too. *Make sure he's the right one, my flower. Don't rush it.*

She'd nearly rushed things once before. Benton had charmed her within days. But then, she'd been confident she wasn't in her fertile time. Was she that attracted to Theo, or was her body betraying her?

"I think you should go." Her voice trembled, bottom lip quivering as she held the storm of emotion inside.

"I think we should talk about what you're feeling," Theo said, stepping closer to her. He reached a hand towards her, then seemed to think better of it and hesitated, his hand hovering like an invitation.

If she took his hand, what would happen? Would he em-brace her? Would she be able to stop herself from taking it farther if he did?

Taking a step back sent physical pain through her chest, especially when she glanced up and saw the hurt look pass over Theo's face, but his hand dropped, and he placed it behind his back and bowed.

His expression neutralized, becoming so calm she thought she might have imagined the hurt look, but the air between them grew strained, and she couldn't believe he didn't feel something for her. She didn't want to believe it. She wanted him to want her, even if that wasn't fair to him when she would never let herself be with him as long as the curse was in effect.

"Tomorrow, we'll find the cave," Bria said, wishing she knew what to say to get back to the warm familiarity that had grown between them over the past two weeks.

"I'll meet you at dawn," Theo agreed. He left the books on the table, taking only his notebook and quill.

Bria watched him leave, regret pooling in her heart.

19

THEO

T HE FOREST SEEMED ALMOST asleep the next morning. Shivering under frost-bitten limbs and pacing to keep his blood from freezing, Theo noticed that everything seemed less responsive, less vibrant than before. The frozen trees were no less beautiful, in fact, they were more so. But some deep part of him that had only woken when he'd started meditating with Bria recognized that these great giants of the forest were getting ready for a long sleep.

What happened to Bria's power when the forest tucked itself in for the winter? Did it, too, grow dormant? Did it weaken? Did *she* sleep like the trees and animals?

He stomped the ground and adjusted the strap of his pack again, then gave into the intrusive thought to check for his notebook and quill and ink to make sure he hadn't forgotten anything. He had his water sack, though it was empty. He'd have to fill it at the first river they crossed.

The sound of Bria's door opening startled him. He jerked his head around, watching the druid as she swayed towards him. She wouldn't quite look at him, instead glancing at the ground, then back up, as if she felt shy.

Bria had never shown any indication of shyness. Bold as the sun on the longest day, as a storm wind, as a brown bear. So perhaps shy wasn't the right word. Reserved? Withdrawn? But she was looking at him, and she hadn't left him behind, so he wasn't in trouble. At least, he didn't think he was. Hard to tell with this stubborn druid woman.

"A bit frosty out," Bria offered in the way of a greeting.

"My toes are frozen," Theo agreed, glancing down at her feet, shocked when he realized they weren't bare. She wore some sort of leather slippers with puffy wool poking out the tops.

"Even druid feet get cold in winter," Bria said in a clipped tone. She fidgeted with the iron clasp holding her wool cloak together at her throat, glancing at him then away again, seeming agitated. Or could it be pleased? A heated blush rose to her cheeks.

"Are you going to gawk at me all day?" she asked.

"If you'll allow me," Theo said.

She looked down at her feet, but her body twisted back and forth, making her skirts twirl.

So she wasn't entirely unaffected by compliments. He smiled to himself, a thrill running through him. Something had given last night, some barrier between them, slowly eroded by the time they'd spent together while he translated the ancient druid texts.

Bria had realized it, too. She'd embraced him, then pushed him away. Whether or not they found the caves today, he had to find some way to open the crack in her wall further, so she'd let him in.

He would get his atheneum and get away from his mother's claws digging into his back, constantly looking for the right opportunity to use him.

The thought sank like a stone in his gut.

Bria didn't notice his inner turmoil. She pulled her hood up and moved ahead on the path, pausing after a few steps to wait for him.

"Are you coming?" she asked.

"Wouldn't miss it," Theo replied, forcing a smile. His skin seemed slimy, his chest hard. The forest closed in around him, like the trees knew his selfish intentions and would suffocate him rather than allow him to use the last druid for his own gain.

Use her, just like his mother planned to use him.

Theo clenched his jaw and his fists. His feet faltered, his steps growing slower until he paused entirely.

He wouldn't do this. He wouldn't be like his mother, the queen. He'd spent most of his youth training to win the heart of the last druid, but he'd never imagined he might actually fall in love with her.

Is that what this was? He was in love with Bria, so he didn't want to hurt her?

"Theo?"

Theo glanced up with a jerk and startled backwards from the woman standing mere feet from him. Stunning in her wildness, beautiful in her determination. She wouldn't tolerate a lie, but the truth would only hurt. *I love you, so I can't be with you.* Who would it hurt more? She might be relieved. But he...he would live his entire life missing her.

Unless he helped her break this curse.

Warmth pierced his heart, and the entire forest seemed to widen, to brighten. The frost sparkled like diamonds across every branch, leaf, and stone. A stream burbled musically, not entirely frozen over, then, and a melodious voice floated into his consciousness.

Choose to serve her and she is yours.

"You're acting strangely today. Are you ill? Did you get enough sleep?" Bria asked, crossing her arms. "I'm not going to keep waiting for you, you know. I can search for the caves without you."

Theo picked up his stride again, this time with purpose and vigor, passing a confused Bria as he went.

Choose to serve her and she is yours, the voice had said. Could it have been...could the goddess of the forest herself have spoken to him? But how, when he was not a druid? Regardless, it wasn't his to puzzle out. He knew the voice was good, and he felt that things were right with the world.

He didn't have to woo the druid, or bed her, or impregnate her. He could forget all of it for a day at least. Today, he just needed to be with her.

He let her catch up to him. "Where do you want to start?"

She narrowed her eyebrows, looking suspiciously at him, but didn't press him for the cause behind his hesitation. "One doesn't march into the deep woods without proper preparation. There's a shrine to Tala I need to visit first. We'll seek her blessing, then we will find the caves."

"What do I need to do?"

"Be quiet. Observe." Bria fell silent.

Theo wanted to break the silence, to bring back the easy conversation that had developed between them over the past several weeks, but he didn't want to break Bria's concentration.

Serve her.

He walked a little ahead of her, moving branches out of her way, until he noticed the branches moved beneath his hands almost before he touched them. His arms fell to his sides as he realized the trees moved out of Bria's way as she passed. He fell back.

Observe.

He watched how the forest seemed to bow around Bria, not suffocating, as it had felt to him earlier, but embracing. Cradling. Like a mother with a baby.

He noted how little moon-white moths fluttered near her face, as if to whisper messages in her ear.

His gaze drifted downward, all the way to her feet, encased in her woolen shoes, and he nearly yelped in surprise.

With each step she left behind, a scattering of tiny green shoots sprouted up.

He adjusted his glasses and crouched down to touch the shoots. As soon as his fingertip brushed them, they vanished back into the dirt. The others gradually did so as he watched, sinking back down into the warm earth. It wasn't the right season for their emergence. He had to wonder if it was the seasons of the Long Days whether these plants would remain and blossom.

"What in the name of tree sap are you doing, you daft lad?" Bria exclaimed. She threw her hands up in the air as she turned to confront him.

Theo stood. "Y-you said to observe, I'm trying to do what you told me."

"Observe *and* keep moving," Bria growled. "Or it will take all day to get to the deep woods. And believe me, we don't want to be in there at night."

Theo swallowed and nodded, then fell into line behind her, trying not to stare at the line of green dotting the ground wherever Bria walked, his heart trying to beat clear out of his chest.

His notes and every record he'd ever read were clear—when plants spontaneously erupted from the footsteps of the last druid, she was...well, to put it crudely, in heat.

Her fertile period had arrived.

He groaned internally, wishing he could run the opposite direction and throw himself in an icy lake. Now that he'd had the thought, he couldn't stop thinking it. Every small bit of her skin that he could see seemed to glow with a soft subtle light, making her even more irresistible than before.

If they united now, right here on this forest floor, the odds were good that she would conceive a child. And she would be more than amenable to his advances, if his studies were correct. Was that why she'd embraced him last night? Had she felt...urges towards him?

He wiped a hand down his face and blew air through his lips. What had he just determined? This didn't change his decision. He wouldn't use her. They would find the caves or...or...

He would return home. A failure. A pawn in his mother's political games, to move, to marry off, to manipulate as she would.

It was Theo's turn to grow stony, serious, and silent.

Bria tried to start a conversation several times, but Theo couldn't manage more than the most basic grunts and blunt answers in response.

They paused near a creek at midmorning, filling their water sacks and snacking on some of the food they'd brought.

Bria offered him half of a bar filled with dried fruit, nuts, and oats, somehow held together with a sticky, honey-like substance.

He ate it gratefully, surprised at how good it tasted. It was similar to the maple biscuits he enjoyed back home.

The food and water restored his energy and his mood, and despite the heaviness of the circumstances before him, he managed to perk up enough to talk.

"So, what is it like to be a priestess of Tala? That's one thing my books don't have much on," Theo said, clambering over a rock. This was farther into the forest than he'd ever gone.

The sun had come out, chasing away the frost. A few birds still remained, trilling their happy songs, perhaps wishing the forest farewell as they flew south to escape the coming cold.

"It's...hard to explain," Bria said, hesitating and staring at a dead tree beside the path that was propped up at eye level. Her fingers traced whorls in the thickly ridged bark, then she pressed her entire hand against it and closed her eyes. "As long as I am close to the Mother of All, I can sense everything. The cracking open of each new seed, the dying breath of every fallen or sick tree, the pulsing aliveness of every creature beneath our feet and in the air."

She raised her head, breathing deeply in.

"It's all muted now, because the Sleeping is coming. Tala casts her protective blanket over everything and sleeps, and I keep watch over the forest, ready to wield her power if men try to harm anything in her domain."

Fierce protectiveness entered her voice, and Theo was reminded of a question he'd considered earlier.

He cleared his throat. "Your power—excuse me, her power, which you can access—is your access to it...limited in the winter? The way your sense of the forest mutes, I've wondered how that affects your ability to channel the Mother."

Bria's gaze fell on him, full of challenge and warning. In it, he could see the charge of a bear, the strength of a grown tree in a storm.

"I do not know your intention in asking that question, Theodore Blackwin, but I assure you I am no less powerful now than the day we met, and if you try to force yourself on me, you will find worms crawling out of your ears and beetles making a nest in your empty gut before the day is through."

He should have felt threatened, but awe filled him instead. "I wouldn't expect anything less from you by now," he replied, shrugging against the strap of his pack. "I would deserve it, if I had any ill intentions towards you. But I think that you know that I don't by now."

Her fierce mask fell apart as she blinked at him in shock. She pushed away from the log—leaving behind a perfect handprint of tiny white mushroom pins—and continued on the trail.

Theo watched her walk for a moment, noting the way the path had all but disappeared, along with the sunlight. The trees were taller in this part of the forest. He jogged to catch up, this time to walk beside the druid. He was confident he had nothing to fear, in spite of her big words. If the voice he'd heard was, in fact, Tala's, surely the goddess would extend some sort of protection to him, especially from her own priestess.

"There's the gnarled silver birch," Bria said, pointing ahead. She dashed down the path, climbing the massive bent roots that rose and fell around the ancient tree. Its trunk would have easily taken four or five men to reach around it.

Theo glanced around with confusion. According to his notes, the first potential location for the caves was somewhere near this tree, but all he could see for miles were trees. No caves, no hills, no rising ground, nothing.

He clambered around the opposite side of the tree, looking for anything that might be interpreted as a cave.

"Do trees in this forest ever move?" Theo asked, so busy searching the ground that he nearly ran straight into Bria as she moved under a branch and stood up mere inches from him.

Her eyes widened, and her breath came in small gasps. She licked her lips—full and rosy pink. At that moment, he wanted to bend down and kiss them.

"Sometimes," Bria replied.

"Sometimes what?" Theo asked, feeling mesmerized by her green-eyed gaze, her lips, her nearness.

"The trees. Sometimes they do move. It's pretty rare and takes an extreme event. But they can move." She ducked under his arm to move past him, and not a moment later, she screamed.

Theo whirled around, ready to fend off a terrible forest monstrosity—a bear, a great horned beast, something ferocious and blood thirsty.

Instead, he found Bria red-faced and completely disheveled, one leg sunk between two massive roots, her arms bracing against them to hold her up.

"Are you hurt?" Theo asked, making his way towards her.

"No, just shocked. I think I found the cave entrance."

Theo reached her and, without thinking, put his arms beneath hers and heaved her up out of the hole with a grunt.

She was heavier than she looked, but then again, she was all muscle from years of climbing trees and living in the woods.

Once she was free, he stepped away to give her space, nearly falling backward himself.

Bria brushed at her hair and nodded his way. "Thanks."

"No problem. You said there's a cave down there?" Theo peered between the massive roots.

"This'll make it easier to see," Bria murmured, waving her hand in an intricate pattern as she chanted some words Theo recognized.

They were ancient druidic, and he suspected her pronunciation wasn't quite right. Not that he would correct her. Something about asking the tree to...move?

The ground rumbled in response, and Theo sat down, hard, as the root beneath him shifted slightly. He gripped its moss-covered surface as hard as he could, knowing full well that if the tree decided to bury him in its roots, he wouldn't be able to prevent it.

Bria balanced on one of the moving roots, somehow not looking even a bit unsteady herself, her arms outstretched, glowing green light moving down her body and into the tree root. The roots covering the hole she'd fallen into spread wide, then settled, and the ground stopped shaking.

Theo stood, wary of things moving again, and stepped closer to Bria to peer down into the hole. He glanced from her to the crack in the earth and back again.

"Is...that it?" he asked. The crack wasn't even wide enough for his slim hips and shoulders to fit through, and Bria was a tad bit wider with her chest and hips. Unless she could widen it with her magic, neither of them would be exploring what lay beyond to discover if this was the cave her ancestor's journal had mentioned.

Bria shook her head slowly. "No, I don't think so. It doesn't...feel right."

"What should it feel like?"

She touched a hand to her chest. "I don't know," she said, her voice barely above a whisper. She closed her eyes and seemed to go somewhere else, lips moving without making a sound, her free hand tracing runes in the air. They glowed, then faded, and she shook her head again, curls falling into her face.

"This isn't it. Come on, we need to get to the next one."

Theo followed her down from the tree's step-like roots. The moment they had both feet on the path, Bria chanted again, and the ground rumbled once more, the roots closing over the cave entrance.

"Well then, it has to be one of the remaining two," Theo said, infusing his voice with cheerfulness he barely felt. He wanted this to work, wanted to help her break this curse. And then maybe, just maybe, she would be free to admit she liked him back, *if* she liked him back, and they could take more time getting to know one another. Exploring one another.

It was decided that they would find the waterfall grotto first, then find the third location on their way out of the southern forest.

They reached the grotto after another hours' hike, stopping near enough to feel the spray from the rushing water.

"I have a good feeling about this one," Theo shouted as they climbed over slick stones to the secret entrance behind the curtain of water.

Bria glanced back at him, her curls darkening as the spray dampened them, her eyes emerald pools of disappointment.

Why did she seem so optimistic the previous night, but so discouraged today? She had been searching on her own for years, and that had to get depressing.

Theo touched her elbow, pausing before the last leap across. "Hey, we'll find it."

Either she didn't hear him, or she didn't believe him. She flung herself across the narrow gap and landed in a crouch behind the waterfall, disappearing behind the water.

Theo sighed, adjusted his pack straps, and jumped.

20

BRIA

Bria stared at Theo as he landed on the stony ledge inside the waterfall grotto, and her mouth dropped open slightly. She couldn't help it.

His white shirt was slick with water, and she could see every curve of his pectoral muscles, shoulders, and arms. Then he took off his glasses, and all rational thought vanished. He looked handsome with them, but without them, his long hair tied back, and the way he looked at her....

"What is it?" Theo put his glasses back on and wiped at the water dripping down his face.

"Um..." Bria couldn't find the words, and she couldn't stop staring. She blinked several times, trying to force herself to look anywhere else, to think about anything other than stripping off his shirt and running her hands...
"No."

"No?" Confusion crossed his face. He glanced around the grotto. "It's not very big, is it?"

Get a grip, Bria chided herself. She swiftly turned and walked to the other side of the small chamber-like cave. It was only four paces, and the rock face was smooth. She ran her hands over it, certainly *not* thinking about whether Theo's chest was smooth or had hair, and tried to concentrate. Surely if this were a sacred place, a source of Tala's power, she would feel something? Energy, vitality, like the forest but stronger?

"There's nothing here," Bria said, her shoulders slumping as she reached the end of the wall. Her stomach pinched, and she realized she was absolutely ravenous,

"Well, it's a good picnic spot," Theo said, sitting cross-legged on the wet ground and opening the top of his bag. He took out several packages, then glanced up at her and patted the ground next to him.

Bria sat down on nearly the opposite side of the grotto, watching him warily. She couldn't let her guard down, not when she was so close to finding the caves. She took out her own meal of a flatbread wrap filled with pungent goat cheese, honey, and sprouts, and her hunger overwhelmed her so thoroughly she hardly tasted it as she took bite after bite.

"It's got to be the last place, Bria." Theo said at last around a mouthful of dried meat.

"I've been searching for these caves my whole life. My father used to take me out to look. My mother looked, and her mother, and so on. Either we lost the knowledge or Tala made us forget. Maybe..." she took a shuddering breath in. "Maybe I'm not worthy, I haven't served her well enough. I failed—"

"Stop," Theo growled so forcefully, Bria choked on the words she'd intended to say next. He crawled on his hands and knees across the grotto floor and gazed straight into her eyes with his brown ones.

After a moment, he sat back on his heels, then inched closer to her and put his hands on either side of her face. "You are everything that is right with this world, Bria Glenraven. A powerful druid priestess, adored by the people who benefit from your stewardship of the forest, fierce and protective. If anyone has failed you, it is Tala herself."

Bria gasped, her throat nearly closing up and tears pricking the corners of her eyes. Her instinct was to bristle and shout. How dare he insult her goddess? But deep inside, where a wound festered, she found herself feeling seen for the first time in her life, something she had yearned for without even realizing it.

"A goddess should protect those who serve her. She should grant them the power to save themselves and their families. She was meant to look after your family, and by all mortal perspectives, she failed. When the humans came and fought in the war that destroyed the druids, she should have been there. If I had been there, Bria"—a sob escaped Theo's throat, and his hands fell away from her face clasping in his lap as he gazed at the ground—"I would have died to defend your kind."

Bria shook her head, fighting the smile rising to her lips. "You would have been taught to hate us, to fear us, as so many in Dunholm still do. The only reason you don't is they need someone who isn't afraid to keep the druid line alive so the forest doesn't perish. But it's failing, Theo. I can't keep it alive myself, and every year new groups of men encroach on Tala's land, cutting trees, destroying life."

"Then she should be the one defending it," Theo insisted, reaching for Bria's hands.

She let him take them, enraptured by his passionate, blasphemous words. Words that she had thought in the most secret chambers of her heart, but never spoken, not even to the goddess she loved so dearly.

Tala, help me, she thought, more out of habit than any expectation of response. The goddess felt so far away, now.

A story passed down from her mother's mother, the echo of a once-powerful deity.

"Maybe she can't," Bria said as the realization struck her. "What if, because the caves are lost, she's somehow lost?"

Theo gave her a sort of blank stare.

It didn't make much sense—how could a goddess get lost? Maybe she was putting too much emphasis on finding the caves. She could find them, and they could be nothing more than this grotto.

"Hey, don't do that, don't send yourself into a spiral again," Theo said, bringing her attention back to him.

How did he know when her thoughts were taking a turn for the worst? Was she so transparent? Or had he made a study of her expressions in their encounters over the past two, nearly three months?

Knowing what she did of him, that was likely.

"What do you propose I do instead?" Bria asked, pursing her lips and straightening her back.

"Come with me to the third location," Theo said. He stood, holding a hand out towards her, and she took it, selfishly wanting to feel the warmth of him again.

It wouldn't be fair of her to keep milking the attention he so freely offered. She knew what he wanted in response, and she couldn't give it. But selfishly, oh so selfishly, she wanted to know what it would be like to be loved by this man. Surely, it wouldn't hurt to pretend for a little while that he was hers, and she was his. So long as she remembered herself, and why she couldn't let him in completely.

They left the waterfall grotto together, crossing the water-slick stones, and hiked back towards the safer parts of the forest. The sun had fallen much farther than she expected while they were in the grotto, and her awareness of the fact that they were still in the deep woods rose to an anxiety-inducing point.

Things came out at night. Things they didn't want to meet. She still had nightmares about some of the things she had seen when she'd dared come here alone.

She quickened her pace, and Theo matched it so he walked beside her. His hand bumped hers several times, and then grabbed hers, as if by accident, but the way his thumb stroked the back of her hand had to be intentional.

Bria reveled in it. Hungered for it, even. Her heart beat faster, not out of fear, but excitement, adrenaline making her hearing and vision sharper, her awareness of his body heat more keen. He caught her looking at him and smiled, his face barely visible in the deepening shadows between the trees.

A hedge appeared in the distance, taller than Theo even if he jumped, thickly grown and somehow looking as if it were cultivated and not wild.

This was how the book had described it, according to Theo's translation. He hadn't been certain, but something about the description had led him to believe it could be a burial site.

But druids didn't bury their dead. Their bodies were claimed by Tala, enclosed in the earth where they became one with the trees and the plants and served their posterity for generations to come.

A shiver ran down Bria's spine. She dropped Theo's hand and clasped her cloak more tightly around herself, tromping around the hedge looking for an entrance. Nearly no sunlight filtered in through the impossibly high canopy above. Night was nearly upon them, and her heart clenched with fear. They shouldn't be here. Not in the deep forest, not at this hedge trying to get in.

Theo came around the opposite corner slightly out of breath. "There's no door."

Bria closed her eyes. Of course there wasn't. If this was a sacred place, the druids would have made certain no one but a druid could enter. She concentrated on the bramble hedge, accessing Tala's power with the words on her tongue and a flick of her fingers as she traced runes in the air.

Runes for opening, for revealing.

Power rushed through her, tentative at first, then stronger. The hedge remained a solid wall of foliage and branches.

Bria drew the runes again. Spoke the words with more strength, more urgency. She invoked her own name, her mother's name, and each maternal ancestor's name as far back as she could remember.

The leaves blurred together through her tears, and she grasped the hedge, rage so strong she wished she could tear the wall down. Thorns pricked at her hands.

"I'm going to look around the other side, see if something happened over there we can't see here," Theo said quietly.

It was no use. She could feel the tight knot of unsatisfied energy gnawing inside of her as the magic she'd cast dissipated without performing its intended design.

Theo's absence made it worse. She had probably frightened him with her display of frustration and anger, but she didn't care. They were so close to finding the caves and possibly a cure for this curse that had banished her to a life lived alone—she could practically feel it.

Almost, but it wasn't enough. She wasn't enough.

She saw Theo's doe-brown eyes in her mind, gazing at her as he had cradled her face in the grotto behind the falls, telling her she was powerful, and wonderful. She basked in the memory of that feeling and readied herself to call on Tala's power again, this time with the goddess's seven names ready on her tongue. If invoking the Mother of All herself wasn't enough, then whatever was beyond this hedge wasn't meant for any mortal to see.

Just before she released the incantation, a piercing cry rent the air, and Bria glanced up to see her doom descending upon her. Wingbeats sent gusts of wind in her direction, golden orb-like eyes glowed like twin moons, and wicked talons larger than her entire body gleamed out of the darkness of the deep woods.

Then those talons grasped her chest and middle and hoisted her into the air abruptly, stealing the scream from her lungs.

21

THEO

THEO FORGOT ALL ABOUT the door when he saw the owl. The creature was the size of Bria's entire cottage, larger, even, and the reflected gleam of its eyes cut through the dusk like twin beams of moonlight.

It hooted as it rose back into the sky, staying below the tree canopy, and Theo realized it had something grasped in its claws.

Not something. Someone.

Bria.

Theo cried out, his words choked and unintelligible. He sprinted across the forest floor, keeping his eyes fixed on the owl's shadowy form in the fading light. Fortunately, its feathers were pale, making it easier to see, but the light had nearly faded from the forest entirely.

Just as he thought how useful a lantern would be at that moment, a light bloomed to his left, a gradual glow forming in the shape of a swirling pattern of fungus on one of the massive tree trunks.

Theo didn't have time to stop and inspect it, he had to keep running if he wanted to keep the owl in sight.

The forest glowed with odd, flickering lights and glowing fungus and insects. Enough that he could see where he was going, which kept him from twisting his ankle on the moss-covered rocks and branches that littered the ground.

Ahead, the owl banked sharply into a tree, and at first Theo thought it had disappeared, but as he craned his neck upward, he could barely make out a crevice in the upper third of the tree's trunk. The owl stood in the crevice opening, fluttering about and making soft cooing noises.

Tiny peeps echoed down to Theo. Babies. The giant owl had babies, most likely as big as Theo himself, and the image of the owl feeding Bria to them wouldn't leave Theo's mind.

He shuddered at the image of her body being stripped to the bone by those sharp beaks and tried to think of a way to climb the massive tree. Its lower trunk was smooth and lacked any branches he could reach even by jumping.

Why had he left her alone for even a moment in the deep woods?

Growing desperate in the barely illuminated darkness, Theo circled the tree. It seemed to take ages to get to the other side of the massive trunk, running his hand along its surface, avoiding the glowing fungus that helped him to not stumble too often on the uneven ground.

He could call up to Bria, see if she were still alive, but he might attract the owl. Perhaps that wouldn't be so bad if it flew him up to be with Bria, but then both of them would be trapped.

Three-fourths of the way around the tree, Theo despaired. He didn't even know what he was looking for. Were the insects in this place as big as the animals he'd seen? He shuddered, and took another step, and leaned in towards the tree...

His hand met air, and he fell on his shoulder, getting a mouthful of rich earth, which he promptly spat out.

A hole of some kind, a hollow in the trunk of the tree. He looked up, expecting pitch darkness, but shock seemed to make his heart skip a beat when he instead saw a gleaming stairway of unusually large bioluminescent mushrooms twisting their way through the center of the tree.

How could that be possible? He'd never read of the like in the natural world. If he hadn't been trying to save Bria's life at that moment, he would have whipped out his notebook and started drawing.

Instead, he removed his pack, tucking it into a shadowy corner where he'd remember to collect it on his way back down, and hefted himself onto the shelf provided by the first mushroom level with his head.

It was as if Tala had created this feat of nature for this precise moment. He never would have considered it before, but the more time Theo spent in the forest, the more he believed in a deity that watched over it and all of its inhabitants. Dare he believe that, after the voice he'd heard, that Tala approved of him as a match for Bria? Or was that a grand delusion created by a desperate mind?

If he'd been fitter, he probably could have made the climb in the span of a few minutes. The tree measured a couple hundred foot-lengths, by his estimation, but he'd spent as little time as possible doing any sort of fighting or strength-building activities. He preferred books over bludgeons, and quills over climbing walls.

He regretted it slightly as he stopped for the fifth time, only halfway to his mark. The cheeps of the owl chicks floated down to him more clearly now. Did they sound extra excited? What was that scuffle he heard?

He kept his ears keen for a scream from Bria, but none came, which gave him pause. Did her magic give her power over these owls? Could he be risking his life for nothing while she made friends with the critters?

The image of Bria stroking downy owlet feathers made him smile and gave him a surge of strength. She'd probably laugh or roll her eyes when he appeared, soaked with sweat and entirely out of breath, and he would join her. Far better to imagine his own embarrassment than the alternative.

The hole through the center of the tree narrowed and became less straight-forward to navigate as he reached the top. He ducked around gnarled wooden ledges and had to jump from one mushroom ledge to another more than once, but at long last his perseverance was rewarded as he reached a hand up and touched a tangled network of branches, conifer needles, and feathers above his head.

He'd reached the owl's nest.

Clambering onto the thin wooden ledge the nest rested over, Theo searched for Bria through the woven mess he could see. She was nowhere in sight, and his heart rate, already stressed by the climb, picked up further.

He needed to get to the nest's surface and look for other signs. He didn't like to think of what he'd find, but it had to be done.

Pushing thin branches aside and spitting feathers from his mouth, Theo started breaking a human-sized hole in the nest. Every branch crackled, and some broke, making a ridiculous amount of noise, but he was beyond caring. Either Bria had fallen to her death from the owl's talons before it had reached the nest, or he would find the remains of her desecrated body dangling from the owl chicks' beaks—

"You dolt!" Bria's voice hissed out of the darkness, startling Theo so hard he nearly fell from his precarious perch on a section of the nest.

He looked down as above him, a curious beak crashed down through the top of the opening he'd been trying to clear.

With a frightened yell, Theo tumbled from where he'd been sitting, landing on a soft, warm, flailing figure.

"Shh! Shhh!" The figure hissed, shoving to help him get right side up and off her lap.

Theo rolled to the edge of the hollow's ledge, stopping himself before he could tumble off into the entrance he'd climbed through moments before.

He crawled on hands and knees to where Bria sat pulling a stick out of her hair and glancing anxiously upward.

"We need to move," she whisper-yelled, shoving his shoulder as he came near.

He ignored her urgency and all propriety, grabbing her in an embrace. It was like hugging a boulder, but he didn't care. She was alive. And he was an idiot. Of course she was alive. She was the last druid. She didn't need a scholar to save her.

He thought she'd pull away, but she didn't, and after a moment her boulder-like stance melted, and she leaned into him.

Until the owls above screeched and their pecking began in earnest. They knew their prey lay below, and they would destroy their own nest if need be.

With a sigh, Theo released Bria, his hand brushing her arm as he did and coming away wet and sticky.

Without any light, it was impossible to see what he'd touched, but he could guess.

"Are you bleeding?" He asked in an urgent whisper.

"It's a scratch," Bria insisted, glancing around him. "How did you get up here?"

"I climbed. There's a sort of path. Can you use your arm?"

She hesitated, and he had his answer.

He turned around, crouching in front of her. "Get on."

"What?" she protested.

"I'll carry you. The owls can't follow us down here, but it'll be hell to climb the first stretch with that arm of yours and I won't risk you falling."

A bird head crashed through the ceiling and Bria screamed, leaping onto Theo's back.

He lunged forward, sliding down from the ledge the nest rested on and onto the first bioluminescent mushroom shelf. The tree shook, making his feet lose their purchase, and he fell into a crouch, feeling his glasses nearly slip off the bridge of his nose. He used one hand to shove them back up, lungs heaving with exertion and fear.

Bria's breath came in quick little gasps in his ear as well, and he dredged up his strength from a realm beyond the fatigue that had overcome him from the climb up. Once he got out of reach of the owl, he could take a break, go slower, but now, he ran.

Run, jump, crouch. The birds' screeches grew more distant, but Theo didn't slow his pace until he tried coming up from a crouch and found his legs contained more jelly than muscle.

Bria slid off his back amid his protests.

"Oh hush. Stay there for a moment. I think I can make this go faster."

He couldn't see her expression in the dim light inside the tree trunk until her magic flared a brilliant blue-green color, illuminating her face. Hair askew, her sleeve dark and glistening, and filth smeared across her face, she looked wilder and more beautiful than ever.

Theo's breath was stolen from his chest. He couldn't muster the words to ask her what she was doing; he could only gaze at her and wonder if a mere mortal like him had ever had a chance with a priestess of the forest like her.

The light around them brightened further, and he glanced down to see more of the glowing mushrooms sprouting spontaneously from the tree and rearranging themselves, growing and adjusting, tilting into a shape with a purpose...

"Slide," Bria said, sitting next to him and bundling up her skirts between her legs. She held her injured arm in her lap. Her face seemed pale. Was it from blood loss or magic use?

Before he could express his concern, she shoved off and slid away from him down the mushrooms that now spiraled evenly around the inside of the tree's trunk.

The more time he spent with her, the more impossible things seemed. If she could do magic like this, perhaps he could work some magic of his own and win her heart. Though not to get her pregnant and perpetuate the druid line, but simply because he *liked* her.

Except his feelings went far deeper than that.

Theo expanded his lungs and, certain he would never be ready, pushed off. Wind rushed through his hair, musty and woody smelling. He picked up speed and clutched his legs in towards his body, wondering whether Bria had really thought this through and included a soft landing at the bottom.

She had, in fact. He saw her ahead. The mushrooms leveled out, and there was one at the bottom shaped like a shallow bowl. Bria slid into it and spun around, falling over, and Theo couldn't stop himself to give her time to move, instead rolling into her in a tangle of arms and legs.

This time, she didn't move right away, making a strange, pained sound that, after a moment, Theo realized was laughter.

He couldn't help but join in. After all, he'd just had the wildest experience of his life—climbing the inside of a two-hundred-foot tree to rescue a druid from a giant owl, then escaping on a mushroom slide.

Bria sat up, still leaning against his side, and glanced at him, merriment making her face flush and glow in the light of the surrounding bioluminescence.

He propped himself up on his elbows, hoping he wouldn't frighten her away.

"You bring so much...vibrance. To everything around you," he said.

Bria ducked her head. "You make me brave in ways I would have never expected. I can't believe you came after me."

Theo snorted. "What would you have expected me to do?"

"I don't know. Sit in the woods and cry? Try to find help?" She shook her head, then reached across her body and touched his hand resting on the mushroom's smooth surface. "I was wrong about you, in so many ways."

His heart thumped, and his mouth went dry. This is where he suspected most men knew exactly what to do. He propped himself up farther, leaned in, and, to his surprise, Bria closed the gap between them.

Her lips melted against his. They were pleasantly warm and softer than he'd imagined. At first, he thought that was it. No sparks, no flame burning in his loins, just her lips against his. And then she reached up and ran her fingers through his hair, grabbing it at the base of his scalp and arched her body into his, letting out the most exquisite moan as her lips parted.

She was in his lap, untucking his shirt with her uninjured hand, exploring his chest, all the while holding him hostage with her kissing.

He left his hands frozen on her hips, wanting desperately to do exploring of his own, but was petrified with a single thought—she wasn't in control right now. And, if she was in her right mind, she wouldn't want this. Not with the curse unbroken. Maybe not even with him.

Theo clenched his jaw and yanked himself away from what she offered.

She made a little sound of protest, tangling her hands in his shirt to hold him close, green eyes pleading with him.

It was torture for him, too. But he respected her too much to let her do this to herself.

His touch trailed from her hips to her elbows and down her arms until he pried her fingers from his shirt and held them.

"I want this. I do. I want you. But not like this."

"I know you've never been with a woman. If you're scared, we can take it as slow as you like, but please—" She licked her lips and swallowed, the movement sending a rush of blood to the root of Theo's body.

He sucked air and shook his head. "It's not that, I swear it isn't. It's that I noticed you trailing flowers earlier today. You're in your fertile time, Bria, and with the curse unbroken...I know it's my duty to the realm, but I *care* about you. I don't want you to do something you'll regret. I don't want to be the reason you die."

Bria turned as still as stone and sat back on her heels.

Then, she let out a cry of frustration and punched the edge of the mushroom bowl surrounding them. It wobbled, and the delicate skin on the surface of the mushroom went dark, like she'd bruised it and the glow dimmed in that spot. She twisted away from him, dropping her head into her hands.

Her back shook against his side, and Theo felt more helpless than ever.

Bring back the owl. He didn't know what to do with this.

"Bria, I'm sorry, I—"

"It's not you!" she burst out, removing her hands from her face. "It's me! I'm a mess. There's a war going on inside of me, and I don't know if I'll ever be able to...to..."

What had Tala's voice told him? *Serve her.*

Theo sat up fully and took her hands in his. "I think I understand some of what you might be feeling. It's...I can wait, Bria."

She glanced up at him in surprise, a tear glistening like a dew drop as it trailed down her cheek lit by the light of the mushrooms.

Theo took a breath, checking in with himself before he said anything more. Was he truly ready to face his mother? To deny her what she wanted—a druid heir to the throne—and break their deal?

"I will wait as long as it takes to break this curse. And we will break it. Together. If it takes thirty more years—"

"Even if...if we never..." She seemed to be holding her breath, her gaze unbroken as she stared at him.

"Even then," Theo promised, and his heart swelled, ready to burst with the rush of love he felt for her.

Her bottom lip trembled, and she slowly leaned into him, letting him wrap his arms around her. She seemed to understand what he'd always intended—she would be safe with him.

He rested his head on hers, relishing in the softness of her hair, though it did tickle his nose. He breathed in, then out, and all the problems of the world outside melted away.

Her head jerked up, and she almost smashed his nose. She gazed at him with a determined fire burning in her eyes.

"We will break this curse and be together, Theodore Blackwin. I'll make sure of it."

The words, more intense and truer than anything anyone had ever said to Theo, sounded like a binding oath.

He swallowed hard, breath shuddering through him. "And I want to become one with you, Bria Glenraven. For the entirety of my existence." The weight of his words settled comfortably on his heart. He meant them, and he knew she meant hers. Now the promises they made had to make it through whatever came next.

"Briallan Glenraven," she said, tilting her chin up in that stubborn way he'd come to recognize.

"What do you prefer I call you?" Theo asked, dropping his voice.

Her eyelids hooded, and a small smile grew on her lips. "Bria."

"Bria it is, then," Theo replied, returning her smile. Heat crept into his body, flaring hotter at the sight of her relaxed body leaned against him, trusting him implicitly. He could control his desire for her, and he would until the curse was broken, and she was ready.

Bria stood, ripping away her warmth. The cold of the forest at the verge of winter made him shiver, and he wrapped his cloak around himself. Bria's cloak was missing, he realized, and he hastily unclipped his and stood to hand it to her.

She waved him off with an understanding smile. "I'm touched, and I would take it, but being a priestess of Tala offers more protection from the elements than your human skin. Keep it. I'll be fine until we're home."

Home. She already implied that he was welcome within her walls. He couldn't keep the goofy grin off his face as he re-fastened his cloak.

"What next? We aren't staying in this tree all night, are we?"

"Actually, I think we should. We're hungry, but I don't think anything can get to us here. That crevice in the bottom of the tree isn't large enough for any big night-time predators."

"It's a bit too cold for sleeping," Theo said, as much as he hated to admit that he couldn't tough out the frigid air. He was already shivering, and even Bria seemed uncomfortable, making him wonder how much of her claim about Tala's protection was true.

"I can grow something to keep us warm. I think I have enough energy left." She tried several times, raising her arms and drawing the druid runemarks in the air. Her magic glowed and faded without any effect, and soon enough she slumped over, energy expended.

Theo caught her, lowering her to the floor of the mushroom. "You've lost a fair amount of blood. Let's find some water and take care of that before attempting any more magic."

Bria told him where he could get water—look in the mushrooms, she said. He cut one open with a knife and used a piece of mushroom flesh to gather it.

Giant mushrooms had many uses, he realized. He cut off her dress sleeve and used another piece to wipe the blood off her arm. The cut, though shallow, leaked a distressing amount. It had slowed to a sluggish oozing, allowing him to clean it, and then he took a strip off the bottom of his cloak and tied it off.

That sorted, Theo considered the sleeping arrangements. He was cold, but not dangerously so. If they huddled together and used his cloak as a blanket, they would make it through the night.

That meant spending the entire night with Bria in his arms.

Theo glanced to where she rested, her back against the upturned edge of the mushroom, eyes closed. He didn't have any issues with the arrangement, but would she?

"May I sit next to you?" he asked.

Bria shifted, eyes opening groggily, and nodded.

He sat down and scooted closer, holding his cloak in front of him, then draped it over both of them.

His mouth went dry. He licked his lips. "I thought this might make us both warmer."

Bria gazed at him with her steely green eyes. The message was clear—*don't even think of trying anything.*

"We'll have to lay sideways to fit underneath," he pointed out, nerves almost undoing him.

Her eyes narrowed. "You turn that way, then," she gestured in the opposite direction.

He complied. Bria backed up against him.

Even through his exhaustion, he couldn't sleep. Apparently, neither could Bria. She twisted and turned, nearly taking all the cloak for herself.

He'd had enough of this nonsense. He turned back towards her, and she yelped.

"Lay still, I promise my intentions are honorable," he insisted, scooting as close as he could get to her, his body cradled around hers. "There's no sense in either of us freezing to death."

"It isn't that cold," Bria insisted, pushing at him, but her efforts seemed half-hearted, and she stopped quickly.

"If you truly wish me to turn back around, I will," Theo said. And he meant it. As much as he enjoyed this, he would always respect her wishes first.

Bria cleared her throat. "I suppose I'll allow it."

"Good choice," he muttered, relaxing his head onto his arm against the wall of the fungus beside him, grateful for her good sense and warmth.

Bria seemed as stiff as a board, hardly moving, hardly breathing, until at long last her body relaxed. Sleep overcame him, and his head relaxed against hers, and they slept, safe in the arms of Tala and each other.

BRIA

Bria's eyes flickered open the next morning, taking in drifting dust motes in the sunbeams that filtered in through the hole in the top and bottom of the tree. The warm surface her cheek rested on moved, and she barely managed to keep from startling away.

Theo. It was only Theo.

His head turned the other direction as he stirred, and Bria moved hers, sitting up as carefully as possible to avoid disturbing him.

He looked beautiful in the early morning light, his chestnut curls free from their usual tie-back and his long eyelashes fluttering against his cheeks. His nose, Bria realized, had a distinct bump she hadn't noticed before, but it didn't detract from his features. Simply made them unique.

She ran a hand through her wild hair, then glanced around again. Her stomach felt hollow. She'd hardly eaten after their lunch the day before, and all of the emotions and fear and escaping made her feel as if she were starving.

Even the deep woods had food her kind could eat. And humans, too.

But first, she had to check the deep scrape on her arm. She unwound the makeshift bandage. Blood and clear fluid seeped slowly from it. She took that as a good sign and rewrapped it, promising herself she would take it easy and not aggravate the wound.

She slipped over the edge of the fungus bowl she'd created the night before and tiptoed through the crevice in the tree's trunk. The forest was a different place after the sun came up, though eerie, and still dangerous.

She found hucklenut bushes not too far from their tree and gathered as many as she could fit in her skirts, then painstakingly cracked each one, discarding the shells. Setting those aside in the tree, she returned to the forest to see what else she could find.

Tala must have been smiling on them that day. Bria happened upon a tangled mass of wild roses, where she foraged bright red, plump rose hips, and nearby, she spotted a crop of curly yellow flock, a jelly-like edible mushroom.

It would make an interesting meal but a near feast as far as she was concerned.

She retrieved their waterskins and went to a small creek to fill them. As she did, she looked over her shoulder at the path she'd taken to get to the burbling creek, and her eyes widened at the obvious, foot-print shaped patches of flowers that bloomed along the ground.

Bria lifted one foot, then the other, spilling some of the water she'd collected. She stepped to the side, pressing her foot to the ground, then bringing it up again. Sure enough, tiny white flowers bloomed wherever she stepped.

Her father hadn't known everything about druid lore, but he'd been well-versed in how to determine if a druid had entered her fertile cycles. Bria considered the past few weeks, the waves of unusual hunger, her sudden illness, and now this. How could she have been so blind?

She'd been so consumed with finding the caves and avoiding letting Theo get close to her, that she had ignored the signs in her own body.

Theo had woken by the time she ducked back through the crack in the ancient tree's trunk.

He clambered down from where they had slept, tugging on his clothes to straighten them and running his hand through his hair. Bria's heart skipped a beat. Had he meant what he'd said last night? Or was he still trying to win her trust so she would let down her guard and go to bed with him?

Her throat locked up, so she didn't greet him, instead plopping herself down to clean the yellow flock and rose hips.

In that mysterious way of his, Theo seemed to recognize she wasn't ready for conversation. He ducked outside, perhaps to take care of personal physical needs, and Bria was left alone with her thoughts circling like condors.

Theo wasn't like that. He didn't plan and manipulate and scheme to get into her bed. And last night, he'd said such wonderful things, promising he would help her break the curse, saying he wanted to be with her even if they were never together in that way.

Besides, she was being silly. They could be together once her fertile period was over. It only lasted a month. She didn't need to be so paranoid.

She relaxed, slightly.

"Good morning," Theo said as entered the base of the tree.

"Morning," Bria said, her tone coming out more clipped than she wanted. She cleared her throat and tried again. "Are you hungry?"

"Famished," Theo said, sitting cross-legged across from her and admiring the neat piles she'd laid out on her cloak. "You've been busy."

"Yes." She didn't know quite what to say to this man who she'd slept with without being intimate together first. Were her feelings even her own, or was her body in control? Did she like him because he was the only man around?

"You know, I think I have something to add to this." Theo stood and crossed to his pack leaning against the inner wall of the tree. When he yanked the flap up, the bag toppled over, sending his notebook, quills and inkpot sliding across the ground along with various other packages and things. "Oops."

The inkpot rolled until it was within Bria's reach, so she picked it up and walked it back to Theo, who took it and thanked her. She crouched down and picked up a metal tin. The unmistakable sound of dried leaves inside peaked her interest, and she turned it over in her hands, reading the writing on the side.

"Oh no, that's not-please don't—" Theo said, grabbing at the tin.

Bria spun around, blocking his attempt, and lifted the lid. A familiar aroma met her nostrils. Golden boxwood...yeraf leaf... and...*what was that?*

"What is this?" she asked, brow furrowing. She didn't recognize at least one of the plants used. It looked like herbal tea of some kind.

"It's just tea. Please, let me put it away," Theo pleaded, as if his life depended on it. As if he wanted to hide something from her.

Bria glanced back at him. "Tell me what it's for," she said, her tone far calmer than she felt. "If you meant anything you said last night, tell me the truth."

She couldn't say exactly why she understood that there was something suspicious about the way he was acting, except by now she knew some of his patterns of behavior, and he'd never shown himself to be particularly good at lying.

Theo's form crumpled. He put his head down, rubbing at his hair, then lifted his head and clasped his hands together.

"I told you the truth. It's tea." He sighed and made eye contact with her. "It was given to me by Master Graymont before I left. He said he'd been studying druids and perfecting a way to—to bring on the fertile cycle sooner."

His lower lip trembled in the silence that followed. A quiet rage built inside of Bria, starting at the root of her core and rising up her spine.

Theo seemed to sense the coming wave of anger. He stood, raising his hands towards her. "I never used it. I swear, I never even considered it. I packed it by accident, but I would never *ever* do that to you."

Her fingernails pressed into her palm like tiny half-moon daggers. How could she possibly believe him? She'd been ill, he'd taken care of her. He'd given her tea more than once. What if he *had* brought on her first fertile cycle in the hopes that it would make her become the delusional, love-sick druid he needed her to be so she would conceive his child?

"How *dare* you come here, pretend to like me, befriend me, and-and poison me with this concoction? You didn't think it was enough to woo me like the others, to make me fall in love with your awkward, bookish charm and sincere brown eyes and your soft looks? You know, it might have worked if you hadn't given up and taken the easy path."

She advanced towards him, tossing the metal tin his way.

He fumbled to catch the tin but missed, sending it thudding to the hard-packed ground. He backed away, hands raised defensively. "I didn't take the easy path, Bria. If you would just listen to me—"

"I'm through listening to you. You can go back to your comfortable castle, your books, and your queen and tell everyone that the next suitor who steps into the Morwood will never be heard from again." She snarled, her voice sounding like the guttural growl of some feral beast rather than her own.

His hands came up, making an exasperated gesture before clenching into fists and falling into his lap. "You never listen to anyone but yourself, do you? No wonder you struggle to receive direction from your own goddess. You're too busy drowning out her voice with the sound of your own! I'm trying to tell you the truth, but you don't want to hear it. I'm tired of you treating me like I'm the one who killed your ancestors. Because I didn't, Bria. I'm not your enemy. I'm glad I found out that nothing could make you trust me before we got into things too deeply."

Theo's chest heaved, and his face held an expression of hurt and rage that made him look like a stranger. Guilt was greased on the fire of her anger, making it flare hotter to protect herself from the discomfort of acknowledging that she might be wrong, that she might be in love with this human, and that scared her because if she loved him, then he could hurt her.

"Go!" Bria bellowed, unleashing the anger that consumed her. A swarm of bees rushed into the tree, answering the call of her unbridled magic.

Theo yelled and covered his face, taking up his bag and sprinting for the tree's opening. The bees followed him.

Bria could hardly think, much less see clearly for the rage that had consumed her. She, too, left the tree and moved through the forest in the opposite direction, heading for the hedges that had thwarted their search for the caves the night before.

No one, not man, not beast, would stop her from finding the caves this time. She would find them, and she would break this curse, and then she would exact revenge for the pain the humans had caused to all of the last druids like her.

THEO

H E SHOULD HAVE STAYED. Should have refused to go. But he could tell that the hurt and anger in Bria's voice and contorting her lovely face went deeper than anything he could see or understand.

She'd been hurt by men before. Her entire existence, her loneliness and her curse, all of it was the fault of his kind. Humans.

In the face of that, his paltry declaration the night before seemed worthless. To Bria, a priestess of the forest, an ant was more worthy company than him.

Maybe it was cowardice that drove him, stumbling, away from Bria, out of the deep woods and down the path that led to his tent.

His heart wrenched in his chest, the feeling so strong he stopped and looked up at the leafless lattice of branches above him, hardly feeling the rain on his face.

He wasn't heartbroken. He'd seen the lads back home get their hearts broken. They moped about and drank too much and ranted about the wicked wiles of women. He didn't feel like doing any of that. He wanted to run back into the deep woods and fall on his knees before Bria and beg for forgiveness.

Forgiveness for the fact that he'd ever considered that he might use Master Graymont's tea. That he had any part in the hurt she was feeling now.

That he'd fallen in love with her, without ever meaning to, and how he wasn't sure he could perceive of a life without her.

But she didn't want him near her right now. And she might not ever want him near her again.

Theo trudged forward, one heavy foot in front of the other, and considered his options.

He could pack up, fetch his horse from where it was boarding and leave today. He'd be back at the castle—and at his mother's mercy—again.

Or he could curl up in his tent, lick his wounds, and hope that when Bria returned, she would have calmed down enough that she didn't send the forest after him.

Neither felt right. He couldn't make a decision like this on an empty stomach. After he scrounged for breakfast, he would decide then.

Theo picked up his pace, energy renewed with his new purpose. He barely saw the forest as he passed, until he crested the hill that overlooked the clearing where Bria's cottage stood like a sleeping giant, windows shuttered and smokestack void of its usual plume.

Had Bria forgotten to close her front door, or had she somehow returned before him?

A chill went up the back of his neck that had nothing to do with the cold.

His sword was back in his tent. If he went back for it, he could lose the advantage of surprise.

His imagination was getting the better of him. She probably hadn't shut it tight, and the wind had nudged it open.

He grabbed a sturdy branch from the top of the wood pile, hefting it as he cautiously approached the door. With one hand raising the branch like a club, he pressed his hand on the door and shoved it open, moving into the room.

Theo blinked, and as his eyes adjusted, his creeping dread intensified to an all-encompassing fear.

His mother, Queen of Dunholm, sat in a chair by a fireplace as ashen and cold as her stare.

"Mother, I-I didn't expect you."

"And I didn't expect such a cold welcome. Empty cottage, no druid, and no son. For all I knew, she'd dragged you into the woods and murdered you."

Theo licked his lips. His instincts told him to keep the club, but he lowered it to avoid looking like he was threatening the queen. He glanced around the cottage, scanning every shadow twice over.

"You're here alone?"

"The important question is *why*, Theodore. Why would the queen of Dunholm, who has far more important things to do than traipse about in the woods to find her most ungrateful son, be here now." Queen Runa's lip curled, and her hands rested tensely on the arms of the chair.

Theo's stomach flipped, then sank. His mind scrambled for a way he could appease her so that she would leave before Bria returned. Because after spending the past ten weeks in the Morwood, he didn't want his mother anywhere near the druid.

He cleared his throat. "I have two weeks left. I can't think of a reason why you'd—" he cut himself off.

His conversation with Rhae. Magnus must have heard and reported to his mother. But then she waited all this time before coming out here...why? Why wait when she heard reports of his incompetence? Why let it drag on like this?

His whole life he'd felt like she was always planning her next scheme, masterful in the art of manipulation. If she had waited intentionally, it was so she could make whatever she had to say hurt more.

"I see those wheels turning in that brilliant head of yours. No matter what they all say, you always were my most philosophical son. You could have been a great strategist, a general like your brother perhaps, if only you reached your conclusions faster."

The compliment wrapped in criticism was a tactic Theo had come to expect from his mother. His old response rose up, ready for him to withdraw and say whatever he had to say to get her to leave him alone.

Instead, he clamped his mouth shut, jaw tensing as he held in his anger. She had given him three months, and he'd be damned before he'd let her take the last two weeks from him, even if he spent them alone in a tent in the snow. He'd rather face the cold than spend any more time in the castle at Dunholm with the queen and her schemes.

So calmly his own tone frightened him, Theo spoke, "Why are you here, mother? Our agreement was for three months."

"There's been a slight change of plans," his mother said, placing her hand on her stomach.

Theo's stomach lurched, and his mind struggled to process the reality created by that simple gesture. It couldn't be. At her age? Wasn't she past childbearing years? He meant to ask who, but he stammered and stuttered until he asked the question he really wanted the answer to.

Footsteps crunched up the pathway to the door behind Theo. He didn't have the reflexes or the thought to raise his club, but he did turn around, facing the arrogant expression of Magnus Ironcrest.

Magnus ran a hand through his hair, then leaned against the doorframe. "Don't look so shocked. She *chose* me." He smirked.

Theo thought he might be sick. The man was his own age, and he'd been with...well, Theo had considered that something might be going on between them before he left. He had never considered that it would—that it could—lead to a pregnancy.

He whirled on his mother, at her hand tracing a swollen abdomen that now seemed very obvious. "How long have you known?"

"Almost two months. I would have told you, but you were too busy chasing that druid. And I thought, why not let you have your chance at glory? You never showed much initiative until you took an interest in the druid suitor role, and I've supported you in it, though I still believe your intellect has been wasted there. I could have sent you anywhere in the world to study with the greatest scholars, but no, you wanted to be a hired whore." Her expression turned ugly.

So, this was what his mother truly thought of him. Theo pushed aside the sliver of pain that slid through his ribcage and into his heart. She had never shown him love, never treated him the way he saw other mothers treat their sons. He'd been a pawn in her game long enough.

He gritted his teeth. "What do you want?"

Queen Runa raised her eyebrows. "Theo, really, is that any tone to take with your mother? Much less your queen?"

The soft ring of a sword being drawn drew Theo's attention to Magnus, who stood at his back. He didn't like that at all. He shifted slightly, trying to get Magnus in his peripheral vision.

"Haven't you missed me? No?" Her sly smile vanished, pursing in a way that Theo recognized meant he was headed for trouble. He hadn't cowered, hadn't done whatever she wanted before she'd even asked.

He'd asked questions, pushed back, and now she circled him with her words like a big cat circling its prey before the kill.

"If not me, then your brothers, surely. I know they haven't come to visit you. Haven't even written you a letter. No, I imagine what you miss most of all is your books." The queen threw her head back and laughed riotously, and then her face snapped back to its cold, hard mask. "I should have them all burned."

Theo shuddered at the thought of all that knowledge, some of it not found anywhere else, drifting on the wind as ash and smoke. His grimace seemed to please his mother, and she chuckled more deeply, more darkly, fidgeting with the gems weighing down her neck.

His skin prickled so uncomfortably, he wished he could climb out of it and hide from his mother's gaze.

"Do you really want to spend the rest of the winter here trying to convince this druid witch to fall in love with you? Unless you've already been in her bed, but I am willing to bet that you haven't. A mother knows." She tapped the side of her nose with one finger and winked at him. "There's no point in these silly suitor games, anymore. The druid has dug her own grave in refusing you. Soon her forest will be no more."

"What do you mean?" Theo asked, clenching his fists and stepping forward.

Magnus brought his sword down in front of Theo, stopping him with its silver edge.

"Tell me!" Theo shouted. He'd never raised his voice to his mother before. Ever.

As her eyes narrowed and she pushed herself to standing, he wondered if he'd live to regret it.

As far as he could tell, she and Magnus were alone, but likely others were hidden in the forest and he hadn't noticed them, like the book-obsessed fool he was.

"The forest has outlasted its usefulness. I'm tearing it down to build a road between Dunholm and Tarnstad as part of your marriage arrangement."

Marriage arrangement? Theo's world stopped spinning for an entire moment, then picked up again, faster than ever before.

"I'm not getting married," he insisted, then winced. Another contradiction. Another mark against him. The thought that he could control this conversation vanished. She was in control. She was always in control. "You're pregnant. You don't need a druid daughter to sit on your throne."

"The infant could still be a boy, you fool!" Queen Runa spat. "The druid's daughter would be insurance, should the worst-case scenario come true. Where is she?"

Theo prayed to Tala that Bria was still in the deep woods. "Far from here. Your son is more of a failure than you ever thought possible." He broke into laughter, the chuckles coming dangerously close to sobs as he did. "I betrayed her trust. She can't stand to have me in her presence. Good luck getting her to agree to have a child with me now."

The queen flicked her wrist and laughed, tossing her head back. "Is that all? Theodore, you're not the only man in the realm. I'll bring the druid back to Dunholm—by force if I have to—and breed her to the first willing man I can find. She won't have a say in the matter."

Anger flooded him, hot and furious at the sight of his mother sitting in Bria's chair, beside Bria's hearth, in Bria's home.

He stepped forward, chest pressing into Magnus's blade. "She is a greater woman than you could ever hope to be," he growled. "How dare you dishonor her with your vulgar intentions. I never should have agreed to this."

The queen's eyes widened at the force of his words, and she held up a hand in defense. "Now Theodore, if you'll uphold our bargain, I have no quarrel with you. Either bed the druid girl and impregnate her or marry the princess of Tarnstad, and you can have your atheneum in the woods."

"Where will you build it if you tear the forest down, mother?" Theo said, calmness leaching through him. The anger still simmered, but it waited, like a serpent looking for the perfect moment to strike. He didn't know what he'd do when he released it, but he had a feeling he'd know when the moment came.

"I'll save a small area for you, dear, you know I would. I don't go back on my promises."

"And yet here you stand, disrupting our original bargain. Two more weeks, you said."

"There are preparations to be made. You can't expect me to let you stay here to perish in the cold. As you said, you've failed. Why waste time you could be using to prepare for a match that could save your realm more than some druid in heat ever could."

That was the last straw. He wouldn't listen to her vulgar insults any longer.

Theo shoved Magnus's sword out of the way so forcefully, the man actually stumbled back, and marched for the door, his mother's unintelligible cries fading into the background. Rage deafened him and nearly blinded him. If he didn't leave, he'd do something he'd certainly regret.

Someone tapped his shoulder as he exited the doorway. He turned around, unable to ignore the reflex, and met Magnus's fist with his face.

The punch sent him sprawling, flat on his back in the mud. He struggled to sit up, and Magnus's booted foot pressed against his chest, pushing him back into the ground.

"Stay down if you know what's good for you," Magnus said.

Maybe it was years of pent-up frustration at what a prick Magnus was, or how the Queen never listened to him, or the awful things she'd said about Bria. Whatever it was, it made Theo shove Magnus's foot to the side, jump to his feet, and land the first real punch he'd ever thrown, square on Magnus's jaw.

BRIA

B RIA REACHED THE SEEMINGLY impenetrable wall of dead leaves and branches, anger swirling inside as agitated as the bees she'd sent after Theo.

Regret tried to grab hold of her anger and water it down, but she stubbornly forced it away. She would not allow herself to regret her actions against the man who had tricked her into drinking that fertility-inducing tea. She should have known that all of his kindness, all of his seeming innocence and sincerity, was an act to get her to trust him.

As she stared at the thick hedge, anger drained out of her and desperation rushed in. She lifted her face and arms to the sky—except she couldn't see the sky, hidden as it was by the giants of the southern forest—and a keening cry erupted from her throat, feeling as if it came from the root of her body and soul.

"What do you want from me?" she screamed. To nothing. To nobody. Because how could Tala, Mother of All, exist and prevent her last daughter from finding the caves that might hold the secret to breaking this deadly curse?

All of Bria's feelings left, leaving her numb with empty questions circling inside of her. She fell to the ground, her knees squelching on damp moss. Her fingers sank into it, holding on for dear life.

What had she done to make her goddess so angry? Why wouldn't she answer her priestess's cries?

She flexed her fingers in the spongy earth, and energy trickled into her, a gift from the moss that carpeted the forest floor. She still had her magic, even if her goddess had abandoned her. If the hedge wouldn't part in the name of Tala, it would part for Bria.

Drawing power from the wound in her heart, she took her anger and fear and channeled it into the ground, telling it to withdraw its support from the hedge, to let it wither and die.

Slowly, with the determination and persistence of a waterfall eroding a cliffside, the earth responded, reversing the life-giving energy it supplied the hedgerow.

Brown leaves showered Bria, cascading to the ground around her. Branches rattled together, like the dying breath of an old man.

Her heart twinged with guilt. As a priestess of Tala, she was meant to foster life, not take it. But she had tried persuading the hedge to move aside, to part, to let her in, and it had refused.

Nothing would come between her and breaking the curse.

When the last essence of life had been sucked from the hedge, Bria stood, wiping dirt and bits of moss from her hands, and grasped the brittle branches, wincing as she encountered the hedgerow's final defense—thorns.

The tiny daggers pierced and scratched, and Bria responded by pulling and breaking. The crack of thicker branches filled the air, and the trees around the clearing groaned, as if pained.

She couldn't deny that they might feel pain. She had, after all, killed the hedges. Murdered them as surely as humans had murdered her family.

Carnage surrounded her, debris scattered on the ground and tossed unceremoniously into haphazard piles as she made a hole in the hedge high enough and wide enough for her to duck through.

Removing the last few stubborn branches, Bria stepped over a ragged stump left in the ground and shoved her way through the arch she'd made.

Her booted foot landed with a loud crunch on uneven ground, and when she looked down, her stomach heaved. Fortunately, she hadn't eaten breakfast after her argument with Theo, so there was nothing for her stomach to reject, but nausea still surged inside her as she looked down at the brittle skull she'd inadvertently crushed.

It wasn't the only one.

Bodies, stripped bare by the forest's decomposers and yellowed with age, lay strewn about with careless abandon. Rusted weapons and armor lay scattered amongst the bones, evidence of the gruesome event that had happened there.

At the center, where the bodies clustered the thickest, twelve uneven stones stood covered in lichen. This was where the druids had taken their stand against the humans.

They had died—hundreds of them—protecting the heart of the forest. Protecting Tala. Against the greed of humans who grew tired of relying on the druids to keep the forests and make sure the creatures of the forest remained where they belonged.

They wanted power and land, and the druids had stood in their way. Were the humans of today any different? They dutifully sent suitors to manipulate the last druid into having a daughter to carry on the legacy of her people, but it was too much work for one woman to bear alone.

Never mind that the druids had started the last war—humans had finished it, taking it too far after pushing a peaceful people over the edge.

Tala had allowed this to happen. She had allowed the humans to wipe out her most faithful priests and priestesses, and she had withheld the secret of breaking the curse that had resulted in the annihilation of the druids.

The weight of the forest pulled on her shoulders, dragging her physically down to the crumbling stones that paved the center of the sacred site. She breathed raggedly, the focus of her vision going in and out as the last bit of her innocence and hope were stripped away.

She pounded her fist on the stones. "Let me in!" she yelled. The sound faded and was met with foreboding silence.

Bria drew herself up, sitting back on her heels, and raised her hands to draw symbols of power. She tried sign after sign, the lights flashing before her eyes, until she paused, panting, on the verge of exhaustion.

Why won't it work? Has Tala withdrawn her power from me? Am I to be disgraced as well as doomed? Tala, answer me!

Her heart cried out to her Mother, and she fell forward onto her hands.

A low-pitched tone rang through the hedge grove. Bria opened her eyes, and immediately noticed a symbol on the standing stone across from her, lit up with a blue-green light that pulsed like a heartbeat.

The stone next to it lit up with another ringing sound in a different, but harmonizing tone. Her breath caught in her throat.

Had it worked? Had Tala heard her at last?

Stone after stone lit up, each with a different color light and a unique tone. Silver, blue, violet, green. They beamed down on Bria, who still sat near the center of the stones.

Awe and fear made her tremble as wisps of light drifted from each stone, until twelve took form around the circle.

Her gaze landed on one of the beings, and her heart leapt with recognition. A lovely woman who looked like an echo of Bria herself.

Sorcha, her own mother.

Then the rest of them, these men and women, were her druid ancestors. If she hadn't been sitting down already, she would have fallen back in shock. Why were they here? Why now? Would they tell her how to enter the caves, or how to break the curse?

Hope rose in her heart, and she stood, reaching out her arms.

"I've come to break the curse on our people. Please, help me," Bria cried.

"We hear the pain of your heart, and we have come," the figure that appeared as her mother spoke with a female voice deeper than Bria had expected, but she could still hear herself in it. Her longing increased, but it only served to fan the flame of rage that burned inside of her.

"Then let it end today," Bria said. "Show me the way forward. I would enter the Heart of Tala and heal the curse."

"You say you wish to end the curse, but you do not understand the cost," her mother-spirit replied, her expression creasing with pain.

"Then help me understand," Bria pleaded, clasping her hands. The clamminess of her skin made them cold to the touch.

The druid man to the left of her mother stepped forward. "You cannot enter the Heart alone."

"Two may enter where one cannot," another druid spirit intoned from behind Bria.

She spun and faced the wrinkled woman. How had she lived to such an age? Had she been one of the last druids to live a full lifespan?

"Two?" Bria said, her mind spinning. "Two druids? Or any two people? Who do I need? Tell me! I'll do anything!"

The twelve druid spirits drew two symbols in the air in front of them, the symbols that meant light and dark. She had never drawn them together like that, the magic weaving in and out in the air, illuminating the hedge grove with light that was somehow also shadow, pulsing and changing. The twelve chanted together.

"The light must unfold in the darkness, beginning what will have no end."

Bria spun around, looking into each face, desperate for a real answer, an explanation of what the vague phrase meant. It had the ring of prophecy to it, and she'd heard it before in the texts that Theo had translated for her. But what did it mean?

Frantically, she drew the same symbols, throwing them into the air to shift and change with the others. She drew symbols for fire, for light bugs, for the moon. Anything she knew of that could mean light, expending the energy and anger inside of her until she felt as if someone had thrown a bucket of water over her. She stood hunched in on herself, her breath ragged and her body damp with sweat.

The twelve stood silently, staring at her.

"Just...tell me what I need to do," she whispered hoarsely.

Her mother-spirit stepped forward. "It must come from you. From your own heart. If we give you the answer, the curse will remain, and the cycle will repeat."

Bria lifted her head. "Can't you give me a hint?" she asked, smiling weakly.

"You have everything you need. The dark is here," her mother pointed to Bria's chest. "But it is incomplete without your light."

Bria wanted to scream at the vague riddles. If Theo were here, he'd have some brilliant idea of what her ancestors were saying. He had an uncanny way of unraveling words.

A hollow place in her core ached with longing to have him beside her. His calm, reassuring personality, like a tree or a stone, seemed to be just what she needed when a tempest raged inside of her.

But her days of admiring him—of longing for him—were done. He had betrayed her.

"The light," her mother-spirit whispered. "It was there, in your eyes, for the briefest of moments. You have what I did not, Tala's daughter. The courage to find true love is a gift, but it cannot last without forgiveness."

Bria blinked as her mother-spirit walked back to her place in the circle, stopping in front of one of the tall stones that stood as a monument to a time long past, but also reminded Bria that she still had a future.

The spirit couldn't be referring to Theo. There was no way a human man—one that had betrayed her, tried to manipulate her—was the answer to breaking the curse.

The thought gripped her mind and wouldn't let go. If breaking the curse was as simple as walking back into this grove with him in tow, was it possible she had made a terrible mistake by driving him away?

25

THEO

ANOTHER PUNCH FROM MAGNUS sent Theo to the ground, and this time, he didn't get back up. His glasses lay cracked on the ground several feet away. His vision blurred and doubled, showing him two figures of Magnus crouching down beside him, rubbing his knuckles and grinning.

"Your head is harder than I expected, Blackwin. You're more stubborn, too. I would have taken you for the turn-tail-and-run or cower-in-the-corner type. Guess you're not smart enough to know your place."

Theo spat blood. More than one of his teeth felt loose. He was shocked he hadn't lost any, getting his face beat to a pulp.

Magnus flipped Theo over with a heave of his booted foot and planted it on Theo's chest. "Let's see if we can make that face any prettier." He raised his foot, hovering over Theo's face.

Theo gazed at the bottom of the boot and wondered where Bria was, what she might be doing. He was glad she wasn't here to witness this. Before she discovered the tea in his bag, she might have saved him. What would she do if she were here, now that she hated him? Would she stand by and watch Magnus kill him?

"Magnus, that's enough, pet. He still has some usefulness for me." The queen's amused voice sent a shiver up Theo's spine. "Get up. Laying in the dirt is a new low, even for you, and I won't have a son of mine looking so disgraceful and pathetic."

Theo wished the ground would open and swallow him. A faint tremor made the ground vibrate. Had he imagined it? He closed his eyes and imagined he was one with the soil, imagined the worms squirming through tunnels and the tree roots reaching deep.

Ever-so-faintly, an image flickered into his mind, mostly blurred colors, but he could make the form out clearly enough to know who was coming.

"What are you grinning about? Get up!" Queen Runa snapped.

Theo pushed against the ground and rose to standing, eyes fixed on the top of the sloped path leading into the clearing.

Sure enough, the last druid appeared, framed by tree trunks that bowed towards her as if beckoned. A green carpet bloomed at her feet, bright colors popping against the frozen soil.

Even without his glasses, everything about her seemed impossibly vibrant, from her wild, flaming hair to her skin flushed pink with exertion to the tiny flowers at her feet.

Did she know how beautiful she was?

"Magnus, quickly," the queen urged from behind Theo, sounding nearer than before.

Magnus acted so fast Theo didn't have time to respond. The queen's lover punched him in the stomach and grabbed his arms, wrapping them behind his back as he forced him to his knees.

Theo cried out and fell to the ground. He suddenly wanted Bria to be anywhere but there to witness the power his mother had over him.

"Greetings, Last Druid. I welcome you," his mother said, her voice carrying over the frozen clearing.

Theo gave in to his impulsive desire and glanced up to see Bria's face contorted into a cold mask of fury.

She hadn't come for him. No doubt she simply wanted to return home and forget all about him. But Theo's heart still leapt at the thought that he'd gotten to see her again. Even angry, she was beautiful. His fingertips brushed something. His broken glasses. One lens was still good, at least. He grabbed them, fumbling to put them on his face.

"You enter my home uninvited, commit violence in my forest. Is this how you welcome everyone? Truly, the pride of humans is a wonder." The Bria he'd met his first week in the forest was back, all of her walls drawn up as tight as ever.

He tried to get her to look at him. No, not merely look, but to *see* him. She barely spared him a glance. If his bloody and rough state had any effect on her, she didn't let it show, and pain pierced through Theo's heart again. He deserved it. Deserved her hate. But if she'd forgive him, let him prove to her how he truly cared, he would never betray her heart again as long as he lived.

The queen recovered from her shock at Bria's sharp reply and laughed nervously. "There has been some misunderstanding. You've met my son, Theodore," Queen Runa gestured to Theo. "I came to retrieve him. He won't be bothering you any longer."

Bria came down the path and stopped about twenty paces away. Close enough that Theo saw every detail of her face, her red-rimmed eyes as if she'd been crying, the creases in her forehead, her hands flexing at her sides.

If he didn't know any better, he would have said she seemed anxious. But she wouldn't waste such emotion on someone who had broken her heart.

"And what if I wish for him to, as you say, bother me longer?" Bria asked, arching a brow.

Queen Runa glanced at Theo in surprise, then back to Bria. "An arrangement could be made, I'm sure. I assumed my son had failed to capture your attention. He has been betrothed to the maiden of Tarnstad. They've offered a great deal in the way of political favors. But if you have something of value to exchange for his hand..."

Theo saw the trap his mother laid. She may not have planned on doing it this way, but she was quick to assess the situation. Bria had shown a hint of regard for him, and his mother would find a way to exploit that.

"What enters the forest is already mine. I will not pay for what I already claim rights to."

Theo blinked rapidly at the insinuation, glancing to his mother to see if she'd caught on. Bria had essentially laid claim to not only the third prince of the realm, but the queen herself.

Queen Runa adjusted her skirts, then clasped her hands together. "I am not used to being insulted. Did your father not teach you courtly manners?"

"No, he did not. He had his hands full teaching me what little he knew of my culture, and how to identify which predators I could live peaceably with and which I should avoid at all costs," Bria replied. She glanced at Theo, an un-readable emotion crossing her face. Pained? Or conflicted? "Though unlike any predator of the forest, I do not think I can trust you to leave me be if I leave you be. You want something. What is it?"

"I told you, I merely came to retrieve my son—"

"I can sense the pulse of every tree in the forest. You think I can't sense your bold-faced lies?" Bria snapped.

The queen lowered her chin slightly, her smile widening. Almost as if she enjoyed having her malicious intentions exposed by a worthy opponent.

"Very well, then. I want an heir for my throne, and I expect you to provide one."

Bria barely batted an eye. "Looks like you have one already," she said, nodding towards the queen's rounded stomach.

"A daughter will inherit my throne, not a son. I will not leave my legacy to chance this time. You will return with us to the castle and conceive. If my son can't get you pregnant, or you don't prefer him, another can be chosen. But you will bear a child, and she will be raised among humans."

"I could have a son as well," Bria replied, her voice faltering. A hand drifted up towards her face, tucking her hair behind one ear.

She was losing ground with the queen. Every moment her confidence faltered was a battle won in his mother's favor. Theo couldn't sit there like a damsel in distress waiting to be saved. He had to *do* something, but with Magnus at his back...

Theo glanced around, from the woodpile to his tent up the hill to the trees. One of the trees moved, then stilled. Theo stared at the place he'd seen the movement, wondering what Bria had planned. He hadn't seen her form any of the activation signs she typically used to animate the forest.

There, again. It wasn't a tree, but a man dressed in dark gray clothing, raising a bow with an arrow knocked towards Bria's back.

Theo snapped his attention back to the conversation, heart pounding with terror and determination. Of course, his mother would have a plan for if the druid didn't respond to her liking. He had to warn Bria.

"But you won't. Everyone knows the last druid bears a female child. It is your legacy, your purpose. If my child is a girl, yours will be raised as her companion. If not, surely you couldn't wish for a better future for your child than to be ruler of Dunholm."

Theo lifted his head, but Magnus's booted foot struck his midsection, and he curled inward, groaning.

"A future trapped in a stone box under your thumb, removed from the forest that is literally in her blood? She is Tala's daughter, not mine or yours," Bria insisted.

Queen Runa's face twisted with displeasure. "You might be the last druid, but you're still my subject."

"I am subject only to Tala," Bria replied, finally glancing at Theo.

Magnus's grip loosened for a moment as he adjusted, and Theo took his chance. He yanked his hands away and spun on his knees, head-butting the man in the stomach. Magnus stumbled back, clutching his midsection.

"It's a trap, Bria! Run!" Theo shouted, sprinting towards her.

The man in the trees released his arrow, and Theo jumped, knocking Bria to the ground.

White hot pain pierced between his ribs, and he went down with a grunt, curled around the arrow sticking out of his side.

"Theo!" Bria's scream sounded far away.

Theo tried to tell her to run again. The man had more arrows, he was certain of it. All he could manage was a grunt as pain washed over him.

Bria touched his cheek, then stood over his body, raising her hands to either side and bringing them together to form glowing rune marks in the air. A sudden wind rose, lifting the curled strands of her hair. She looked ethereal and deadly and more beautiful than he'd ever seen her.

"If you want him, you'll have to go through me," she said, and then she released the runes.

BRIA

THE MOMENT THEO SAVED her life and nearly lost his, Bria knew she loved him. Her feelings went far beyond the yearning of her body, or the convenience of keeping other suitors at bay. He might have been an idiot for keeping the herbs in his pack, but he was her idiot, and she wouldn't let the queen take him from her.

The rune she released shot into the ground and created vines that acted like extensions of her hands. She didn't want to hurt anyone, just prevent any more arrows from being shot.

Some of the vines wrapped their curly tendrils around Theo, then her feet and lower legs, anchoring her to the earth.

To Tala.

Bria glanced from the dozen men and women with arrows knocked who had appeared when Theo had yelled, to Magnus, who held a sword outstretched in front of him, then to the queen, whose expression suggested she thought she had already won.

What should I do? Bria sent the thought to her goddess. The advice of her ancestors at the standing stones suggested she needed to forgive. But how could she forgive humans for what they had done? Their ancestors had attacked and killed her people, and this woman wanted to take Theo and force her to bear a child for the realm.

Bria raised her hands slightly higher and vines burst from the ground about two feet high, then paused, waiting for her command. She had a vine for every person who wished ill towards her, and then some. She could crush their weapons, break their bones, cut off their access to air so they could never bother her or Theo again.

They belong to me too, the voice of her goddess pressed into her skin with a sensation like tree branches rustling past, leaving the taste of spring water in Bria's mouth and the scent of flowers in her nostrils.

Bria bit back a sob at the sensation of love flowing through her. Love for the wicked queen and the men and women waiting for her to give the word to attack. She looked at the queen with tears in her eyes, and spoke the words that Tala put in her heart.

"I am not yours to remove from the forest. People are not dolls to be played with, or puppets you can control. The world does not belong to you."

Queen Runa hefted her skirts and stepped closer to Bria, Magnus tailing her like a shadow.

"I will burn this forest to the ground if you do not return my son to me!" Queen Runa snarled.

"You could," Bria said, the calmness of Tala coursing through her. "But then what will your people eat? Many of them rely on the forest's bounty to survive. If you succeeded, they would starve. And the creatures held within the bounds of the forest would escape. You cannot remove the druid, and you cannot control your son. Your desire for control is a curse in itself."

"You're the one who is cursed. Your purpose is to bear a child for the realm and then die!" Queen Runa shouted, her shoulders heaving, a desperate sort of fear in her eyes.

Bria knew why the queen had come to the forest herself. She tugged her feet out of the grip of the vines, closed the gap between herself and the queen, and reached out. "I have carried your same burden, Runa Goldenvane."

The queen eyed her offered hands with disdain. "You know nothing about the pressures of ruling a realm, of bearing child after child without hope while your people grow restless, your own counselors plotting your demise because of the one thing you cannot control."

Bria held her head high. "I do know what it's like to go through life with the expectation of bearing a child that will become everything to your people. I know what it's like to let uncertainty and fear fuel hatred and misunderstanding. The real curse is the hatred between our people. Despite all of it, I forgive you, and I forgive those who came before you."

The words flowed out of Bria's mouth, and emotion moved like molten lava inside her, melting her heart, cracking her wide open like a geode revealing precious crystals. On her right and left, faded images appeared, growing stronger with each passing moment—her ancestors from the standing stones, smiling at her. Proud of her.

Bria returned her attention to the queen.

"Let it go! Let the Mother of All heal you as she has healed me," she cried, reaching out again.

For a moment, she thought the queen would accept Tala's offering of healing. But the queen's expression hardened, and she pulled away from Bria.

"Take the druid and collect my son!" She waved a hand with all the confidence of someone who is used to being obeyed without question and walked away, towards two horses tied to some low-lying branches near the far side of Bria's cottage.

Magnus grinned, wagging his sword in her direction. "I bet you're wishing you had taken me when I offered."

Bria bit her lip, glancing at the soldiers that closed in on her and Theo. *Theo.*

She glanced down and noticed his eyes were open, though his face was pale and pinched with pain, and crimson blood had spread across his vest around the arrow still stuck in his side.

She had to get them out of there, had to protect him somehow without putting the other humans' blood on her hands.

Surely Tala didn't expect her to *let* them take her and Theo on the queen's orders? Even if Bria drove them off, what would keep the queen from returning and burning the forest as she had promised?

She raised her hands, urging the ivy vines she'd summoned to bind her enemies' legs and arms. Shouts of shock and anger echoed through the clearing.

Tala, help us, she prayed.

THEO

B LOOD COATED THEO'S FINGERTIPS, and his heart beat a rapid staccato, each pulse causing more of his precious life force to leak out into the ground.

He took a sort of morbid comfort in the fact that his blood, and later his body, would nourish the ground and any plants that grew there. Would Bria be able to sense his spirit in whatever grew? He couldn't hope for anything grand like a tall oak or a fresian pine, but a little currant bush perhaps, that would feed her for all her days.

He hoped they were long and joyful and that she found a cure for her curse before the end.

Theo closed his eyes, drifting off for his last sleep on his way to the afterlife. Except there was an awful lot of shouting in the afterlife, and he didn't much care for that. He'd thought it would be quieter.

A booted foot kicked his uninjured side, and his eyes flared open, meeting Bria's frantic glance.

"You can't die now! Hang in there!"

A sword whistled through the air, flashing in the dismal daylight.

Theo cried out, too late, his response sluggish as the blood leaching out of him into the dirt.

Vines twisted around Bria's ankles, crisscrossing over Theo's chest and legs, anchoring them together as the tops of the vines caught Magnus's sword and trapped it.

He had to get up, had to help her, but all he could do was struggle weakly against the vines holding him down. Bria was trying to protect him, but he couldn't lay there and watch her fight off the queen's men alone.

His struggling slowed as his energy waned, and his eyes felt heavy. He fought as long as he could, but eventually, he gave in and drifted close to unconsciousness, aware of the fight happening above him in the way that he had often been aware of a dream that had happened just before waking up.

Our druid daughter has finally found a man who will put himself aside. Someone worthy to share the burden as a steward of the forest.

The voice of many voices, the Mother of All, spoke to him through his shifting dream-like consciousness.

He had died. How else could he hear her so clearly? Though she'd spoken to him before...

You are not dead yet. My daughter has need of you.

Even if he wasn't bleeding out on the ground, he had no fighting skill and no way of convincing his mother to stop and leave them alone. He would get in the way.

Theo, the voice pronounced his name with a hard 'T' sound, and the dissonance of his name being pronounced wrong jerked him out of the deeper unconsciousness he'd slipped into.

Theo, wake up. Serve her.

Theo gasped as if he'd emerged from water and sat straight up in the middle of a battle zone. The first thing he noticed was his vision—his glasses lay broken on the ground, the bridge snapped and the glass shattered, and yet his vision was clearer than it ever had been.

He moved his arms and the vines fell off, and when he felt his side he found it damp with blood, but the bleeding appeared to have slowed or stopped.

Even more shocking, his hands were glowing.

Brilliant golden light crept down his arms. He tried to shake it off, but the light remained.

A *gift, so you may serve her better*, the echoes of Tala's voice whispered in his mind.

Theo stood, and, not knowing the first thing about commanding the forest, simply observed.

Bria wielded a sword made of branches that were somehow strong enough to withstand blows from Magnus's sword, and better yet, it trapped the blade in its various branch-like notches, yanking it away from him while vines trailed on the ground and tripped him up.

Several other vines acted as shields, whipping out to stop arrows coming from soldiers in the trees.

She could clearly have killed all of them within moments by calling on the beasts of the forest or burying them past their heads in the ground, but she seemed to be trying to avoid killing them.

He admired her respect for life, but her magic seemed to be having a hard time keeping up with every opponent she faced. The vines would go inert, allowing the archers to free themselves, and Magnus's iron blade chipped away at hers, forcing her to regrow it every few blows.

A horse whinnied in the distance, and Theo caught sight of the biggest enemy of them all. His own mother, Queen Runa.

She rode away on her gray mare, not even looking back at the men and women giving their lives over her selfish desire for a druid heir.

The queen would be back. And when she returned, she would return with fire.

The image of Bria battling flames that licked at the ancient trunks surrounding them was too much to bear. Anger rose inside him, hot and righteous. He spread his arms out on either side, fingers forming like gnarled claws that pointed at the sky, and he spoke words that he'd only ever read, words that would wake the ground itself.

The dirt beneath his feet waved, lifting him up and then growing solid where he stood. He circled Bria in his thoughts, stilling the dirt beneath her feet. She spun around, looking at him in shock when she noticed him standing very much alive, rather than dying.

Theo brought his hands together and pulled them apart, making the waves in the earth intensify. Magnus lost his sword and his footing, rolling across the ground, his body lifted and lowered and tossed about none-too-gently.

Theo reached out farther with the command, encompassing the land the cottage stood on and making it stand still, then pushing out farther until the ground beneath the horse his mother rode wobbled strongly enough that the horse danced anxiously sideways, and its rider fell off.

He caused the ground to rise up and meet her as softly as he could, not wanting to harm the infant in her belly. He let her legs, hips, and arms sink deeply, and then he stilled the ocean-like ground, locking her and her soldiers into place.

"How did you do that?" Bria asked over the sounds of the soldiers panicking.

Theo walked towards her, the wound in his side making his progress slow, but not preventing him from moving. He took her hands in his.

"It would appear that Tala thinks I'm a good suitor for you," he said.

Bria rolled her eyes. "She's been telling me that since the beginning. I ignored her."

"Well, now you can't," Theo said, teasing. He leaned in, hesitating, asking, wanting to sweep her into his arms in a passionate embrace and kiss her until their lips were numb.

Bria cocked her head and smiled mischievously. "Are you going to leave them all like that? Or should we deal with them first?"

Theo groaned. Why couldn't she just let him kiss her? "If you think we must," he said with an exaggerated sigh. "What's an ideal punishment, do you think? Turn them to stone? You could use a few statues placed strategically to ward off unfavorable visitors."

"Nah, I don't want to look at their faces the rest of my life," Bria said, making a disgusted face of her own that served to make her look cuter, somehow, with her dirt-smeared cheeks and brightly gleaming eyes. "Let's summon the bears."

"The bears?" Theo asked, raising his eyebrows.

"Oh, you'll like them. They won't, of course, but it's been a while since we had a mauling in the forest. Spread the word and it'll do just as well to keep unwanted visitors away."

"But the mess," Theo said, and to his satisfaction, he caught the slightest gasp from his mother's direction.

Theo offered his arm to Bria, and together they walked over to the queen, her crown lost in the dirt and leaves, a twisted, terrified expression on her face.

"Theo, my baby, please, don't do this to your mother!" she begged, offering him a quivering smile.

To his surprise, her words had no effect on him. Before meeting Bria, he would have been overcome with guilt and done his best to appease her. Now, he felt like a parent facing a child who needed a bit of discipline.

"There's no need to pretend you suddenly like me. I've never wanted your approval less than I do now. I've moved on, mother, and it's time you did as well."

Queen Runa's face changed, morphing from her pleading mother act to one Theo had seen many times—the one she wore in her political dealings. Conniving, cold, self-assured. Perhaps the truest face she had ever worn.

"Come now, Theodore, you wouldn't kill your own mother. Not with child, as I am." She didn't even glance down at her belly, currently being cradled by the earth.

"The child is innocent, and I won't cause harm to come to it," Theo agreed. "But you are not without your crimes, here. You've attacked the Last Druid in her home and threatened the forest she watches over. It is not me you answer to, but to her." He nodded to Bria, who stiffened as he brought attention to her.

She glanced up at him, as if to be certain he wanted her to pass judgment on his mother. Insecurity twinged, but he brushed it away. He trusted her. She had forgiven him. She would choose the queen's fate with fairness, more a queen than his mother ever was.

"Runa Goldenvane, you are henceforth banished from the Morwood. You, your progeny, and anyone bearing your insignia will be restrained on sight as seen fit by any druid occupying the forest. If passage is required by your people, they must first seek permission from the druids by making an offering at a location at the edge of the forest to be set forth in writing hereafter."

Theo smiled. A fitting punishment, if a bit lenient. He would have added a dramatic flair and used the phrase "on pain of death," to be sure there was no misunderstanding, but by the look of horror on his mother's face, he presumed the message had gotten through.

He shifted his expression from one of admiration for Bria, to one of cold neutrality. "Do you understand the terms?" He didn't know what to call her, but he knew he would never again call her mother again. She didn't deserve the title of queen of the realm, either, but that was, perhaps, a fight for another day and by someone other than him.

Queen Runa pursed her lips. "I understand."

"You will sign a document witnessing your understanding, two copies, one for each of us. You will leave us to govern our realm, and we will leave you to govern yours. As long as you do not violate the agreed-on terms, we will leave you in peace," Theo added.

The queen's lip curled. "Very well. What might those terms include, other than my banishment?"

Bria's grip crushed Theo's hand. "You will release Theo from any marriage arrangement you have made regarding him. He is his own man and free to choose whom he marries and when."

"You think he intends to marry *you*? He intended you for breeding and nothing else—"

"Silence!" Theo bellowed. Vines, not called by him, wrapped around the queen's mouth.

To his right, Bria smirked, and he assumed they were her doing.

He continued. "You will not speak such vile words here. Your time in these woods is finished. If you do not answer our missive to meet at the edge of the woods and sign the treaty when it comes, you will find the forest a much less forgiving neighbor. There are things living deep in these woods that you have only heard of in stories, things fit for nightmares," Theo said. He had to force down a smile. His mother had threatened and manipulated his emotions all of his life. It was too amusing that the tables had turned so far that he found himself saying such things back to her.

Bria elbowed him. Perhaps she didn't appreciate his flair for the dramatic.

"We will release you now," she said. "You will leave now, and never return. Oh, and Magnus Ironcrest?"

Magnus grunted, and Theo realized the man was buried to his chin, unable to move any other part of his body.

"This banishment extends to you. As the queen's lover and someone who tried to kill both of us, you are not welcome here." Bria's smile was sweet as a poison berry, and Theo hoped he was never on the receiving end of it.

"Should we let them go now?" Theo asked, feeling the strain of holding the earth in such an unnatural position. It seemed to object to being held out of place for so long.

"Yes," Bria replied, the muscles in her arms tensing and betraying her nerves.

He relaxed his hands, urging the earth to heave up one final time and release the bodies he'd captured. Fascinated, he watched as the once-trapped forms re-emerged on the earth's surface, rubbing dirt from their arms, shaking it from their clothes, and scrambling for their horses.

The queen didn't wait for any of them, lurching and grasping the reins of her horse and heaving herself upward. She didn't even spare a glance back for her youngest son, the third prince of Dunholm.

"That poor infant," Bria muttered, turning towards Theo and leaning her head against his chest and sighing.

Movement at the corner of Theo's vision made instinct kick in, and he twisted, shoving Bria behind him. He fell to the ground with a grunt, holding his injured side.

Magnus lurched past, a sword still in his hands. Theo had asked the earth to swallow them all, but he must have missed one.

"You will pay for your disrespect, Blackwin!" Magnus bellowed, pivoting and reaching out a hand. His fist tangled in Bria's hair, yanking her towards the ground. She screamed and clawed at his hands, then twisted in his grip and kicked him away from her.

Theo's hands formed claws as he commanded the earth again. This time, he held nothing back.

As Magnus swung the sword down towards the two of them, the earth beneath his feet opened, and he fell, screaming, into a hole that became his grave.

Queen Runa didn't stop her horse. She didn't even spare a glance over her shoulder for her supposed lover, the man who had gotten her with child.

Bria scrambled on hands and knees over to Theo, shoving her curls behind one ear to better see him.

Theo leaned his head against hers, relishing in the warmth of her body pressed beside him.

"Erm, Theo? You're still bleeding," She backed away from him as quickly as she'd come, one hand glistening red.

"Am I?" he asked. The blissful, carefree state he was in wasn't just contentment at his mother leaving or being with Bria. He had lost so much blood he had become delirious.

The adrenaline rushed out of his body, he swayed back and forth, falling into Bria's arms as he lost consciousness.

BRIA

B RIA COLLAPSED WITH THEO in her arms, unable to hold up his limp body on her own. Rage and sorrow and confusion tangled inside of her.

Why had Tala ever let this man into her forest? And why, if she had chosen him for Bria, had the goddess allowed him to get hurt?

She was sinking further into the darkness of her own soul, falling fast and hard away from the place where she could feel Tala's comfort.

Theo still breathed, but for how long? She couldn't bear to think of the light in his eyes going out forever, of letting the forest claim him and use his body for nourishment.

It's not his time! Bria thought, clutching his body close to her, not minding the blood that was surely soaking into her dress. She didn't feel it. Her mind was in too much turmoil to be concerned with something as trivial as a stain.

If Theo died, she would be alone. Completely, entirely, utterly alone. She doubted the queen would send any more suitors after what had happened.

Bria could leave the forest and seek out a companion, but the more she considered the possibility the more she realized she didn't want anyone else.

Theo was kind. He looked at her with admiration and treated her with respect. He thought she was beautiful, and he always wanted to learn more about who she was and what she believed. He had taken care of her when she was ill and had been concerned for her safety when there was danger.

He hadn't said it, but he loved her.

His face blurred through the tears that welled up in her eyes, and she gasped, breathing through the tight emotion in her chest.

She needed him. She didn't want to be alone anymore. Even thinking about him dying made her realize that the loss of him would leave a hole in her life that would be hard to fill.

Is this what falling in love was? Digging a hole in yourself to make room for another? She hadn't realized it was happening, and now it was too late.

The face of her mother's spirit form floated into her mind's eye, a memory of the encounter Bria had had earlier that day.

"You have everything you need…You have what I did not, Tala's daughter. The courage to find true love is a gift, but it cannot last without forgiveness."

Bria bit her lip. She had forgiven the queen, but that wasn't enough on its own. She had to forgive Theo. She had to forgive herself.

And she had to get both of them to the grove.

"You cannot enter the Heart alone," one of her ancestors had said.

Bria didn't know what they meant by the Heart, but it had to be what she'd searched for all this time to break her curse.

She blinked away her tears and took a deep, shuddering breath.

"Theo?" she asked, shaking him.

He groaned and moved his head, eyelids flickering. He must be in pain, and the realization struck Bria that he was hurt because of her. That arrow had been meant for her. And if she hadn't fought with him, hadn't gotten so hurt she couldn't see that it might have been a simple mistake, they would have arrived at her cottage together, faced the queen and Magnus and the guards together, and possibly fought them off sooner.

If he died because of her, she would never forgive herself.

Bria crouched and grabbed Theo under his arms, heaving him up the path leading away from her cottage. She had climbed trees, chopped wood, and stayed fit her entire life, and she still wasn't strong enough to drag him more than a few feet.

She stopped a short distance from the tree line, panting, her arms and legs growing heavy already with fatigue. The cold bit at her fingertips.

The sacred hedge grove was an hour's walk. It would take a full day to make it like this, and Theo could be dead by then.

Bria set her hands on her hips and considered the forest around her, her breath puffing out in a cloud around her face.

Desperation was making her act like a fool. She had magic; she might as well use it.

She could ask the trees to carry him, but many of them were now sleeping for winter. To wake even one up would take an enormous effort, and she would need to wake multiple to pass him along.

How had Theo made the ground move to capture the queen and her guards?

She frowned and put her hand out over the ground, sketching the rune for "rise" in the air with her fingers. The ground slowly domed where she concentrated, and once she'd practiced a few times, she could make it raise and lower at will. She found it more stubborn to persuade than the trees. Sometimes it refused her entirely. She would have to ask Theo how he'd done it when he woke up.

The fact that he had magic at all still stunned her. She considered how it might be possible as she moved him along beside her. She took the same path back to the southern part of the forest, where the trees became giants and the eldritch beasts walked. It was still daylight, fortunately, and she didn't see any creatures, but she heard their deep lowing and the eerie calls of birds far up in a canopy that blocked out the sky.

Once the frozen dirt path changed to moss, the air warmed up and her magic flowed more readily. The moss responded to her urging with an eagerness the dirt didn't have, confirming Bria's feelings that while plants and trees and animals listened to her well, the earth simply did not.

Could that be a difference in the magic of a female and male druid? Had Tala gifted Theo with the abilities that a druid priest would have had?

Excitement filled her, and she pressed on with more energy than before, despite her empty stomach and the exhaustion of fighting the queen's men.

The hedgerow appeared. The entrance she had forced through before had already grown back over itself.

She wouldn't force her way this time. Either her ancestors would let her enter, or they would not. If they didn't, she would take it as a sign that she had gotten it wrong, and Theo wasn't the light that had come into her life and changed her heart.

Bria brought Theo closer, letting him rest on the ground beside the hedge. She nudged his hand to touch a branch and rested her own hand on the leafy surface of the hedge, breath catching in the back of her throat as she waited.

The leaves quivered, and branches creaked, then peeled away, forming an arched doorway in the hedge.

Relief flooded Bria, and she thanked Tala in her mind, then turned and grasped Theo under his arms, bringing him into the grove under her own power.

It didn't take too much effort to drag him to the center of the standing stones. She crouched beside him, checking his wound, which was still seeping blood. An alarming amount of his shirt was soaked with it. His breathing was ragged, and his face far paler than normal.

Bria swallowed against her rising panic and stood, addressing her ancestors and her goddess for the second time that day.

"I have returned. I understand now. I have to forgive, and I do." She swallowed. "I forgive Theodore Blackwin, for his betrayal of my heart and trust. I forgive Queen Runa for her hatred and threats. I forgive all humans that played a part in the destruction of our people."

Her voice broke, and hot tears streamed down her face. Saying the words had opened a waterfall of emotion that eroded the walls she'd built up to protect herself against disappointment, loneliness, and pain.

But she was ready. She was ready to heal, to be free of the curse and restore her people.

She released her tightly clenched hands, and raised them in the air on either side. "I forgive myself for my narrow-mindedness, for my bitterness and sadness, and I plead for forgiveness from all of those I've wronged, but especially Theo, and my Mother."

Her voice trailed off to a hushed whisper that somehow still echoed around the grove, the last word ringing with a low musical tone in her ears as it was chanted, over and over.

Chanted by the spirits that rose from the glowing stones, the familiar faces of the ancestors who had greeted her before. Mother, grandmother, great-grandmother, and with male druids brought from farther back in her bloodline.

Twelve spirits, all smiling at her, their faces no longer serious and grim.

No one stirred, except Theo, moaning quietly at her feet.

"I need to heal him. He's dying," Bria said, gesturing downward.

None of the ancestors spoke or came forward.

"The light must unfold in the darkness, beginning what will have no end," Bria repeated from memory. "This is what you wanted, isn't it? For me to forgive others, to forgive myself, and to bring the one who brought life to the darkness of my life with me to this grove? You must save him!"

One by one, the ancestors bowed their heads and faded from view, ending with her mother, who smiled sadly before she, too, disappeared.

Bria's hands fell limply by her sides. She had failed. They would have done something, said something if she'd succeeded, wouldn't they?

She sank to her knees beside Theo, resting a hand on his chest, a lump forming in her throat.

"I'm sorry," she whispered to him, absently rubbing her hand against the soft fabric of his shirt.

His hand covered hers, and she startled at the touch, gazing into eyes that glistened with pain and what was probably disappointment.

"Don't...be," he said, forcing the words out. He braced himself and tried to sit up, but Bria held him down.

"You'll hurt yourself. Stay there," she pleaded. What could she do? She couldn't heal him, and her ancestors had gone. Would Tala answer a prayer from her failed priestess?

She was almost afraid to cry out, lest she anger the Mother of All further, but she couldn't stop the tiniest, most faithful part of her heart from reaching. She reached for the deity she'd grown to know and love, the invisible companion she'd had all her life, the one who had taught her about the forest.

Warmth rushed into Bria's chest, filling her to the brim with a love so deep and complete that she thought she might become one with everything around her and cease to exist as herself.

Theo's grip tightened on her hand, anchoring her back to the center of the standing stones. She squeezed back, and as she did the ground beneath them rumbled and rotated.

A ledge appeared around the circle as the center platform sank. They were descending. Somehow. Impossibly.

Bria laid herself protectively over Theo. His hand stroked through her hair, as if to reassure her. He didn't seem to have much strength, even to speak, but his touch dispelled some of her fear, and Bria sat up straighter as the platform came to a shuddering stop at the bottom of a deep pit.

Tiny pinpricks of sunlight, appearing as golden stars twinkling in a sky of dark green, came through the canopy far above them.

Bria brought her eyes down to look around them. Glints of purple and blue caught her eye everywhere she turned, and as her vision adjusted, she realized they were surrounded by crystals that stood taller than any mortal she had ever known.

Aside from its ethereal beauty, it seemed like any other cave. Why had the humans wanted it? And why had the druids protected it with their lives almost to extinction?

Theo's hand moved away from her hair and he sat up, propping himself on his elbows to gaze at the crystals.

"I'm sorry about your glasses," Bria whispered.

"It's all right," Theo said, touching her hand. "I can see."

She wondered how it was possible, but before she could ask, the crystals lit up from within one-by-one. Each one let out a harmonizing tone that she recognized. They were the same ones the standing stones had emitted before her ancestors appeared in spirit.

Here, the sounds combined into a song that reminded Bria of the forest. It brought to mind the spark of life in every living thing. The sound washed over her and through her and a new tone emerged, one she recognized as coming from her own soul.

The tones rebounded off the crystals, filling the cavern with their vibrations. The floor shivered and trembled, sending the pulsing rhythms through Bria's body. She rocked and swayed with them, barely conscious of Theo doing the same beside her.

A single high, piercing tone interrupted the never-ending flow. Everything went still, even Bria's breath. A brief pain struck between her eyes, and the cavern flooded with colors she hadn't noticed—or been able to see—before.

She had been gifted with a new kind of sight, and now each of the massive violet-blue crystals had an image moving across its surface.

Bria stood and spun around, watching each silent moving picture as long as it lasted before it shifted into something else.

One crystal showed her a young druid, face contorted with effort as she curled around her swollen, pregnant belly and birthed a baby. She scooped it into her arms and held it for a moment before her eyes closed, and the baby was removed from her arms.

Another flashed with the terrible image of the forest burning, animals and eldritch creatures fleeing, spirits unable to escape their chosen vessels writhing in pain.

Her gaze landed on a wide, short crystal that revealed her own face, smiling down at an infant in her arms, and a man with long brown hair kissing her on the cheek and tickling the baby. Their baby.

It was Theo.

"What is this place?" Theo asked in a hoarse and breathless whisper.

Bria shook herself out of her stupor and circled once again, more slowly, feeling dizzy at the vast array of scenes being played out on crystalline glass.

"These images...I think they reveal the past and the future."

"Present too. Look," Theo said, pointing over her shoulder.

Bria turned in time to see her own face reflected like a mirror in a simmering crystal surface, with Theo's face visible behind her, then a bright light flared, and the image was gone, shifting into dozens of other histories and potentialities.

"Everything that was, is, and could be," Bria said in awe. She closed her eyes against the flashing images, suddenly overwhelmed.

"What can we do with this knowledge?" Theo asked. He sounded stronger, and Bria wondered if he had been healed by the crystals or if he was fighting against pain and weakness.

"I'm not sure we're meant to do anything. Just to realize the enormity of it all and the impossibility of controlling any outcome," Bria replied, sadness creeping back into her heart. She turned to Theo, eyes brimming and making the light of the crystals look like shooting stars. "I can't prevent it, can I? I couldn't stop myself falling in love with you, and I won't be able to stop us from having a child, and I can't cure the curse to stop my death—"

"Whoa, whoa there," Theo said. "Come here,"

Bria obeyed, stepping closer and sitting on the floor beside him.

He pulled her into his arms, holding her gently and stroking her hair. "I think the point is that you don't know any of that is true. You might stop your own death. Maybe that's what we're here to do. Or you might not. The question is, can you accept it?" He lifted her chin with a finger, urging her to look at him.

She did, staring past the crystal visions surrounding them, really seeing him for the first time.

He wasn't the same suitor that came knocking all those weeks ago, more comfortable with his books than with a woman. There was a new confidence, a new light in his gaze.

Again, Bria was struck with the longing to be with him, whether it was a few more weeks or years, she didn't want to face them without him, whatever they brought.

She breathed deep, releasing her fear before she spoke. "Are you asking me if I can accept my fate, curse or no curse?"

"Will you choose to *live*, curse or no curse?" Theo clarified, his eyes searching hers.

Bria glanced away. "I don't see how any of this is relevant. You're the one who is dying."

"Hearing you say you love me, being with you here, now, makes it less terrible somehow," Theo said.

"Does it hurt?" Bria asked, wishing she didn't feel so helpless.

Theo nodded, then pushed his hand through her hair, cradling the back of her head and pulling her in towards him. Their foreheads pressed against each other.

"Not as much as knowing I won't be there for you to see how it all turns out."

"I don't want to do it without you," Bria cried, twisting her fingers into his shirt and holding on for dear life. His heart still beat in his chest, but for how much longer? "I wasted so much time being angry at you for something you hadn't done. I wish I could go back and tell myself I was being an absolute fool."

"Now that's something I'd like to see. Two Brias, one scolding the other."

His ability to joke at a time like this astounded her.

"What would you tell yourself, then? If you could go back?"

"I'd tell him to throw that wretched tea canister away," Theo said. He reached a hand up to her face, tucking a curled strand behind her ear. "I'd tell him it will be both harder and better than he can ever imagine, winning the love of a woman like you. That it's the greatest honor of my life to be chosen for this."

Bria's heart leapt to her throat, and her entire body flushed with warmth. She both wanted to look at him and to look away, embarrassed by the sensations gathering inside her, passion coiling like a serpent in her belly, not to strike at her, she realized, but at her fear.

With a sigh, she released it and gave in to her longing. She threaded her fingers through Theo's tangled hair and tilted her chin upward to brush his lips with hers.

He gasped and leaned in closer, their bodies pressing up against each other, arms reaching, wrapping, grasping, lips pressing firmly together and moving as one. They parted, breath heavy, then came together again, and again, until they barely came apart anymore, each kiss flowing into the other.

Bria's hand traveled down Theo's shirt and moved to go under it, to explore his skin and take their passion to new heights. Her fingers roved up his chest and across his side until they touched something swollen, hot and sticky.

Theo shouted in pain and coiled in on himself.

"Theo!" Bria cried, hovering over him anxiously. She had hurt him. She hadn't meant to, but it brought reality crashing back down over her.

She lifted her head to the opening above, where the dim green canopy let so little light in it seemed like it could be night, and the final barrier of bitterness and pride fell.

"Please! Tala, Mother of All, heal him!"

Silence followed. Theo, gasping for air, turned his face up to meet Bria's gaze, tears glistening in his eyes.

She couldn't bear to see the truth spelled out so plainly in them. He was dying, and she could not control it. Could not change it. She was at the mercy of her goddess, who had plans she could not see and reasons she could not know.

Bria fell into his arms. "Why let us meet at all if this was going to be the end?" she sobbed.

Theo leaned back onto his elbow but held her steady, kissing her head and stroking her hair. "Because our lives were empty without each other, and now they're full. Full of light that wasn't there before."

Bria withdrew slightly, her breath quickening in surprise. "What did you say?"

"Full of light that wasn't there before. Bria, you brought me out of the darkness I couldn't even see I was in. From the moment we met—"

"That's it!" she exclaimed. "Light unfolding in the darkness, Theo, this is what the text was talking about."

"The curse? You think this might break the curse?" he asked, sitting up and then falling back again with a grunt.

Bria glanced upward, brow furrowing. "But if we've met all the requirements, why hasn't anything happened? Why don't I feel any different?"

"Maybe you'll feel the difference when you meet the next man lucky enough to get to spend the rest of his life with you," Theo said.

"Don't say that. I don't want anyone else," Bria replied, fiercely wrapping his hand with hers and kissing it.

She glanced at the crystals, noticing that they all showed the same image, one that had happened only moments before—her kissing Theo on the hard stone ground, her hand on his injured side, both of them...glowing?

Light poured down on them from the opening in the ground, splashing around them like water, filling the cavern.

Bria's words of surprise were swallowed as the light reached her head and filled her mouth, her ears, her nostrils, consuming her senses and plunging her into light so whole and complete, her mind interpreted it as darkness.

She understood nothing, was aware of nothing, but the slightest sensation on her hand told her she still held onto Theo. They anchored each other to the world, keeping them from getting swept away in the maelstrom that was a deity's embrace.

Tala had answered their pleas.

Bria was filled with the sense of her, though her mortal brain could hardly comprehend all that Tala was and did.

The darkness seemed to expand, holding Bria, cradling her, and all around a great pulsing sound reverberated through the air.

She was back in her mother's womb—no, she was in the Mother of All's womb. The embrace of the earth, the beginning and the end.

Now she knew why the druids referred to this place as the Heart. It was the heart—her Heart. The Heart of Tala herself.

Bria knew what came next. She waited, allowing herself to simply be, until a sensation like pressure squeezed her entire being, compressing her, expelling her back into the living world.

She fell forward, gasping, laughter bubbling from her mouth as her first cry reborn into the world. She felt lighter than air, all worry and trouble from before vanished as the light drained from the room.

Theo's laughter echoed with hers, and she sat up, meeting his gaze, and looked across him to see that his wound was gone...and he was entirely naked.

She glanced down, face flushing with embarrassment, then realized that she, too, was naked. Naked like the day she was born.

Her eyes flicked back up, drinking him in as his eyes roved across her, and then he crawled across the floor towards her.

She rested back on her heels, kneeling before him, fully aware of every inch of his physical presence and the warmth radiating from him. Desire, molten hot and somehow contained inside her, urged her to lean forward, to touch him, to explore him.

"I think," Theo said, licking his lips and tilting his chin in a tantalizing way. "I think that means the curse is broken."

"And you're not dying," Bria replied, closing the gap further, until their breath mingled and excitement flooded her at the prospect of what would happen next.

Theo dodged her lips and slid his face alongside hers, putting his mouth next to her ear. "I don't know about you, but I don't want our first time to be on this stone slab."

Bria giggled, cupping his cheek with her hand. "How does a warm bed of moss sound?"

He turned his face towards hers, lips trailing down her jawline, down to her neck, then back up to her lips.

"That sounds divine." He pressed himself against her, and Bria arched her back, hands sliding along the stone floor as she willed the soft, tiny plants to multiply beneath them until a thick cushion rested between them and the floor. Theo pushed her down onto it, a tender, yet fiery gleam in his eyes that she met with her own.

They came together as one beneath the standing stones, promising their souls to each other with the blessing of the goddess of the earth and with the trees of the forest as their witnesses.

EPILOGUE

BRIA

THE HARDEST WORK AND greatest joy of Bria's life came the next Warming season as she birthed twins—a boy and girl, both with the reddest of hair and the heartiest of lungs. Elowen and Thorne, tiny stewards of the forest.

She rested in bed and nursed the babies while Theo cooked and cleaned and doted on her every need. Never once did he complain, and never once did he seem to regret his choice to leave his cushioned, princely life behind to be with her, though he confessed many times that he missed his books and only regretted not bringing more with him.

When the twins were a bit older, clinging to her in a colorfully woven wrap gifted by the women of one of the neighboring villages, Bria encouraged Theo to visit the surrounding people and write their stories.

"Start your own atheneum. It'll be bigger and better than anything the queen is hoarding," Bria reassured him, while she secretly set to work on a project of her own—restoring the druid ruins to their new purpose in the Morwood.

With a new roof and repaired structure, as well as a thorough cleaning, the building stood tall and proud. It was made of druid-grown stone bonded with the surrounding trees, so it looked like the forest had literally grown its own library.

Passers-by were invited in to browse the sparse titles, and pretty soon word spread of the books in the woods. People came from all around with donations of their own, growing the collection by the hundreds.

Theo had gotten his atheneum after all.

He spent much of his day there, though he took plenty of time to roam the woods with Bria and the twins.

Around the time the twins took their first toddling steps, holding onto the great, grandmother-like trees for support, Bria and Theo found themselves contemplating their children's futures.

"The forest was enough of a teacher for me," Bria argued, countering Theo's not-so-casual suggestion that the children needed to attend one of the nearby village schools.

"You couldn't even read your own language when I met you," Theo replied.

"No one could. It was a dead language. Only stuffy scholars like you could translate it. A village school isn't going to teach them that. Besides, I've picked it up quickly. I can teach them now."

"But they need to be with other children of all ages and backgrounds. Even you have to admit you would have benefitted from more social interaction."

"Not stuck in a box I wouldn't have," Bria retorted, scrubbing her fingers deeper into the ground, her irritation bringing forth an errant mushroom.

She sat cross-legged on the mossy earth in front of the atheneum, her intention on encouraging tiny fern fronds to uncurl their heads from the ground. She found growing sources of food around the atheneum to be most beneficial to weary travelers passing through and needed to increase foraging sources as quickly as possible.

They had more visitors every day. Soon they would need help managing the books and the patrons.

Theo held onto their little girl. Her bitty fist gripped his finger, and she took a mighty, unsteady step forward, then tottered on with glee-filled giggles while her brother sat near their mother, sticking dirt-covered fingers in his mouth.

Theo sighed, helping Elowen over a large tree root, swinging her a little in the air to induce another fit of giggling laughter.

"I know that druids belong in the forest. Maybe we can invite other children here for lessons. History, geography, letters and counting, and how to listen to and respect the forest." Theo's voice took on an energized, hope-filled note, and Bria smiled, recognizing the signs of another one of his passion projects.

"That sounds like a good start," she said, sliding her little boy closer to her, gently taking the fingers out and wiping at them with her skirts. A little dirt never hurt, but the child ate it like it was an essential part of his diet.

"We ought to have named you mud instead of Thorne," Bria chided with a smile on her face, bringing him into her lap and kissing him on his chubby cheek.

"Hail!" A male voice called from up the road.

Bria's head shot up, the voice tickling a memory in the back of her mind. She craned her neck, trying to get a better view of the traveler through the trees. His thick mop of brown hair had streaks of gray in it, but still she knew him.

She stood up abruptly from her seat on the ground, Thorne in her arms, feet frozen in place as she gaped at the man she'd called father coming up the pathway, followed by more than a dozen people.

"Hail, Bria!" her father cried, waving frantically, his expression already choking up as he recognized who she held in her arms.

Bria met him at the edge of the road, beneath an arched entryway she'd grown from the wood herself and handed Thorne to him, her throat threatening to close as emotion bloomed in her chest.

"Is this...is he yours?" her father asked breathlessly, bouncing the little boy who stared at his grandfather with bright and curious eyes.

"Yes, and his sister as well," Bria said, gesturing to Theo, who had picked up Elowen and came to stand at Bria's side.

"Twins!" her father's eyes bulged, and he burst into joy-filled tears. "You broke the curse!"

Introductions were made, and embraces had, and then her father turned to the people gathered quietly behind him.

They wore long robes in earthy tones of pine and soil and buttercups and rust, their braided hair clicking and clacking with wooden and glass beads every time they moved their heads. Men and women and even an adolescent.

"Where have you been?" Bria breathed, taking them in. She could sense them the way she sensed Theo, the way she sensed Tala. There was a kinship between them, distant, but there. She could practically smell their home forest on them.

"Across the Tarnstad mountains and across the Mulbalm plains, I searched for years to find the people spoken of in your mother's books. One of your ancestors in particular mentioned another grove of druids that they traveled to visit once in her lifetime, to trade and to marry and to share techniques and magic and stories. I wondered if they'd met the same fate as your people, or if they might still live, and if I could perhaps bring you to them, or them to you, so you might not be alone..."

It was Bria's turn to burst into tears, and then another round of introductions and embraces was had. Bria and

Theo welcomed the Niannàn druids into the atheneum and their home, sharing bread and stories and magic and wonder together.

In the space of a year and a day, Bria's life had expanded beyond her wildest dreams. She had a partner who loved her, beautiful children, her own life granted to her, and now an entire extended family to share their culture and their life with her.

She knelt on the ground, placing her forehead to the soil, and felt Tala's pulse in the earth far beneath. The same rhythm echoed in Bria's heart and in the hearts of those she cared for. The rhythm of love.

Delve into nine worlds of magic, fantasy, and romance with the Of Dusk And Dawn books, each written by a talented author who has created a story with a broken curse that contains the prophecy of Dusk and Dawn!

Those Who Seek Vengeance - **Christy Kenning**
| Secret Identity, Fairytale Retelling |

Forgotten Retribution - **Leigh Fields**
| Star-Crossed Lovers, Greek Mythology |

Broken - **Ada James**
| Forbidden Love, Secret Twins |

Sacrifice for the Standing Stones - **Bree Moore**
| Enemies to Lovers, Nature As Ally |

Blade Upon the Vein - **ASF DeWeese**
| Hidden Royalty, Enemies to Lovers |

Web of Echoes - **Courtney Davis**
| Tragic Past, Second Chance Romance |

Sky Stitcher - **A.C. Guess**
| Enemies to Lovers, Forced Proximity |

Starlings in the Dark - **Forest Moria**
| Gods and Mortals, He Falls First |

Brightless - **Teshelle Combs**
| Fated Mates, Light and Shadow Magic |

Special Thanks

T HIS BOOK WOULDN'T EXIST without all the other ODAD authors and their advice, support, and humor. I'm so grateful I got to participate in the Dusk and Dawn Collection!

Thank you to Beth, Amy, Lee, Megan, Sam, and Emily for being this story's first readers. Your advice and feedback was invaluable.

Jenny, Heather, and Kaylee, thank you for being my sounding board!

Special thanks to my husband for holding down the fort and managing our crew while I finished this book. You're seriously the best partner I could ask for.

Bree Moore lives in Iowa with her husband, seven children, and two cats. When she's not busy homeschooling or folding laundry, she sneaks off to write more fantasy.

Bree writes urban and epic fantasy to explore different worlds with amazing creatures and magic systems. She enjoys giving her readers a story that is both entertaining and emotional, with a healthy dose of romance. When she's not writing, Bree can be found foraging for edible plants, watching fantasy shows and movies, or hanging out with her husband and kids.

Published works include: *The Shadowed Minds* series, the *Lost Souls* series, and *Shadows of Camelot* series. She's currently working on *The Plague King Chronicles*.

Visit www.authorbreemoore.com for a FREE fantasy book!

 tiktok.com/@breenovels

instagram.com/breenovels

www.ingramcontent.com/pod-product-compliance
Lightning Source LLC
Chambersburg PA
CBHW061757190726
48289CB00007B/1991